Life Belongs to the Living. War Belongs to Dog.

LANCE CORPORAL JOHNNY ABLE—He's a nineteen-year-old Okie, a U.S. Marine, and the most feared sniper in Vietnam. The VC call him Ghost Dog. While other snipers zap, ding or waste, this kid *kills* . . .

MIKE KRAGEL—The Korean War veteran and Pulitzer Prize–winning war correspondent is hopelessly drawn to the dark side. He becomes Johnny Able's celebrator, surrogate father, unmasker, and possibly his ultimate target . . .

THE 100TH KILL

"The mystery element is compelling, the sense of place rings absolutely true, and the combat scenes are riveting . . . a terrific book."

—Allen Appel, author of *Time after Time*

CAPTAIN BILL LANGE—Commander of Johnny Able's Marine sniper platoon, he has one job to do: create a cadre of killers. It's a job he does well, and, in Johnny's case, perhaps too well . . .

COLONEL "STICK" STEINKE—The head of the 2nd Battalion of the 9th Marine Division, he believes that snipers don't win wars—troops and firepower do. Johnny Able's personal mission is to prove him wrong . . .

"Grisly and gripping . . . Sasser has caught the essence of sniper warfare in Vietnam. More twists and turns than a mountain road . . . technical accuracy coupled with a brilliant plot . . . The sights, the sounds, the smells took me back to Vietnam. I once again felt the hot steel of the bolt handle in my palm and looked through the crosshairs with eyes stinging from sweat."

—Craig Roberts, Marine sniper, Vietnam,
and author of *Combat Medic-Vietnam*

BRIGETTE NGUYEN—The young Vietnamese B-girl fits Mike Kragel as perfectly as a Hong Kong tailor-made suit. In Johnny Able's war, she'll be forced to choose sides and risk the little she has left . . .

CARL CAN'T—The teenage civilian answers the phone, writes the heads, and tells the girls in Da Nang he's a war reporter. He's as young as Johnny Able and, like Johnny, earns a hero's rep too soon . . .

"Well written and makes you feel like you are right there where the action is."

—Chet Hamilton, U.S. Army sniper, Korea

"*THE 100TH KILL* brought back a lot of memories from my own time in Vietnam. The tension doesn't let up. I couldn't put the book down until I'd finished it."

—Gary Edwards, Marine sniper, Vietnam

Books by Charles W. Sasser

Smokejumpers
Last American Heroes
  (with Michael W. Sasser)
Shoot to Kill
Always a Warrior
Homicide!
The 100th Kill
One Shot—One Kill
  (with Craig Roberts)
The Walking Dead
  (with Craig Roberts)

Published by POCKET BOOKS

THE 100th KILL

A Novel of Vietnam

Charles W. Sasser

POCKET BOOKS

New York   London   Toronto   Sydney   Tokyo   Singapore

This book is a work of fiction. Names, characters, places and incidents are either the products of the author's imagination or are used fictitiously. Any resemblance to actual events or locales or persons, living or dead, is entirely coincidental.

An *Original* Publication of POCKET BOOKS

 POCKET BOOKS, a division of Simon & Schuster Inc. 1230 Avenue of the Americas, New York, NY 10020

ISBN: 0-671-72713-3

First Pocket Books printing May 1992

10 9 8 7 6 5 4 3

POCKET and colophon are registered trademarks of Simon & Schuster Inc.

Cover art by Steve Gardner

Printed in the U.S.A.

This book is dedicated to people who have made a difference in my life: To my sons, David and Michael, of whom I am justly proud; and to my wife, Nita, who has made my life good.

Part One

Part

One

1

THE KID'S FACE FRAMED THE FIRST TIME IN THE NIKON'S viewfinder. It was like the 135mm lens magnified and brought out something not readily apparent to the naked eye.

I dropped the lens from my eye.

He became just another kid of thousands swept across the Big Pond since LBJ started his buildup by landing Marines at China Beach. Maybe his face was even a little more boyish than most. I doubt if he had even shaved before he enlisted in the Marine Corps, the Crotch, the by-God U.S. Marines. He was blond and high 'n tight on the sides so that his head looked almost bald around the pulled-low patrol cap.

I swept off my boonie hat and wiped the Vietnam sweat out of my eyes and off my face.

The kid remained perfectly motionless. He lay prone behind a log, posing for the camera, the sling of the 30.06 Winchester Model 70 wrapped snugly around his forward arm to steady the 8X sniperscope through which, unblinking, he peered directly at me. It seemed a natural position for him.

Through the camera lens again I saw the smile that really wasn't a smile. His face and his arms up to where he rolled up the sleeves of his jungle utilities were baked brown, but the eyes probing mine were paler than the tropical sky, as though the sun had bleached them out along with his smile and his hair.

The camera's automatic wind whirred.

The rifle made me nervous.

"That goddamned thing *is* unloaded?" I asked him.

"Of course, sir. I would never point a loaded rifle at someone I didn't intend to kill, sir. Would you?"

The other snipers *zapped* or *dinged* or *wasted.* This blond kid *killed.*

Capt. Bill Lange chuckled in the background where he waited for me to finish. I framed the kid and shot film until I was satisfied. His eyes never wavered. Finally, I stood up and let the Nikon hang against my chest with the Canon SLR. I took out a notepad and ballpoint. I jotted down the date, military-style with the day of the month first: 9 Sep 67.

"What's your name, Marine? And your hometown?"

"They call me Dog, sir."

"Dog?"

He stood up. The utilities hung loose on his skinny frame.

"I walked point in the Three Nine—Third Division, Ninth Marines—before I came to sniper school," he explained. "They said I could sniff out the gooks like a bird dog. My real name's Johnny Able. I'm an Okie from Muskogee, sir. You know, like *The Grapes of Wrath.*"

"You read John Steinbeck?"

"Ol' Dog reads, sir," he said.

I looked at the kid. This was a little different bird here. Captain Lange stepped up.

"Thanks, Dog. That'll be all," he said. "The others are down on the Five Hundred Range."

"Yes, sir."

Dog started to walk off with the rifle hanging from the end of his arm. He paused with his back to us. He appeared to be studying the open field that snugged against this finger of

Hill 55. His head lifted until his eyes were on a level with the distant jungle that fringed the river.

"Sir?" he said. "I didn't catch your name, sir."

"Mike Kragel."

"Which publication is the story going to be in, Mr. Kragel?"

"I work for the wires—the INS, International News Service."

He remained studying the field and the jungle.

"Sir, do you know who Pablo Rhoades is?"

"He was a sniper. I understand he's in a hospital in Japan now."

"Pablo had ninety-three confirmed kills before the gooks fried him in an ONTOS, an amphibious track. During one mission he low-crawled on his belly across an open field just like this one in order to kill an NVA general. It took him three days to crawl one thousand meters."

He looked back over his shoulder with those bleached eyes.

"I'm going to get one hundred kills," he said.

2

CAPT. BILL LANGE'S SNIPERS HUNG OUT AT THE BOONIERAT Club, so Lange hung out there too. He never felt comfortable with other officers, he said. Too much ass kissing and ticket punching going on. His small eyes popped in surprise when he took the first gulp from his beer.

"Goddamn!" he exclaimed.

The kid behind the bar was bare from the waist up. Sweat glistened on his torso. We were his only customers. It was the middle of the afternoon.

"Where in hell did you get ice, Rafter?" Lange demanded. "The officers' club hasn't had any for weeks."

Rafter grinned and winked. "Suck ass don't get ice in this man's Crotch, Cap'n," he said. "You gotta be a Snuffy to know how to work the system."

The cold beer cut the dust going down. I relaxed and stretched my legs underneath the makeshift table constructed of old rocket crates. A glance took in the hootch.

The lower half of the club was plyboard, including the floor, while the upper half and roof were canvas pulled from around the sides to let whatever breezes stirred in the camp drift through the bug screens. A lone jeep passing by kicked up red dust that clouded and drifted slowly as it settled on the rows of military-dressed hootches. Everyone seemed to be out on patrols or operations. I had picked up scuttlebutt that elements of Two Nine were moving to Khe Sanh to reinforce against an expected invasion from the North.

"Another round?" Rafter called from where he leaned across the bar.

The bar itself, like almost everything else inside the hootch, had once contained 81mm rockets and M-60 ammo. Rafter attempted to give the club class by tacking cloth cut from old fatigue shirts over the front surface of the bar and draping an OD cargo parachute across the ceiling. He brought two more beers sweating from ice.

"What can you tell me about your high school dropout?" I asked Lange out of idle curiosity.

"Dog?" he said.

He downed half his fresh beer and then made wet rings on the rocket crate table with the bottle.

"So you saw it too, eh?" he asked.

"I'm not sure if a photo will show those eyes."

Lange downed the rest of his beer. Beer and snipers were the two things that aroused the captain's passion.

"When Dog first showed up here from Three Nine I almost sent him back and told 'em to keep him until he grew up. Christ, Mike, he looked like *such* a goddamn baby. My kid's fourteen and *he* looks older'n Dog."

The lines etched around Lange's mouth and into the forehead between the graying crew cut and the small dark eyes seemed deeper than since I last choppered out.

"Lots of men can kill in the heat of battle," he said. "Everybody's shooting and if you point your M16 and happen to hit and the gook goes down, well, then, you and your buddies can slap each other on the back and tell each other, '*We* got the slant-eyed little gook bastard.'"

I settled back. A journalist learns to be good at listening. Lange's way of getting to a point was to circle around and around it warily, like the bulldog he was, then strike for the kill.

"It's different for a sniper," he went on. "It's just *you*. The first thing you see through the scope are the eyes. You put the cross hairs on him and the eyes pop right out at you. A lot of men can't do it then."

He paused for us to drink beer. He lit his cigar, puffing his cheeks like a bellows until the cigar caught.

"Mike?" he said through the smoke. "You ever kill a man? I mean, where you see his eyes?"

I had killed, but not like that. The Eighth Army and the Chicoms fought back and forth across the Yokkokchon Valley while the peace talks went on and on at Panmunjom. It didn't bother me now, if it ever had, but I didn't think much about it.

"In battle," I said.

"You'll still understand what I'm talking about when I tell you about Collins," he said. "Mike, whenever I get a new sniper student in, I bring him over to the Boonierat here to get to know him over a few beers. I want to make sure they're suited for the job. Not many of 'em manage to slip past me. Collins was one who did. I found out later his platoon commander bought the farm on Operation Starlight and a Bouncin' Betty killed his best buddy. The reason Collins wanted to be a sniper was so he could shoot gooks one at a time and see 'em die—to get even.

"Collins got even for his platoon commander. He got even for his best buddy. He got even for himself. He had eleven confirmed kills. One morning he didn't show up for equipment inspection when One Nine was making a hammer-and-anvil sweep out toward Giang Dong. They were going to use my sniper platoon as a blocking force to catch the gooks when they slipped out the back of the ville. I sent Sergeant Rhoades to find out what was wrong with Collins. Pablo came back and goes, 'Skipper, I think you'd better come see this for yourself.'

"I found Collins at the back of his hootch sitting on the floor underneath his poncho. The boy had gone catatonic. It was like the only thing there was his body. I sent him to the air base at Da Nang where they have a psychiatrist. I heard he was starting to come out of it pretty good until one day they let some journalists talk to him. One of them asked him, 'What does it feel like to kill a man?' He just flipped out again. I guess he's back in the World at some nursing home or something, just sitting there because I didn't pick him out right and he saw too many eyes through his sniperscope."

I was beginning to see why Bill Lange was starting to look so old.

He didn't have a chance to go on with his story. There was a disturbance outside. Seven or eight dusty young grunts in field gear came swiftly down the road between the lines of hootches. One of them shouted something into the Company CP as they passed it. A minute later they were stacking arms outside the Boonierat Club. A red cloud of dust surrounded them as they stamped inside. They were all slapping and roughhousing one of their number.

I figured he must have made a winning basket or something.

"We been lookin' for you, Skipper," the grunts greeted Lange. "Sonofabitch, Skipper. Ol' Deke the Geek here broke his cherry today, his first day out."

Deke the Geek wore the wide lopsided grin of some Iowa farm boy. He leaned out of the group toward the captain. Some of the others had their arms around him, and he had his arms around them. I saw a smear of dried blood on his utility shirt front.

"Zapped that motherfuckin' dink, sir," he exploded. "Right here, sir, in the ten ring."

He freed an arm long enough to tap the center of his chest with a thick forefinger. He seemed on a high, like a hunter who has just bagged a trophy buck.

"One shot—one kill, wasn't it, Geek?" someone shouted.

"Yessir, Cap'n. Just like you said: one shot—one kill. Hey, Rafter. Beers all around on me."

Lange jumped up.

"Rafter, these boys' scrip is no good here. The beers are on me, gentlemen. And they're *cold.*"

Rafter was busy for a few minutes. Beers started disappearing; they made the grunts even looser.

"My first gook, Skipper," Deke roared. He killed a beer with each fist. "You know that little ol' ville down on the Tuy Loan where Hotel's been takin' fire? A couple of gooks holed up in that schoolhouse on the outskirts and zapped one of our guys. We zapped them back with bloopers. Then me an' Sergeant Norman set up on the schoolhouse roof an' waited. We figured they'd do like always an' try to sneak out across the rice paddy to the river.

"That's what happened, Skipper. This ol' boy comes runnin' out drivin' a water buf across the dike. But, Cap'n, that water buffalo had somethin' *wrong.* It had *too many legs.* Charlie was usin' it to cover his *di-di.*

"The range was about seven hundred yards. The distortion wasn't bad for that time of day and there was almost no wind. I shot the buffalo and it tumped down on its side right where it was. The farmer took off across the water like a duck tryin' to fly, but that fuckin' crazy dink, Cap'n—the buf fell on his rifle or somethin'. He's tuggin' away at it an'—"

He stopped, looked hard at Lange.

"Skipper, you're right. That's what you see when you put the scope on 'em—their eyes. He didn't kick around or nothin'. He died in place."

One of the grunts grabbed Geek in a headlock. "It don't mean nothin', Geek. You shot the motherfucker. He deserved it. That's all it means."

The snipers scuffled off across the plyboard floor, stamping and pummelling and laughing. Somebody poured a beer down Geek's back. I watched.

"It don't mean nothing," Lange echoed wryly. He was quiet for a while, drinking and smoking his cigar.

The snipers crowded around another table and got down to some serious drinking. The more they drank the quieter they got. They were doing some hard talking. Deke the Geek got quieter than the others.

Lange said, "I know how to make killers out of these boys. The question is—can they turn it off when the war's over?"

The bastard was starting to get maudlin on me.

The students from the Five Hundred Range, including Dog, drifted in a short time later. They went through the macho ritual with Geek of slapping and shaking hands and rough-talking before they settled down to drinking. Dog was with them, but he wasn't. He solemnly shook Geek's hand, then drifted off to sit alone at the end of the bar on an upended four-deuce mortar crate. He drank one beer slowly, savoring it while he carefully watched the others. He made no effort to join them and they didn't offer him a place at the table. He drank his beer, looking a little like the last kid chosen for sandlot baseball. Even Rafter pretended to be busy at the other end of his bar restocking and wiping down.

Some time passed before Lange blinked and returned to his story.

"Geek there, look at him," he said. "He's a simple ol' boy, just wants to be accepted as one of the troops. Tommy Hands there"—nodding toward a tall kid with high shoulders and long arms—"he thinks he can save gyrene lives by killing gooks first. Carson over there is a lifer. War's a game and he likes to play it. I can read them all like an old issue of *Stars & Stripes.*"

Dog got up to leave. As he walked by, I said, "Buy you a beer, kid?"

He stopped.

"I only drink one, sir," he said.

His bleached eyes shifted to Captain Lange.

"Next week, sir?" he asked.

"Next week, Dog."

"I'm ready, sir."

The screen door of the Boonierat Club sluffed shut behind Dog as he left. Deke was the only one who looked up from drinking; it was only a glance. I watched Dog's slender figure walking away between the hootches, loose jointed and light treaded. He carried his rifle in its case. A heat devil of red dust tornadoed across behind him, creating a little vortex of turmoil.

"I'm sending him out for his first kill next week," Lange explained, watching the kid too.

"Him," Lange said, "I can't read at all."

Lange and I were both getting a little drunk. The captain chewed on his cigar and leaned across the table toward me, as though to confide a secret. Our faces were only inches apart.

"When the kid first got here I asked him what about the killing, could he do it? His expression didn't even change. It always looks like he's about to smile. 'I can do it, sir,' he said. Just like that. He's a born natural at shooting, and he moves through the woods like a ghost. Only . . ."

"Only what?" I prompted after a minute.

He sat back.

"I keep thinking about Collins," he said.

3

MIKE KRAGEL DISPATCH (WITH POSED PHOTOGRAPHS OF LANCE
Cpl. Johnny Able and Capt. Bill E. Lange), 11 Sep 67:

Vietnam (INS)—It is a different kind of war than
Americans have ever fought. There are no fixed battle
lines, no set piece actions, no ground to take or hold. It
is a war of small group and individual actions. It is a
personal war.

And to no soldier is it more personal than to the
sniper.

The dictionary defines *snipers* and *sniping* as: One
who shoots an enemy from hiding. . . . To shoot at or
pick off individual enemies from hiding . . .

Vietnam is not the first war in which Americans have
used snipers. Snipers date back to the Revolutionary
War and before that to the French and Indian War.
They were used in the Civil War. Capt. Herbert W.
McBride made sniping an art and a science in the
trenches of WWI.

Although snipers have been utilized throughout
their history, Americans still express an aversion to
such unsportsmanlike conduct. They believe in Gary
Cooper or John Wayne who walk down the middle of a
dusty street to shoot it out face-to-face with the bad
guys. To bushwhack an enemy, even in war, is considered unfair and underhanded. It is wrong to kill, but if
we do kill we must kill in a fair fight.

Still, even though we are ashamed of the snipers

12

and what they do, each war of this century has produced a need for them. They were used at Salerno and Normandy and Pork Chop Hill. After the need for them was over, we corked them back into their bottles, as though they never really existed, as though sniping were morally wrong and unfit for a role in the United States armed forces.

However, men like Capt. Bill E. Lange, commander of the U.S. Marine Corps sniper platoon and school on Hill 55 near Da Nang, South Vietnam, are uncorking the bottle. The first sniper school in Vietnam was started by the marines in mid-1965, shortly after President Johnson began his troop buildup. Since then, according to Lange, the sniper has proved his value in this new kind of war. Lange says the sniper is the bravest man on the battlefield.

"When you look through the rifle scope," he explains, "the first thing you see are the eyes. There is a lot of difference between shooting at a shadow, shooting at an outline, and shooting at a pair of eyes. Many men can't do it at that point. It takes a special kind of courage."

Lange trains his snipers to believe in the philosophy of *one shot—one kill.* The most deadly weapon on the battlefield, he says, is the single, well-aimed shot; one bullet costing a few cents is more effective against an enemy than a ten thousand–pound bomb dropped indiscriminately.

During WWII, the U.S. infantry fired an average of twenty-five thousand bullets to kill a single enemy. That ratio rose to fifty thousand in Korea. In Vietnam, the ratio of bullets fired to bodies counted may exceed two hundred thousand.

It takes a Marine sniper only 1.3 bullets to kill an enemy. In one six-month period, snipers of the 9th Infantry killed 1,039 enemy soldiers, more than any battalion in the 3rd Division.

One of Captain Lange's newest snipers is Lance

Cpl. Johnny Able, twenty, a self-described "Okie" from Muskogee, Oklahoma. Able, nicknamed "Dog," has the shy good looks of the boy on the block who took your daughter to her high school prom last Friday night. He will graduate from Lange's six-week sniper school in eight days. Graduation ceremonies consist of his proving himself by going into enemy territory with an instructor-spotter and shooting a Vietcong soldier.

Able says he intends to prove himself the best sniper in the war. The previous Top Stick was Marine Sgt. Pablo Rhoades, who logged ninety-three confirmed kills before he was wounded and evacuated home to the United States.

"I will get one hundred kills," Able promises.

4

BY VIRTUE OF POKING AROUND IN OTHER PEOPLE'S LAUNDRY AS part of his business, and by his nature, too, I suppose, your average journalist is a cynical bastard. That is especially true of journalists who go to war to witness and report on man's greatest folly. Add on top of that a big dose of fatalism and you have your average combat correspondent. He won't believe you if you swore on a stack of prayer books as high as the Citadel in Hue that LBJ was going to have the troops home by Christmas, and he'll be convinced he'll die of the Saigon clap or something even if he survives the hyped-up commies running around in the bush in their black pj's.

Take Brigette Nguyen. I always suspected Brigette'd be gone in less time than it took a cowboy in Da Nang's Dog

Patch to razor the wallet out of a GI's pocket if she got a better, more permanent offer.

Brigette was a nineteen-year-old B-girl when I picked her up at the French Fuck, which is what we called the lounge in the Continental Palace Hotel on Duc Phon Street. We had a room on the third floor that made it harder for a sapper to get to you and blow you out the double French window-doors and over the balcony. It wasn't the best hotel in Da Nang, but it was okay if you could stand the legless war victims who crawled around in the lobby like crabs whining and tugging at you for money.

I kept Brigette okay. She used to wriggle around in stretch jeans and tight blouses with all the other Cinderellas, but then she took to wearing the traditional *ao dai* with pants because she said it was dignified and suited her as the paramour of a famous American newspaper writer. Judy Wong was the only one of the other girls she saw anymore. She said Judy Wong was jealous of her because Judy Wong wanted an American paramour too, maybe somebody from the U.S. MilGroup or a diplomatic clerk.

"Biness," she said. "Girl must make biness when sun shine, for goo'ness sake."

"Business," I corrected. She spoke pidgin when I found her.

"That what I say—biness. *Biness.* You not hear good, Big Shoot."

"Big Shot. Oh, I hear you. You're like a raven. You talk all the time. I should have taken Colonel Giap's offer and sold you to him."

We were in bed, naked. The ceiling fan slowly stirred the morning's humidity. A lizard the size of an iguana crouched on the balcony railing outside waiting for flies and playing voyeur through the glass doors. Brigette propped herself in bed on one elbow. The sheet fell away from her small, upright breasts. The nipples were dark, the color of her lips. When her face with the delicate scar across its nose went serious, she resembled one of those Oriental dolls that cried real tears.

"You not sell me, Big Shoot Mike. I too good to you in bed. Where you find 'nother girl like Brigette, for goo'ness sake?"

"If I weren't so kindhearted, you'd be gone on the next offer."

"Biness. Biness for you, biness for Brigette Nguyen. I sell *you.* You forty year old. You old, wore out. I trade you on new model. Just like America men do."

She was a dazzling creature when she giggled.

"Big Shoot, Mike, Brigette find 'nother paramour when you go to you wife in 'Nited States. Girl must be— how you speak it?—*practical?* Yes, practical, for goo'ness sake."

Even if I weren't already married back in the States, Brigette would be just another slanteye brought home from a foreign war. They were all right to have over here, even delightful, but they never worked out back home. So like she said, it was *biness* while it lasted. You had to be *practical,* for goo'ness sake.

I didn't tell her I was due for reassignment back to the World, maybe even as chief of the Chicago office. I wanted our *biness* to last until I hopped aboard the bird homeward bound.

Anyhow, I'd face that when it came up. At the INS office I ripped the piece on snipers out of the old Royal typewriter with a ratchet sound and handed it to Hank Baylor. Hank was INS Bureau Chief. The Bureau wasn't much, not like the AP or UPI. It was just one room on the second floor of the old French Ministry Building. There was Baylor and Tom Stoud and me and a pimply-faced teenager named Carl from Duluth, Minnesota. Carl answered the telephone and wrote heads and kept his journal and told the B-girls on Duc Phon that he was a war correspondent. I could never remember Carl's last name, but it didn't matter. Everybody who knew him got to calling him Carl Can't, as in "Carl can't do shit."

Baylor read. He said, "Good piece. Give it to Carl to headline, then wire it. What about this Able kid?"

"He'll die," I said. See what I mean, cynical? "Haven't you seen *High Noon?* Some gook with a faster gun and a truer aim will blow him out from underneath his *Semper fidelis.*"

Baylor tapped a pencil eraser against his front teeth. He had the greatest handlebar I'd ever seen. My mustache ran straight across the upper lip and blunted off at the corners of my mouth.

"Follow that kid for a while," Baylor said. "Let's see what happens."

"What do you want? His obituary?"

Baylor strolled across the closet we all shared with our desks. He gazed out the window. He stood to one side of it though, a habit we had all acquired.

"The Top Stick angle will appeal to the folks back home," he said. "Mom and Pop and Sister Sarah on the old farm need a hero."

"Even if he dies?"

"Especially if he dies. Dead heroes are the best kind."

This war did seem to have a shortage of heroes.

5

I THOUGHT I'D GIVE DOG A COUPLE OF WEEKS AND IF HE WASN'T dead by then I'd catch a Huey flight back out to Hill 55 and see if he, like Deke the Geek, had made his first kill. In the meantime, Operation Cedar Falls started. About thirty thousand U.S. troops flooded Binh Duong Province to root out a reported enemy stronghold near the Cambodian border. It had all the earmarks of a big operation, the kind that generated Pulitzers. Aircraft started bombing hamlets and dumping herbicides on rice fields and jungle.

Baylor told me to take Carl Can't with me; he and Stoud were going to Khe Sanh.

"That little shithead?"

Baylor grinned. "He can carry your camera bag."

"I'll carry your camera bag," Carl Can't said, eager for his big chance.

"You got a pimple on your nose," I said. "Go mash the sonofabitch."

You couldn't hurt Carl's feelings.

"You won't be sorry for taking me, Mike. You'll see."

"Just don't do anything unless I tell you to."

"Mike, I'll be the best partner you ever had. I want to learn everything I can."

"Yeah."

"You'll see, Mike."

I caught a pedicab to the hotel and shoved extra underwear, a razor and toothbrush, and a fresh set of camouflage jungle utilities into my camouflage day pack. I loaded up on film and made sure both SLRs were working. I slipped on my armband with Press written on it in both English and Vietnamese. Brigette watched, her lower lip trembling.

"Famous news writer dangerous biness," she said.

"*Business.* I'm not famous."

"You famous, for goo'ness sake. Ask people. Everybody know Mr. Mike Kragel, paramour of Miss Brigette Nguyen."

I grinned. Sometimes she was like a child.

"Mike?"

"No," I said.

"Don't say no till you know what I ask."

"You always ask. Judy Wong can find her own paramour."

You couldn't help laughing when her dark eyes popped wide.

"Mike, please? When you in Saigon you see other famous news writers from Associate Press. You think Judy Wong pretty, yes?"

"Judy Wong is very attractive."

"Well. Not pretty like me, but pretty. Judy Wong *deserve*

big shoot paramour, for goo'ness sake. Please, Mike? Tell big shoots Judy Wong pretty, good in bed, and she most loyal too. Just like me. Good biness girl. Okay, Mike?"

"Brigette . . . ?"

"Please, Mike?"

I gave in. "You never know."

She grabbed me and kissed me and pressed her firm body hard against me.

"Promise me you be careful, Big Shoot Mike," she whispered. "Brigette Nguyen not want do biness with nobody else."

I picked up Carl Can't at the office on my way to the airfield where a C-130 Hercules was waiting to fly correspondents to Saigon. It was that kind of war; the military went out of its way to get good press back home. I tossed Carl my canvas bag full of photo gear and other equipment and led the way down the narrow steps to where I left a pedicab waiting in the street. Carl Can't stumbled on the stairs and ended up at the bottom in a tangle of skinny arms and legs. I rolled my eyes and jerked him to his feet and took my camera bag back. He whimpered like a whipped alley cur.

"Shithead."

But I relinquished the camera bag again. Carl clutched it and wagged like a puppy and heeled. When I stopped suddenly, he ran up my legs, then backed off and grinned sheepishly.

"Walk three steps behind me," I instructed.

"Even when we get to where they're fighting?"

"Especially when they're fighting."

"Mike?"

"What now, Carl?"

He didn't say anything.

The C-130 engines were already revving when we got to the airfield. The airplane's back ramp was down on the tarmac and about a dozen men in various mixtures of fatigue uniforms were proving their credentials to an air force liaison officer. They were shouting at each other above the engine roar and rechecking equipment. I recognized Horton and Johnson from AP, Whipple from *Time,* and a few others from *Newsday* and *Commentary.*

"Mike?"

"Goddamnit, Carl."

"Mike, I don't want to be afraid."

I looked at him. He was already afraid.

"I just can't be a coward," he said, whining, and it grated on me. But he was so damned pitiful that I gave in a little and slapped him on his bony shoulder. I hadn't realized before how small and young he was; he looked about as young as the kid sniper, Dog.

This was a war of kids.

"Everybody's afraid sometimes, Carl," I said.

"Even you, Mike?"

I looked at him. "Let's catch that goddamn plane before we miss it."

His face beamed with sudden relief. "Yes, sir, Mike. Thanks, Mike."

We sprinted across the boiling tarmac, Carl Can't keeping a respectful three steps behind, just like I told him, our backpacks and camera bag flapping. The tail ramp was already starting up. The liaison officer recognized me and spoke into his helmet mike. The ramp froze.

"Going on another one, huh, Mike?" he said as Carl and I jumped for the ramp.

"Back into the valley of the shadow, Bobby."

I dropped into the webbing next to Horton from AP. Carl Can't's eyes were bugged out and dark. I showed him how to belt in. The plane vibrated and inched forward. There was no insulation in the aircraft, except gray pads to protect some of the hydraulics. It was so noisy you had to thrust your faces close together to talk.

Horton thrust his face into mine. He wore a trimmed gray beard that always smelled sour like garlic and Korean *kimshi.* He was living in Da Nang with this cunt from Inchon.

"Who's your cherry boy?" Horton shouted as the plane started its runout, engines throbbing.

I introduced Horton and Carl. Carl was gripping the bar on the forward edge of the webbing. He let go to shake hands quickly across me, then grabbed the bar again. Horton laughed. Carl watched wide-eyed the line of grunts strapped into the opposite webbing. Some of them, the old-timers, were already asleep. The FNGs—Fuckin' New Guys—were as wide-eyed and staring as Carl.

"Mike, this is the beginning of the end," Horton shouted.

"What're you talking about?"

"The war. I predict this is the last year. We're winning."

"Shit we're winning," I said.

"I understand we're going through them at Binh Duong like a dose of salts through a goose. Uncle Ho's finally coming out to fight and our boys are kicking ass. It's Katy bar the door."

"You AP hotshots speak in cliches just like you write."

"Mike, know what's wrong with you? You're cynical."

I knew that.

"These little people can't stand up to a modern superpower like the United States," he went on, still shouting. "I believe LBJ when he says we'll have the boys home for Christmas."

"He said that last year too."

"That was when the VC were sneaking around shooting from ambush. Now they're trying to match us man on man."

I thought of Captain Lange and his snipers. "Now *we're* sneaking around shooting *them* from ambush."

"What? What did you say?"

"It's a fucked-up war," I said.

There was a standard rejoinder for that. Horton came back with it, grinning, "It ain't much of a war, but it's the only one we got."

It was too much strain to keep the conversation going above the engine roar. I dropped my chin on my chest and closed my eyes.

Carl shouted into my other ear. "How can you do that?"

"What?" I kept my eyes closed. He still hadn't mashed the pimple on his nose.

"How can you sleep when we're about to . . . you know . . ."

"About to what, Carl? Die? Go to sleep, Carl."

The crew chief said we received ground sniper fire on final approach into Saigon. He seemed upset. You expected sniper fire at Da Nang, but not at Saigon.

At the AP motor pool I persuaded Horton to check out a jeep to me and charge it to the INS account.

"Goddamnit, Mike. It's my ass if you get bullet holes in it."

"I'll treat it better'n my granny does her nineteen fifty-seven DeSoto."

"Maybe I should go along to make sure."

I jerked a thumb at Carl. "I already have one cherry."

"I don't know why I even bother with you, Kragel."

"Drop by the French Fuck some night when we get back and I'll repay you. I know this gorgeous cunt you can trade in ol' Kim Kimshi for."

He ignored it. I understood he was going to marry his slanteye and take her Stateside. That was a mistake.

"Kragel, I don't see why you don't go in the chopper pool with the rest of us," Horton complained. "It's suicide to try to reach the fighting in a jeep. The road's probably blocked. I ought to have my head examined for giving you a jeep."

"I'm leaving you my granny's DeSoto for collateral."

Carl Can't tossed our gear into the open backseat and grabbed his seat and hung on. I popped the clutch and shot out into the traffic on Tu Do Street, the main thoroughfare through the capital. It was jammed and noisy with bicycles and pedicabs and motorbikes and carts and small autos, but there were signs, too, of the fighting going on in the Iron Triangle north of Saigon. Refugees looked battered and weary and out of place in their peasant garb.

One peasant blocked traffic with his water buffalo. The honking was driving the beast insane. It whipped around and around hooking with its massive horns. It wounded a Peugeot and two Renaults and a Honda scooter and had a black marketeer trapped in the gutter before a policeman shot it with a .45 Thompson. A bunch of motorists jumped from their vehicles and dragged the animal out of the street, leaving a bright wide streak of blood. The traffic resumed while the peasant who owned the buffalo sat on the carcass and cried into his hands.

Like Da Nang with its Dog Patch, the outskirts of Saigon had an almost medieval cast to it from all the refugees shunted into makeshift camps. The squalid shanties with their beggars and hawkers—*everything* was for sale—were like fresh scabs on a burn wound. Sewers bubbled with effluvia drained off the corruption. I caught Carl Can't trying to hold his breath. I laughed at him and whipped the wheel in time to avoid a kid chasing a squawking chicken.

I took the road out toward Bien Hoa. At first there was just a trickling of refugees fleeing the bombers and the ground fighting. Gradually the trickling became a stream, then a river, and then we barely made headway against a current of bicycles loaded with baggage, pushed by their owners, old trucks carrying pigs and chickens and kids, top-heavy wheelbarrows, pedestrians with everything they owned piled onto their bent backs, carts pulled by water buffalo.

There were many wounded, too, in dirty bandages, some still in shock. A blind woman had a bloody rag wrapped around her eyes; her husband led her with a piece of rope tied around her waist. A dazed prepubescent girl wandered along in the stream, carried by it. Her clothing had been burned off by white phosphorus, known as Willie Pete, in a bombing raid; some of the charred cloth still stuck to her blistered skin. Every few steps she paused to bleat like a goat.

"You drive," I snapped at Carl Can't.

I framed the girl in my lens. I recorded the blind woman on a rope. I went through a half-dozen rolls of black-and-white Tri-X and then started on Kodacolor. The automatic wind whirred.

A lot of journalists thought all there was to war was

combat troops and airplanes and the other machines of war trying their best to annihilate each other. But *this* was a face of war too, these players on the periphery of the fighting. The unusuals like these refugees, the peasants who tried to keep on with their lives, snipers like Dog and Bill Lange— they had always attracted me more than the generals and the campaigns and the search-and-destroy missions. The unusuals gave a human face to war.

I looked at Carl Can't. He sat hunched behind the wheel, gripping it tightly with both hands, looking straight ahead with a look like a deer caught in headlights. His pimply face was wet with tears. I turned away, back to the camera. The lens showed things that you ordinarily did not see. It also sterilized things in a way and kept them at a distance.

The jeep bogged down against the current. Humanity parted around us, like water around a boulder in a stream. We sat in the open jeep beneath the sun, our clothing turning dark from sweat while the river of flesh flowed. Once, several Vietnamese in black pajamas carrying AK assault rifles slipped by. They pretended to ignore us, and I didn't try to take their picture. Carl Can't looked the other way.

"M-Mike?"

The corner of his lips barely moved.

"Aren't . . . aren't they Vietcong? They'll shoot us, Mike."

"Don't panic, shithead. Mixing in with refugees is an old VC trick."

He still wouldn't even glance at them. "Are they gone, Mike? Are they?"

"Why the fuck did you ever come to Vietnam?" I asked in disgust.

He thought I really wanted to know. He took a deep breath when the VC vanished.

"My dad was a Marine in Korea," he said, "but the Marines wouldn't take me when I tried to join. I had a hernia. Every time I looked at Dad I saw he was ashamed of me, and I was ashamed of myself. So . . ."

"Carl, no foxhole confessions, okay? We got a job to do."

"Sorry, Mike. I didn't mean anything."

"Just fucking drive this thing," I said. "I want to reach Bien Hoa before dark. Those cocksuckers in black won't bother us as long as the sun's up, but they'll goddamn sure cut our throats after dark if they can."

I saw that reassured Carl Can't immeasurably.

I ran point, parting the waves by thrashing in front of me with a long stick, while Carl Can't crept the jeep along in my wake. We couldn't get off the road. Diked rice paddies filled with water snugged against both sides. Where there wasn't rice, there was jungle.

"Mike, can we make it before dark?" Carl called out once in his reedy voice.

I ignored him. Sweat burned my eyes. It was already midafternoon. The stream of refugees gave no signs of slacking off.

Events occur in war which can immeasurably alter plans and lives. When I first spotted the sun glinting off the metal skin of the two warplanes swooping above a distant mountain, I gave them no more than a brief glance. I saw they were WWII AD-type fighters—each a stocky prop job with a cockpit and wings mounted to a giant recip engine—that the U.S. had probably delivered to the ARVN to fly against the commies. Taking a break from parting the waves to drink water and wipe sweat, I watched idly as the lead plane chandelled off the mountaintop and started losing altitude. It lined up on the road choked with Vietnamese. Its engine throbbed, pulsating in threatening waves out of the burning afternoon sky.

It didn't occur to me what was happening until the refugees stampeded in panic. They dropped their loads and abandoned bicycles, wheelbarrows, and other vehicles to splash headforth into the rice paddies. They were trampling each other.

Carl stared in confusion. I dived for the side of the road. While mixing in with refugees was an old VC trick, strafing the refugees in order to discourage the VC was an old ARVN trick. Their American Air Force advisers discouraged it, but the ARVN did it anyhow.

I looked up and back from where I sought cover. Carl Can't still sat behind the wheel of the jeep, as though mesmerized by the sight of the plane bearing toward him. It wasn't a hundred feet above the earth. It grew rapidly larger and more threatening. Its wing guns opened up on the crowded road, exploding a swath of blood and flesh and bone.

"Carl Can't! You shithead!"

I lunged for Carl. An instant after I yanked him from the jeep and threw him to the ground and dropped beside him, the jeep vibrated like it had been shot with a bolt of lightning. Machine-gun bullets riddled it, left it smoking. The passing AD was so low it seemed to suck my breath away. My clothing flapped in its wind. Through the crook of my elbow I glimpsed the Vietnamese pilot's face.

Then I heard screams and the wailing of the wounded.

The second plane would be making its run. We had to get the hell away from the road. I reached out for Carl Can't. Carl Can't was already up and going. But he was going the wrong way.

At first I thought it was blind terror. He was running toward the center of the road. Then I saw a dark peasant cloth in shreds, bright with blood in the sunshine. The body was writhing in horrible pain. The young girl was screaming. It appeared one of her legs had been ripped off at midthigh. Her cone hat lay near her, the straw ripped like a village hootch fragged by grenades.

Who could figure it? Carl Can't had been scared shitless since we caught the C-130 at Da Nang, and now here he was risking his ass for a gook girl.

The drumming of the second plane's engine drowned out my cry of warning.

Carl was bent over the wounded girl, trying to pick her up. She was fighting him, mad from the pain.

I bolted toward him.

As I dived for Carl, a trail of bullets chewed the earth

around us; we were the vortex of a vicious storm of metal and dust and smoke. I snatched Carl and rolled with him away from the Vietnamese girl. The bullets finished her off. I rolled with Carl, shouting at him for being such a shithead. I had him by the chin and throat, dragging him, although the plane had already sucked by.

I smelled the metallic odor of fresh blood.

My hands were wet and warm and sticky.

I stopped and stared at Carl. He was bloody from the crotch up. His arm twisted oddly backward so that his hand seemed to be gripping the back of his neck. A shard of bone protruded from the skin above his elbow.

"M-M-Mike . . ." Carl stuttered weakly.

"Goddamn you, Carl Can't!" I raged, furious at him for getting shot.

How many times had I told this shithead that journalists were *observers?*

I glanced up wildly, scanning the sky for more airplanes, but the sky was clear and pale blue and empty.

"M-Mike . . . I couldn't let her . . . Not again . . ."

"Not *again?* What are you talking about? Damn you, you shithead, why did you have to do *this?*"

A shadow fell over where I was kneeling next to the wounded boy.

"He's a shithead, sir, and intent on getting himself killed," a strangely familiar voice said. "But we'd better stop the bleeding. The planes won't be back."

Lance Cpl. Johnny Able stood looking calmly down on us, his sniper rifle hanging from one hand. A second American Marine in jungle utilities materialized behind him.

"We've been watching you," Dog said. "From over there."

He pointed to a stand of green jungle beyond the nearest rice paddy.

"He tried to save a gook cunt," I said in frustration.

Dog looked long at Carl Can't's face. "Yes," he said.

Some peasants were gathered around the dead girl keening and gnashing their teeth. Similar scenes were being enacted all up and down the road. Almost immediately, the others started to move again, accepting this latest blow as stoically as they accepted everything else in this war. They were used to it.

How could anybody get used to this shit?

6

I LOOKED AWAY FROM CARL CAN'T'S EYES, THEY WERE FILLED with such terror of dying. Dog and I splinted Carl's arm in place with his hand still gripping the back of his neck. Some of his guts bubbled out through perforations in his belly.

Dog stood so that he shaded Carl's face. I knew what he was thinking. I had seen men die too. Frothy blood bubbled to Carl's lips. He stared at Dog's face. He kept burbling and the fingers of his good hand lifted off the ground. They were smeared with blood already dried. They tried to point at Dog.

Dog stared calmly back at him.

"He's trying to say something, sir," Dog said.

I wet Carl's intestines with water from my canteen and wrapped his torso with strips torn from my T-shirt, then wet them too. Carl moaned deep in his throat, burbling, trying to speak. He reeked with the odor of stuff leaking from his guts.

"He your buddy?" Dog asked politely.

"We're out of the same office."

"They always want to talk when they're dying," he said. "Sir, it's like they have to get everything said before it's too late."

I glanced up at his face.

"But by then," he finished, "it's already too late."

I grunted. "You're a cheerful bastard."

I couldn't tell if he was smiling.

"This is a cheerful place," he said, and it was almost like he meant it *was* cheerful.

"Christ," I muttered and finished with Carl's bandages.

The two Marines helped me carry Carl to the shade of the disabled jeep, jostling through the refugees, while I thought of what to do next. The grunt with Dog said they broke their PRC-25 radio earlier that morning when the snipers were setting up on the roads for exfiltrating VC.

I squatted in the shade at Carl's feet to think. The other Marine—Sgt. Roger Norman, he said, one of Lange's sniper instructors acting as Dog's spotter—rested with his back against the jeep's front wheel. He packed chewing tobacco into his jaw. Shattered glass from the jeep's windscreen lay on the ground around him, reflecting the sun like mica. Horton would be pissed about his jeep.

Norman chewed and spat a gob and sprayed the passing legs of the Vietnamese. Dog remained standing. He appeared relaxed, but his restless eyes constantly scanned. The scoped Winchester hung from his left arm like an appendage. He was wearing twin .45 pistols in holsters slung low, gunfighter style, one on each side of his web gear. His patrol cap shaded his eyes like before, but, also like before, his eyes pierced the shadows like pale ice.

"None of this shit touches you?" I asked, irritated because I was letting it touch me.

The pale eyes shifted to me. "I don't let it interfere with my job, sir."

I snorted. "And how's the job going? Got your hundred kills yet, Top Stick?"

The sarcasm was unwarranted, but Dog didn't seem to notice.

"I'll get there," he said.

I wouldn't let it go.

"Maybe you'll end up gut-shot instead like this poor sorry sonofabitch."

Those ice-pale eyes again. "Maybe."

When he turned slightly I caught sight of tiny bloody objects, like folds of skin, hanging from his web belt on a piece of parachute shroud line. They didn't register.

"Forget it, kid," I said. "It's not been a day I'd write home about."

He shrugged casually. "At least you have someone to write home to."

Just for a moment I thought I glimpsed something human in the kid, some sadness, some nostalgia, *something*, but then it was gone. Instead, there was that smile that wasn't as his eyes lifted to gauge the sun.

"You don't want to be here when night comes, sir," he said. "Charlie is as thick as lice on a cur out here."

I was sweating. I wondered how long it would take Carl to die. I couldn't walk back to Saigon carrying him, and I couldn't leave him.

Sometimes Carl's eyes almost closed as he fought unconsciousness. Then they sprang wide again, staring at Dog, continuing their vigil. It was like Carl had fixated on the kid.

"What's his name?" Sergeant Norman asked from his place by the jeep's front wheel.

"Carl."

Norman waited for me to go on. It occurred to me that a man ought to at least remember a dying man's name. It was bad enough to die, but to die unknown to those around you, among strangers as it were, that was something obscene. Carl the unknown war correspondent. He wasn't even that. He was just a kid.

"We call him Carl Can't," I said, and looked away.

The sun made shimmers on the water in the rice fields. The new green rice was starting to shoot up. The refugees kept floating by, like silent ghosts.

"Do you know him, Dog?" Norman asked. "He keeps staring at you."

Dog shrugged. "Dying men do weird things."

I couldn't resist another poke at him. "You've seen plenty of dying men, Top Stick?"

Dog shrugged again. He refused to take the bait. For all

the expression his face registered he might have been a dropout back on the block hanging out.

Sergeant Norman spat tobacco juice at passing tire tread sandals. He grunted. "Saw two today. Show him, Dog."

Dog merely stood there with his pale eyes reflecting the equally pale sky. He shifted slightly when he felt my eyes prying for the folds of skin on his parachute cord.

I realized what they were.

"It's a way of keeping count," Dog explained patiently. "Take the total number of ears and divide by two. That's confirmation enough for any count."

I couldn't help asking. "How many?"

"Six."

"He got two kills today. Four ears," Sergeant Norman said, neither approval nor disapproval in his tone. "He collected the other two an hour after the first time he went out. The kid's a natural."

I pictured Dog the day I took his photo on Hill 55—peering down the scoped barrel of his Winchester. I watched him now, waiting to read some emotion in his face, some reaction to what he had done today. Hard as I searched, however, I saw nothing in him past his eyes.

I didn't understand this kid.

The kid looked at me. I thought he was smiling.

"'There is no hunting like the hunting of man,'" he quoted, "'and those who have hunted armed men long enough and liked it, never care for anything else thereafter.'"

"Hemingway," I said. "I know. Ol' Dog reads."

"Ernest understood what it was like. To kill, I mean, sir."

The journalist in me wanted to continue this, to probe this kid's cold psyche, but Carl Can't interrupted. Gurgling like a sick baby, he tried to reach Dog with the claw of his remaining good arm.

"What're you going to do with him?" Norman asked.

I had to do something. Maybe Carl would live if I could figure out how to get him back to Saigon and the military hospital.

* * *

My searching gaze happened to fix upon an ancient Mercedes truck working its way very slowly forward with the human stream. Its flatbed was piled high with women in cone hats and their children and bundles. Legs protruded everywhere from the truck like quills from a porcupine. Another dozen children rode on the fenders and hood, all but obstructing the graybeard driver's vision.

"The Saigon Express," I murmured.

I jumped up and shoved my way through the Vietnamese and held my arms up in front of the rattling old truck. Papa-san understood English, but he pretended not to know what I wanted. I motioned for the Marines to bring Carl. They appeared from behind the wrecked jeep, Dog carrying Carl's feet and Norman supporting the shoulders. Carl kicked feebly, trying to get free. A thin trickle of blood dripped from his arm.

Papa-san started wailing in a thin singsong voice. "No more room, GI. No more room. Numbah ten, GI. We go, we go."

It wouldn't do any good to argue.

"Give me your fucking pistol," I told Dog.

I cocked the .45 and pointed it at the driver's head. Papa-san stared ahead, but the passengers on the flatbed cleared a place for Carl. That meant several had to get off and walk. The Marines hoisted Carl onto the truck and I climbed on behind. The other passengers crowded toward the front and onto the truck cab from where they dispassionately watched the crazy Americans. I cushioned Carl's head on my thighs. The truck inched forward with a scraping of gears.

"Keep the forty-five," Dog shouted.

I intended to.

"I'll bring it back," I called.

I kept the pistol clenched in my fist, just in case. The Marines left behind the truck turned and started to buck the current to reach the roadside, heading back into the rice paddies and jungles from which they had emerged. Carl's body trembled. He was trying to sit up, his eyes straining to maintain contact with the young sniper in the road. It took an extraordinary effort on his part for his head to spring off my legs. Words burst from his throat with a violent spewing of blood. The screech reached out like the slap of a sniper's bullet.

"It's you!"

Dog switched ends like a cat.

Carl was mad from the pain and from shock. His body relaxed and fell back.

"It's you."

His babbling made a froth on his lips. I looked from him to Dog standing behind the truck. Dog watched a moment, then he turned and with Norman forced his way through the refugees.

Those were the last words Carl Can't ever spoke. He died on the road to Saigon. I continued to hold his head in my lap, looking away, until it was a good way toward midnight and his body had stiffened so that when two MPs outside the embassy compound in Saigon lifted him off the old rattle-trap truck he hardly bent in the middle.

I wondered how it was that Carl Can't seemed to know Johnny Able.

7

MIKE KRAGEL DISPATCH, 3 OCT 67:

Vietnam (INS) — Yesterday, Carl Can't died a hero on the road to Bien Hoa in the Iron Triangle — and no one with him when he died knew his real name.

His name was Carl Anthony Dubose, twenty-one.

He listed his hometown as Duluth, Minnesota. A war correspondent for International News Service, he was the fifth newsman to have died in this war so far.

Everyone knew him as Carl Can't, a shy midwesterner from a U.S. Marine family. He elected to come to Vietnam anyhow when he was rejected for service in the armed forces because of physical reasons.

He had been in Vietnam four months.

Carl Can't was young and inexperienced in his trade. That earned him his nickname, as in "Carl can't do . . ."

Yesterday, Carl Can't tried.

Aircraft from the Republic of Vietnam, U.S. allies in this strange war, strafed a column of refugees fleeing bitter fighting that had erupted around Bien Hoa. The enemy often mingles with refugees to conceal his movements.

Eight people were known killed and an undetermined number wounded in the air attack on what were largely unarmed civilians.

One of the wounded was a Vietnamese girl of about fourteen. She lay in the open in the middle of the road when a second fighter aircraft roared down the stream of panicked refugees with its wing guns blazing.

Carl Anthony Dubose sprang from cover and raced across the road in an attempt to rescue the Vietnamese girl from certain death. He was cut down in his attempt.

Two U.S. Marine snipers were in the area blocking escape attempts by Vietcong trapped by elements of the 9th Marine Regiment. Lance Cpl. Johnny Able of Muskogee, Oklahoma, and Sgt. Roger Norman of Macon, Georgia, helped a second INS journalist load the critically wounded correspondent aboard a refugee truck crammed with Vietnamese. That was the only way left to get him to medical aid.

It took eight hours for the truck, slowed to a snail's pace on the road, to reach the outskirts of Saigon. By then, Carl Anthony Dubose was dead.

The Vietnamese girl also died.

But Carl Anthony Dubose tried.

INS Bureau Chief Hank Baylor cited him for heroism and valor. The Vietnamese government has also recommended him posthumously for the Vietnamese Cross of Gallantry.

His name on the citations will not read *Carl Can't*.

——————————— 8 ———

I WASN'T PARTICULARLY PROUD OF IT, BUT IT WAS A PART OF MY nature to procrastinate, to put off things that were disagreeable on the presumption they'd resolve themselves at the proper time and go away. Like, I kept putting off telling Brigette about my pending rotation Stateside. I likewise knew if I mentioned the divorce papers to her it would just further complicate matters.

I didn't like my life complicated.

The divorce papers from Sharon's Chicago lawyers, *Greed, Avarice, and Sloth*, arrived while I was getting Carl Can't's things together to send to his next of kin. I was going through his desk and the old army footlocker he kept underneath the bunk he slept on in a corner of the office. Baylor had allowed him to sleep there in exchange for his being available to answer the phones and the wire twenty-four hours a day.

Carl didn't leave much—a pitiful little pile of such as his wristwatch, some old letters, a girl's chain and locket with a photo of a plain-Jane in it, his wallet containing a wad of Vietnamese piasters, and a few other pieces of junk, including the journal he was always writing in. We called it his Great War Novel.

The mail came and Hank Baylor sorted it and dropped the letter in front of me. I looked at the envelope and knew what it was without opening it. Sharon had threatened it often enough. But knowing what it was, even expecting it, and then finding it had happened were different matters.

I hadn't left much back in Illinois, unless you counted Sharon, and she stopped writing me more than six months ago. I stopped writing her too. Twelve years of marriage, no kids, and what we'd had left gradually faded like the inked stamps that filled my passport.

I stared at the envelope and then cleared my throat of the sudden knot. I shoved the letter away, trying to be nonchalant, to let Baylor know none of this old shit the world dished out bothered me.

I had seen all the shit there was and lived through it.

I'd read the fine print later.

Baylor was still standing there.

I picked up Carl's wristwatch and wiped off a smear of dried blood. His family didn't need to see that.

I murmured, "The shithead didn't leave much, did he?"

"A ditty bagful," Baylor said. "That's about the most any of us gypsy types'll leave."

He just stood there.

"Trying to save a slant-eyed cunt," I said.

"Mike," Baylor said. "Mike, it's okay."

I splayed my hands on the desktop and looked at them. They felt like they were vibrating.

"Why the fuck shouldn't it be okay?"

The motherfucker got himself killed being stupid. The grunts said it all the time: *It don't mean nothing.* He was a shithead.

It don't mean nothing.

That was what I told Brigette when I got back to the Continental Palace after Carl Can't died. She was wearing a black silk dressing gown that sleeked out her gentle curves and made hollows where hollows ought to be and turned her eyes into large fluid ink spots. Most of the time you didn't notice the scar across the bridge of her nose and under one eye, but now I did because she started crying when she saw Carl's blood on my utilities. The blood was dark and crusty and dried, but Brigette murmured, "For goo'ness sake!" with feeling. She came and held me and cooed like she did and tried to rock me like she would a baby.

She was a living thing, and warm, and she smelled like a woman does when her hair is clean and has been in the sun.

"It don't mean nothing," I gasped into the long black hair and against her slender neck. "It don't mean nothing."

Her hands were all over me, feeling for injuries.

I burst out with it: "The stupid bastard went and got himself killed for no reason. He was a shithead, but he was a kid and he didn't have to do that."

"Baby-san, oh, baby-san," cooed Brigette, and I had never let Sharon talk to me like that.

It was like I couldn't get enough of her, of having something *alive* in my arms after Carl. I emptied my juices into her in a savage kind of lovemaking, as though taking it all out on her. But she took it and came back for more. All night even when we weren't making love I held onto her tightly and wouldn't let her turn out the light. When I finally slept and awoke and saw the lizard on the outside balcony catching the first rays of sun, Brigette had not slept. She was holding me close to the warmth of her naked body, watching me sleep.

She smiled. "For goo'ness sake," she said.

The night was over at last. I got up and shaved and showered and stepped out the French doors onto the balcony and looked down into Duc Phon Street already crowded with vendor carts, boom-boom girls, kids and bicycles, and GIs and pretty Vietnamese women on motorbikes. Brigette slipped up beside me and interlaced her fingers in mine.

"Last night," she said, "not biness, Mike. Last night come from heart."

Her face wore an earnest expression. She patted her breast.

"From heart," she said. "For goo'ness sake, Mike, you not notice Brigette have big heart? Brigette have heart big enough for both you and me."

I wouldn't look at her. I was ashamed of how much I had let myself need her last night. You couldn't let yourself need people, especially in war. Life was so goddamn uncertain.

"I've got work to do, Brigette," I said, breaking away from her.

It don't mean nothing.

At the office Baylor kept standing by my desk.

"Let's mosey over to the French Fuck and I'll spring for a cool one," he said.

"Stoud's out. Who'll watch the office?"

"Screw it for now. We'll get us another boy Friday."

"Let me get Carl's stuff together first."

Carl had always said he was from Duluth, Minnesota. That was why it surprised me when I rifled his W-2 and insurance forms from the files and started to write his folks' address on the brown package that was all that remained of Carl Can't. I frowned, thinking, as I addressed the package to Mr. and Mrs. Frank Dubose, 106 Flint Circle, Vinita, Oklahoma.

"Nobody ever listened to Carl," Baylor said, rolling the ends of his handlebar mustache in that unconscious habit he had. "It does seem to me though that he said he was born in Duluth but his folks moved somewhere else when he was about ten or eleven. I guess maybe he grew up an Okie."

"I wonder how close Vinita is to Muskogee."

"My plane laid over in Tulsa once, but I've never even heard of Vinita. It's probably some little crossroads of three or four Podunks with some inbred hillbillies. Why?"

"Nothing. I'll take that drink now."

We started out of the office, the package underneath my arm.

"Aren't you going to at least open your mail?" Baylor asked, nodding at the lawyers' letter I left on the desk.

"I'll wait until some night when I'm drunk."

"That bad? Sharon?"

"I guess the bitch is going ahead with the divorce. Fuck her."

9

EVEN ON MY COLLEGE NEWSPAPER, THE ILLINOIS STATE *Clarion,* I had had a second sense for a good news story. Someone would drop a careless word or I would pick up some gossip at the cafeteria or at one of the pubs on The Strip the college bunch frequented and things would start clicking and clicking until I put it together. Old Prof Beardsley always said I'd either get a Pulitzer for investigative reporting or I'd end up dead from sticking my nose where it shouldn't be stuck.

"I'm going to be a novelist," I told him.

"You're a muckraker," he said, snickering. "You have that something all good muckrakers have. Ol' William Randolph Hearst had it. You always have to see what's on the back side of the human face. The dark side."

Anyhow, something was clicking and clicking. It kept me from worrying about the divorce or having to tell Brigette I was leaving. I couldn't help pondering Carl Can't's fixation on the kid sniper when Carl was dying. That both turned out to be from Oklahoma seemed more than a coincidence.

I sent word through a chopper pilot I knew out to Capt. Bill Lange on Hill 55 that I'd buy him lunch the next time business or pleasure called him to Da Nang. I wanted to ask him some more questions about Dog. Brigette immediately insisted she and Judy Wong be included in the date. I mounted a token resistance, just to see to what depths

Brigette would go for her friend, then laughingly relented when she, "for goo'ness sake," promised to massage my back every night for a whole month.

I kept busy in the meantime with Sharon's divorce papers, a sortie out to a Special Forces "A" Camp where Stone-Age Montagnards were battling any Vietnamese, North or South, who crossed their jungle path, and in correspondence with an old college and former INS buddy turned lawyer in Chicago. Dennis Fry warned me that I ought to arrange to come home for the divorce if I wanted to save my pension and a little parcel of land I owned on the Kankakee River that I was holding for retirement. Sharon had a prosperous real estate business of her own, but she was still asking in the divorce for *everything*.

Who could figure them? They said they loved you, and maybe they did, but then they went ripping and tearing for your balls and throat.

I shoved the divorce thing to the back of my mind and the back of my desk until I could concentrate on it and make a decision. I didn't think I'd miss Carl Can't, he had been such a thin shadow around the office, but once the little shithead was gone and I had to write my own heads and get my own coffee and attend the Five O'Clock Follies, the news briefings at the airbase, I realized how much he had always done. A time or two I started to call his folks, just to talk—someone who lived Carl's last minutes with him ought to reach out and touch them—but I kept putting it off.

I had almost forgotten about my invitation to Captain Lange until he appeared at the office one morning in pressed jungle utilities.

"You're not getting out of lunch this easily, Mike. The best beer and the best French cuisine in Da Nang. Wasn't that what you said, or are you welching?"

Lange had a simple honesty in his bulldog face that I liked. I gripped his hand as firmly as he gripped mine.

"Bill, my man, not only am I not welching, I'm going to

arrange for the prettiest dinner companion you've ever had."

"Round eye or slanteye?"

"Does it matter? The opening that counts runs the same way in all of them."

Lange grinned around his ever-present cigar. "I haven't been with a woman in so long I'd be overjoyed if she's under ninety and can get from her wheelchair to the bed under her own steam."

After I managed to get through to Brigette on the telephone, she became so excited that she ran her words together. She promised to dash out immediately and find Judy Wong and they'd get dressed.

"Cap'n Lange, he officer? Very, very good, Mike. You do good. He make fine paramour for Judy Wong."

"Brigette! Brigette, we're on our way over."

"Mike, for goo'ness sake, no dare see Judy Wong and me before we dress."

"It's just for lunch, Brigette."

"I not want new paramour of Judy Wong see her until she stunning."

"He's not her paramour," I protested.

"Wait till he see Judy Wong."

I sighed. What the hell.

"Will Judy be as stunning as you?" I teased.

"No Da Nang lady stunning like Brigette Nguyen, for goo'ness sake. Not even Judy Wong."

"The most stunning to ever leave the city of Hue?"

"Yes, for goo'ness sake."

"Okay, Brigette. We'll wait for you downstairs in the French Fuck."

"Mike, lady not meet gen'lemen in place call French Fook."

"Brigette, we'll meet you in the *lounge*."

I hailed a pedicab in the street. On the way over to the French Fuck in the little man-powered vehicle, Lange smoked a cigar and talked about his snipers and the war and I briefly filled him in on what happened on the road to Bien

Hoa. I gave him Dog's .45 to return and he stuffed it in the back band of his trousers, along with his own pistol.

At the French Fuck something explosive called a Singapore Sling turned into three or four while we waited for Brigette and Judy Wong. The lounge was a pleasant place though. Heavy stucco walls beat back the tropical heat while slow-turning ceiling fans kept the air from getting stale. The white-coated dink barman was a friend of Judy Wong's and always went out of his way for me, but I still suspected him of being a VC spy. But what the hell. If the truth were known, half the boom-boom girls and bartenders in Da Nang and Saigon were spies. What mattered was they served you well and you kept your mouth shut around them.

Lange and I talked. He said he had had Dog transferred to the sniper platoon as permanent party.

"The kid's a natural at the business," he said.

I recalled the ears on his belt.

"He's dead set on duplicating or exceeding everything Pablo Rhoades accomplished as a sniper," Lange said, smoking. "Were you in-country, Mike, when Pablo and his spotter wiped out the company of NVA recruits in Elephant Valley? They pinned 'em down in an open rice field for five days and knocked 'em off one by one."

Lange said Lance Cpl. Johnny Able had had his own Elephant Valley. Lange pieced together the story from After Action reports and from what Dog's spotter, the same Sgt. Roger Norman from the road, had told him.

10

THE DINKS WERE BUSY AND PICKING UP THEIR ACTIVITY ALONG
the network of supply trails generally lumped together
under the one designation—the Ho Chi Minh Trail. B-52s
wiped out a seventy-bicycle convoy loaded with rice and
bullets north of Hue, the ancient capital. Horton at AP, who
was still harping about his lost jeep, was correct when he
said the NVA were feeding more regular soldiers into the
fight to beef up the VC guerrilla fighters. I Corps reported
more than thirty contacts with NVA regulars during the
previous month. Even company-size GI patrols were assured of contact on operations that had formerly been
nothing but long walks in the sun. Intel reported concentra-
tions of NVA in Cambodia along the border, waiting.

The trails that supplied the enemy were like rat tunnels
through the jungle. Vietcong forced the villagers along the
routes to maintain a latticework of live vegetation above
trails often wide enough to handle trucks and tanks and still
remain unseen even from low helicopter surveillance. When
B-52s dropped defoliants in some of the valleys, turning the
dark green of the forests into a pale, gaseous mist, the enemy
simply burrowed their tunnels elsewhere. The only way to
find and interdict the supply network was by ground troops.
Or . . .

"Snipers," said Capt. Bill Lange.

A gathering of marine brigade and battalion commanders
in a smoky operations tent at the Da Nang air base watched
as the stocky sniper commander drew a cigar across his

upper lip, savoring the rich dark aroma. His eyes raked the high-ranking officers.

"If I had *one company* of experienced snipers," Lange continued, "and the authority to use it properly in support of your infantry operations on the Ho Chi Minh Trail, I could bottle up enemy supplies and reinforcements from now until the Second Coming."

He lit his cigar, his cheeks working like bellows.

"Gentlemen, for the past year we've been training snipers for you. Most of them we send back to your units to become the eyes, ears, and trigger finger for the battalion commander. Some we've built into a platoon—actually a reinforced squad—that can be used upon request by any commander in I Corps. These snipers, gentlemen, are the most effective and cost-efficient weapon on the battlefield. Gentlemen, we must learn to use them."

Everyone had his pet formula for winning the war. Lange's was snipers. Everybody knew it. Col. "Stick" Steinke, commander of the Two Nine, got up to leave. His chair scooted into the legs of the officer behind him. A thin sheen of sweat glistened red on his face. Everyone knew his formula too. Snipers didn't win wars. Troops did. Firepower did. Bomb the gooks' asses back to the Stone Age. *That* won wars, not a handful of Daniel Boones playing at big game hunting.

"Fuck this shit," the colonel snapped.

Instant silence descended, followed by the uneasy scuffling of boots on the dirt floor, the uncomfortable clearing of throats. Lange realized that the others, officers being officers and natural suck asses, would rally around whoever had the most weight on his collar. He also realized that if he couldn't get past brigade level, his proposal to consolidate snipers into a full company under his command would never reach General Westmoreland.

Lange doggedly pursued his quest. "If you want to strike fear into the little peoples' hearts," he persisted, "if you want to make 'em cautious, if you want to slow down infiltration from the North, if you want to make the enemy travel at night when progress is slower and more hazardous across the mountain passes, then the answer is to sic snipers on 'em. You let the enemy know like the Spanish partisans did Napoleon that nowhere along the supply line is he safe from the crack of a hidden rifle. *That's* the way to stop the infiltration of supplies and troops—by the judicious use of the most deadly weapon in Vietnam. Snipers, gentlemen. Snipers."

Lange was always harping on that. Colonel Steinke watched, a scowl slashed across his broad Hun's face with its blunted features.

"Your prima donnas, Captain," he scoffed. "They kill a gook now and then and—"

Lange cut him off.

"My *reinforced squad,* sir, killed more Victor Charlies last month than your entire battalion."

The colonel was a man hewn large, an Annapolis man being contradicted by a Mustanger captain who had started off as a goddamned *private.* Steinke glared.

"Screw your body count, Captain!" he roared. "Body count doesn't mean squat when it's collected one or two at a time all over the AO. Your little gunfighters and their boasting about getting a hundred kills might get headlines, but they aren't dog shit in winning this war. We can cut those trails with troops, Captain. Bomb the little yellow bastards until their balls fall off and then send in *real* troops and mop them up. This is *war,* Captain. This isn't Dodge City or the OK Corral. A *company* of snipers! I'd as soon support an ARVN sweep on Hanoi."

Lange saw his argument smoking toward earth.

"Steinke is one stubborn sonofabitch," the One Nine commander apologized to Lange after the meeting broke up, "but he's tough and the higher brass listens to him. He makes more enemy contact than any other commander in I Corps."

"He also has the highest casualty rate. Snipers can help save lives and accomplish the mission at the same time."

"You're preaching to the choir, Bill. I'm too short to do anything anyhow. In three weeks I'm out of here and back to Camp Pendleton. I'm history."

Lange bit his cigar almost in half.

"That's why we won't win this fucking war by Christmas, or next Christmas either," he growled. "Everybody does his year and leaves. There's no commitment to victory. Officers thinking of their careers punch their tickets and *di-di* out of here. Kissing ass instead of kicking ass."

That was the way it was. Lange cut his staff, leaving only enough instructors on Hill 55 to train the sniper students who trickled in from the battalions. The rest of his platoon he hurled against the infiltration routes from the North. The ring of ears on Cpl. Johnny Able's belt grew. He seemed tireless in his obsession. He volunteered for every mission while the other snipers grew weary and less ambitious. They took to drawing straws to determine who *had* to go out with Dog. Even Sergeant Norman, who alone among the snipers had developed at least a tolerance for Dog's eccentricities, complained to his skipper.

"He gives me the fucking creeps, Cap'n. When we're out there, it's like I'm with an evil spirit or something. Maybe I'm supposed to be on watch when we're in a hide and he's supposed to be sleeping or resting, but he ain't, Skipper. He's just sitting there in the dark and you can feel his eyes. He don't think about eating or sleeping or pussy. I don't even think he shits. All he lives for is to shoot gooks. One hundred kills won't be enough even if he lives long enough to get them. Then he'll want two hundred, then four hundred. The war'll be over and he'll still be out there somewhere slipping around in the woods zapping slopes. He's a psycho, Cap'n."

"Maybe that's what it takes."

"He just sits there in the dark waiting and fingering that string of gook ears, like he's doing the rosary. I'll partner with him, Skipper, if that's what you want. Nobody else will. But he scares the shit out of me. Cap'n, if there weren't gooks to shoot, he'd be shooting *us.*"

Lange hoped he never regretted not having sent Dog back to the Three Nine when he showed up that day for sniper school looking like a high school sophomore about to letter in first year track. He studied the kid. Dog remained soft-spoken and deferential to everyone, not just to officers. Yessir, nosir, three bags full, sir. He possessed that same depth of concentration and singleness of purpose that marked the really good shooters, like Pablo Rhoades. But there was also something else about him. Something.

"You deserve a stand down," the captain encouraged Dog. "You pull more missions than the others. Go fishing in the Tuy Loan. You like fishing. Catch the next mail truck to Sin City and knock off some pussy."

"I'm better off in the bush, sir," Dog said in his soft voice. "That's where I belong."

Dog had his gear laid out on his bunk, cleaning and repacking it for his next mission. Both canteens were full of Kool-Aid to kill the taste of the chemicals the engineers used to kill the taste of the human shit in the water. The 100-round bandoleer was studded with fresh 30.06 172-grain boat-tailed cartridges. Dog carefully stuffed socked tins of C-rat peanut butter, jam, cheese, and crackers in his pack around the PRC-25 radio so they wouldn't rattle in the bush. He slapped full magazines into each of his .45 pistols, the one he had carried since the Three Nine and another he acquired to replace the one he gave the journalist on the road. He worked the slides with deadly, oily sounds, chambering rounds, and slid the thumb safety On. The scoped Winchester rested spotless in its protective case.

Satisfied that all was ready, Dog straightened slowly. He had been working methodically. His expression remained flat, pleasant but flat, unreadable. Lange couldn't help shifting his gaze to the string of ears attached to the kid's web belt. Some of the ears were turning black and withering, while the more recent ones were still brown-pink and scabbed with blood.

Dog kept careful count. Eight kills so far. Confirmed. Sixteen ears.

Lange cleared his throat.

"Kid," he said gruffly, "you don't have to prove anything."

"I know, sir."

"You're a good sniper. I don't want you to burn out."

"I won't burn out, sir."

Dog waited, his sun-faded jungle utilities loose on his lanky frame, his pale eyes like a sky without depth. How could a mere kid make Lange so goddamned uncomfortable?

"Don't wear those ears into town or anything," Lange said to cover up his discomfort.

"I don't go into town, sir."

The captain fished out a cigar and bit off the tip, snapping his teeth. You tried but you could never get anywhere with this kid. He never opened up.

Lange studied the kid through the smoke as he lit his cigar, puffing.

"Be on the flight line in six zero minutes," he said, giving up. "The Two Niner is going out again. You'll be with Hotel Company. Norman'll be your spotter. Steinke is battalion CO, but he won't give you any shit."

"Aye, aye, sir."

Lange turned and started out of the hootch.

"Sir?"

Lange paused.

"Thank you, sir."

Lange didn't ask him for what.

11

A PAIR OF HUEY GUNSHIPS WORKED OUT WITH MINIGUNS ON A draw where the hill jungled down deep into a valley. Smoke popped and puffed as the ratcheting guns vibrated the helicopters in the air, like men over jackhammers. The

H-34s had already made several false insertions to confuse the enemy, but this one was *it*.

The helicopters slicked in to the hilltop that had been bombed to make an LZ. They came in fast and darting like green locusts to unass the Hotel boonierats, then pulled pitch and leaped back into the air from the reduced weight. Sergeant Norman sprang out the door and hit the ground right behind Dog. He stumbled in the tall knife grass and went to his knees. Dog waited in the tree line for him. The snipers had their faces mottled green and black with camouflage paint.

"Murder Incorporated," one of the grunts snickered.

Horrible Hotel, as the company called itself, was on the ground and ready for action. It lined itself out and crept off the hilltop through the thick jungle toward the wide flat of the valley. First Platoon took point, Third drag, and Headquarters and Command joined Second in the middle of the caterpillar.

Elsewhere in the hills that surrounded the valley, Foolish Foxtrot and the other elements of Two Nine were also inserting. The objective was to cut the supply trails from the North and drive the enemy out and make him fight. The only problem with the plan was that it was the little people, not the Marines, who chose the place and the time for contact. If they chose no contact, then the Marines found nothing except abandoned hootches, rice caches, a few Red Balls still rutted from traffic use, and sometimes tunnel complexes.

Snipers were the only friendlies with the luxury of choosing the place and time for contact.

Dog and Norman tagged along with the company until they knew the enemy had pinpointed Hotel and its direction of travel. Then Norman dug a little hole with his boot heel, got rid of the quid of chewing tobacco in his jaw, and tamped the earth down again. He rinsed out his mouth with canteen Kool-Aid. In the bush you didn't smoke or chew or even fart or the gooks smelled you.

Before the snipers slipped off from the main body Norman grasped Dog's arm and said in a low warning growl

"Kid, I'm getting too short to get my ass shot off. Sixty-two days and a wakeup and I'm out of here. No fucking chances this time. If shooting gooks is your bag and you get your rocks off on it, that's your business. But when you hang my ass out and it ain't necessary, then that's *my* business."

The kid's eyes gleamed like shards of glass in his camouflaged face. He seldom spoke in the bush. He turned silently and led the way with his compass. The two snipers, hunting, were alone in the jungle. The soughing and sway of vegetation marked their passage.

In the rear at the Tactical Operations Center, Captain Lange kept his snipers pinpointed on a map from their radio checks. He had six teams out on the Two Nine operation, including Dog and Norman. When they slipped into their hides to wait for targets, he coordinated cover mortar fire and had it on call for them in case they had to cut out and *di-di.* He ate and slept in the Ops Center whenever his snipers were out, *if* he ate and slept. He left the bank of radios, manned by NCOs and lower-ranking officers, only long enough to slip outside for a piss or to study the distant hills where helicopters buzzed like flies over a corpse.

Mostly the Marines swept an AO and the gooks moved out ahead of the advance, then moved back in when the Marines were gone again. The Marines swept the area again and the same thing happened. It had been going on like that since China Beach.

This time it might be different. The little people were choosing to make contact.

Echo Company took six rounds of incoming mortar at midmorning. A sniper kept Foolish Foxtrot pinned down for over an hour. Horrible Hotel's point sprang an L-shaped ambush shortly after it finished a break-in-place for noon rations. Net radios crackled and spat with the excitement and confusion of fighting in the jungle where all you saw were shadows mostly. You could be shooting at each other almost point-blank and still not see anyone. NCOs and officers at the Ops Center stopped whatever they were doing to listen to the radio activity.

"Black Rover, this is Rover Four. Contact! I repeat—Contact! Over."

"Six, this is One. Smitty's down! They got Smitty! Dustoff! Dustoff!"

"One, this is Two. They got a machine gun three o'clock yours! Goddamnit, Actual, get some men and neutralize that goddamn gun."

"Rover Four? Captain, I thought we had air cover. Where the fuck are those choppers?"

Radio procedure broke down in the excitement. Everyone was screaming and yelling and asking questions over the air. You didn't have to be there to feel the confusion. Colonel Steinke's voice wedged itself into the bedlam, inserting itself from his command helicopter hovering five thousand feet above the valley.

"Rover Four, this is Black Rover, over."

"Black Rover, they broke contact. We have blood trails, over."

"Rover Four, get on those trails. I want those little fuckers hurt. Get in there and hurt them. Do you read me? Over."

"Black Rover, we need a relay for Dustoff, grid coordinates . . ."

"Rover Four, leave a rear guard and get on those gooks. I want a body count. . . ."

". . . two friendly Whiskey Alphas, one enemy Kilo Alpha confirmed. . . ."

"Rover Four, what the fuck are you doing? Goddamnit, move! Do your job or I'll get somebody who can. Over."

Lange listened. "Cocksucker," he muttered to himself. You could afford to get apoplectic if you were in a chopper out of range and it wasn't your ass down there getting shot at. Everyone in the Ops Center looked at each other. A couple of officers shook their heads but wouldn't say anything in front of the enlisted men. A gunny who had been around too long to give a damn said, "One of these days that colonel'll explode and there won't be nothing left but shit to sack up and send home."

"Gunny, don't you have something else to do?" a lieutenant rebuked mildly.

"Yes, sir."

"Gunny . . . ?"

"Yes, sir."

"He's your superior."

"Yes, sir."

Lange's snipers made their radio checks and the team of Deke the Geek and Tommy Hands made one hit, then packed up and moved to another hide. At 1500 hours the sniper radio band broke squelch, interrupting a long silence. Dog's voice sounded matter-of-fact, as though he had rung up for time or the weather report: *"Armageddon, this is Spartan Three. Bingo two. Over."*

Two more sets of ears for the kid. Lange grabbed the mike. "Spartan Three, this is Armageddon. Over."

"Platoon-size element in the open," the kid radioed. His voice, though low and terse, was laced with triumph. *"Armageddon, we have Charlie pinned down. Over."*

"Do you request Sparrow Hawk? Over," Lange shot back.

The ready reaction force remained on standby whenever the units were in the field.

Dog remained silent for a long minute. When he keyed the mike again, Lange heard Norman in the background. It sounded like the two men were quarreling.

"Negative, Armageddon," Dog said. *"Will keep you advised. Spartan Three out."*

Lange couldn't help it. He grinned around the Ops Center. It seemed Dog had Pablo Rhoades' Elephant Valley going all over again. He hoped Dog could pull it off. Steinke's battalion out there had one pitiful little enemy KIA and at least two friendlies WIA while Lange's snipers had already accounted for three enemy dead and were about to add to that.

"Steinke, jam *that* up your ass," Lange hooted, and the gunny who had been around too long to give a damn grinned at Lange and gave him thumbs-up.

12

DOG HOOKED THE MIKE BACK TO THE SET AND HIS GAZE RAKED across the grim set of Norman's jaw. They were among good cover and concealment in an old bomb crater that had grown over again. Norman had a hard time holding his tongue, but now wasn't the time to let it loose. He glared across the seven hundred yards of abandoned rice paddy that stretched between them and the dilapidated scattering of grass- and tin-roofed hootches which was all that remained of Thieu Bien. The peasants had left months ago, driven out by the combined efforts of the VC and the B-52s.

Norman sweated heavily. It burned his eyes and blurred the sun reflecting in the muddy rice water. He stewed, but he kept his silence. He repositioned the spotting scope on its tripod legs and peered through it. The rotted hootches leaped out at him. He slowly swept the village with the glass, the scope picking out old camp fires and a rusted kettle and rags flapping disconsolately in the breeze around a hole blown in the thorny bamboo fence that ran parallel to Norman's right along the south side of the village. He looked at the two fresh corpses sprawled in the open, both in NVA khaki with their pith helmets lying nearby. One of them—the officer—wore a sidearm with a red star on the grips. The other had been carrying a radio. The relentless sun and the weight of the radio on his back were already starting to sink his body into the earth.

Norman's scope moved on. It was the first chance he had had to take a really good look at their situation.

Beyond the village rose a hill sparsely studded with palms. Undergrowth was starting to sprout again among the

53

palms where the peasants had kept their little gardens, but there was still barely enough to provide a man concealment.

Norman checked the north side of the village. The old rice field extended around to that side. The rice plants that remained were still green and only about shin high.

The sergeant realized finally that the NVA platoon was trapped in the village between the bamboo fence and the rice paddy and the rising open hill at the rear. The enemy soldiers were scattered out and hiding in hootches or in what remained of an old VC breastwork. Their only escape route lay across one hundred yards of open field to a tit of forest that bulged out toward the village from the far right flank of the ribbon of jungle in which the snipers had burrowed their hide. And Dog, like a patient predator, was watching.

When the NVA platoon first entered the abandoned village from the rear and Dog began to draw a bead, Norman grabbed his arm and shook his head vigorously. It was suicide for two men to fire on an element that large. But Dog had already read the situation. He snatched his arm free and squeezed off his first round, nailing the officer in the ten ring and sowing confusion. His next shot crumpled the radioman. That left the platoon leaderless and without communications, unless someone had a second radio.

Norman now glanced at the kid with grudging respect. The kid looked back and gave that flat nonsmile before he scrambled forward on his belly to a tree whose low over-hanging branches cast a black shadow hard to penetrate with the naked eye. He used a felled tree trunk as a rest for his rifle. Norman crawled up beside him with the spotting scope and his M14 rifle. The open sights of the M14 made shooting at this range difficult, but they might need its firepower if the trapped gooks got organized and rushed them.

Dog pointed at the first hootch on the left and then on to the next, numbering them: "One, two, three . . ."

Norman nodded. He wiped sweat and glued his eye to the spotter scope. He didn't have to wait long.

"Movement in seven," he whispered presently. "Low and

to the right of the door. Looks like the gook is thinking about making a try for the radio."

"I have him."

The kid waited. The next time the soldier stuck up his head, Dog's Winchester cracked and the gook's head evaporated in a pink cloud.

"Hope I didn't destroy his ears," Dog said nonchalantly, bolting in a fresh round.

The sun beat down. Heat devils shimmered on the surface of the rice ponds. Dog ate some peanut butter and crackers and drank Kool-Aid while Norman kept watch. Then they switched off.

"We'll call in arty on 'em before nightfall and *di-di*," Norman suggested.

"We have them trapped like flies in a spider's web," Dog replied. "I'm going to send them to hell one by one."

Norman's temper flared. "Goddamnit, Dog. It ain't my idea of fun to be out here in the dark with a bunch of pissed-off gooks. I told you I'm getting to be a short-timer."

Dog lay there, looking relaxed, his cheek resting lightly on his rifle stock. Ready.

"This is fucking crazy. You know that!" Norman hissed. Their faces were inches apart.

Dog settled the rifle butt more comfortably against his shoulder. Overcome by his anger, Norman grabbed a handful of Dog's utility jacket. Dog's head slowly turned. The flat blue eyes reached out of the camouflaged face. They were like a blow. Norman released him.

"Goddamnit," he said, with real feeling, but he lay there on the moist jungle floor behind the log.

When he cooled off, the sergeant had to admit that holding the situation like it was made sense in a crazy sort of way. If they called in artillery on the village, most of the soldiers would escape. If Sparrow Hawk sliced in, they'd have to attack across open ground. Some of them would die. The open fields around the old ville that trapped the gooks also made the position highly defensible.

Dog rested silently, looking through his scope and fingering the gook ears hanging from the parachute cord at his belt.

"Let the one-hundred-fives blast what they can and then we get the hell out of here," Norman insisted.

Dog watched the village through his scope.

Men hunted are like squirrels. They have no patience. Shoot one and the others suck in, but it won't be long before heads start popping up again to look around. A sniper who has learned patience can work off that.

The rice paddy and village against a great red setting sun resembled a scene from an Oriental postcard when three gooks made their bid for freedom, suddenly rushing from hootch four nearest the tit of forest. Dog methodically dropped the leader before he was a third of the way across the clearing. That turned the others back. Dog killed one of them, but his third shot, hurried, ricocheted off a rusty iron kettle as the survivor swan-dived over it and disappeared in a low place.

"Five," Dog said, and relayed the number to Captain Lange on his next radio check.

Sergeant Norman grew more sullen with the fall of night. It didn't help his mood any when the trapped platoon opened fire from the village. Muzzle flashes winked. Vicious fireflies. Lead scythed through the jungle—but it was all fifty yards to the snipers' right flank. The gooks had no idea where their persecutors were hiding. It was too dark to catch Dog's reaction, but Norman could feel the kid's flat nonsmile.

The snipers waited, holding fire. You only shot when you were assured of a hit. Anything else was waste.

Norman took over radio watch. He radioed for illumination as soon as the firing from the village stopped. The guns had already been laid on and were waiting. Rounds from a 105mm battery exploded over the village, bursting into brilliant miniature suns suspended from tiny parachutes. The parachute flares bathed the hootches in an eerie pinkish light that flickered the world into an old black-and-white horror movie.

"One o'clock, to the rear," Norman snapped, eye to the spotting scope.

The gooks were like rats running out the back of the village. Dog knocked down the lead Vietnamese soldier. He wounded another in the gut. This one sat down hard and grabbed his belly. He rocked himself in pain and terror. Dog let him sit there. The others abandoned their suicide mission and scurried back to the hootches.

The wounded one sat bleeding and writhing in the strange glowing light of the parachute flares. Norman watched him through the spotting scope. The soldier had lost his helmet and dropped his rifle. He threw back his head and his mouth hollowed into a cavern and the veins on his neck stood out like cords. He was howling at his comrades to rescue him. Norman couldn't hear it, but he could imagine it.

"Put the poor sonofabitch out of his misery," Norman said.

"Wait."

"Look at him. Put an end to it."

"Wait," was all Dog said.

Artillery shells kept popping in the sky, replenishing the old suns as they set. The wounded gook's screaming played on his hiding comrades like an exposed nerve. Finally, one of them could stand it no longer. He sprang up and sprinted around the back of a hootch and dashed toward the casualty. Dog's patience paid off; his rifle cracked. The rescuer's body skidded into the wounded one like Joe DiMaggio stealing second base.

Then Dog shot the decoy. Norman watched. One instant the face filled his scope, horror written on it at seeing his comrade dropped dead virtually in his lap. The next instant the man's face exploded. It disappeared, leaving a kind of pinkish haze in the air for a second. Norman withdrew from the scope and rubbed his eyes.

"Oh, fucking Christ," he said.

* * *

Dog remained silent. He remained silent as the night wore on and the constant evil suns played in the sky. Survivors of what was turning into a massacre cowered fearfully in their decaying hootches away from the little suns and the threat of fire so accurate it had already claimed eight of their number. They must have thought they were surrounded by Marines. Every hour or so either Dog or Norman fired one round to let the gooks know what still awaited them.

Twice the snipers changed positions to keep from being pinpointed. They took turns on watch, but Dog never slept. He was a predator. He waited for another kill. Sometimes he ate, but the rest of the time Norman felt his eyes watching. He wondered if the kid's eyes turned black at night like the sky.

At 2330 hours the radio crackle-whispered into the darkness. It was turned low, but it was still startlingly loud. Dog shifted slightly. Norman grabbed the mike and acknowledged with two clicks of the mike switch.

"Spartan Three, November Victor Alpha platoon reported proceeding your direction. ETA sometime tomorrow. Over."

There was nothing they could do about it now. It was too dark. If they tried to slip away, they'd sound like a tribe of feeding monkeys. Besides, a tiger mauled a guy from the One Nine when his platoon moved at night, and two or three guys in the division had died of snakebite. Tigers and snakes and other creatures fed at night.

They were awake like that goddamned kid.

Norman clicked the mike three times to acknowledge the message.

"Spartan Three," Lange's mechanical voice whispered back. There was a long pause. *"Spartan Three . . . Armageddon out."*

Norman low-crawled up next to the kid and spoke directly into his ear to keep his voice from carrying at night.

"Did you hear?" he asked. "Charlie'll have *us* trapped. We're hauling ass outa here as soon as we can see."

The kid lay silent.

"Motherfuck it, Dog. We're *didi-ing* at first light."

Norman dropped his head onto the moist humus of the jungle floor. It smelled of decay. It smelled of danger.

"We're getting out."

He spat out the words in uncontrolled frustration.

"You ain't getting me kilt just to dangle some more ears on your belt," he whispered bitterly. "Fuck you. And fuck Pablo Rhoades."

He slithered back to his spotting scope.

13

CAPTAIN LANGE AT BASE CAMP SWEATED OUT THE LONG NIGHT. As each hour passed he clicked his mike twice and received three clicks of assurance in return.

Radios around the division began switching to Armageddon's net as word spread. Wherever Marines could, from Hill 55 to Da Nang air base, from the bridge watch over the Tuy Loan to the PPBs in the scrub pine flats, they found radios to gather around to wait for the drama to unfold. It was more exciting than the serial cliff-hangers that used to play at the movies on Saturday afternoons. Two snipers had an entire NVA platoon trapped. The snipers had already killed nearly half the platoon and had the survivors shitting their pants.

But Charlie was on his way to pull a rescue.

Col. Stick Steinke towered over Captain Lange inside the Ops tent. Lange was built like a bulldog, Steinke like a Great Dane. The jittery light from the generator-powered lamps gave everything the quality of a schizophrenic light show.

"You *will* request Sparrow Hawk at dawn," Steinke raged. "I've already advised them to stand by for action."

Lange looked at him.

"With all due respect, Colonel," he said levelly, knowing he held the upper hand, "the sniper platoon is *my* command. My men have everything under control."

Lange knew Steinke. He knew the type. Steinke didn't want to be shown up by two *gunfighters* after the stand he took against snipers in front of everyone at the S-3 in Da Nang. It would save face for him if he could show that the Ready Force had to go in and pull the snipers' bacon out of the fire.

Lange almost said it: *What is your battalion's body count so far on this operation, Colonel? One?*

Instead, he said, more restrained, "Colonel Steinke, Spartan Three has accounted for eight enemy KIA so far, with no friendly casualties."

Steinke glared.

"There's no percentage in getting Marines killed by sending in troops," Lange argued, "when my snipers can accomplish the same thing with far less risk. Let it go on like it is for a while. They're doing okay at the OK Corral."

He couldn't resist getting in the jab. Steinke's head snapped back. Outside the Ops Center the generator chugged noisily along, creating power surges that made the weak electric lights throb yellow against the colonel's angry features.

"Your *Top Stick*," Steinke sneered, "is about to have boo-coo gooks rain down on him like a tub of shit."

"We don't know for sure those gooks are heading for Thieu Bien," Lange countered.

Colonel Steinke grinned thickly. "Where else but there? We don't know their exact position right now, but they're on their way," he predicted.

"In the meanwhile, Colonel, I trust the judgment of my men. Will that be all?"

Lange didn't want the kid coming out without finishing what he started. Not with that idiot Steinke watching and waiting for someone to make a mistake.

Stay in there, kid, he cheered. *Run up the score.*

14

THE FIRST MAUVE LIGHT OF DAWN SEEPED INTO THE ABANDONED village like leaking water. The 105mm battery ceased planting its little suns. The day promised to bring brassy skies and temperatures of above one hundred degrees. Norman was already sweating even in the cool of the morning. Gook corpses scattered among the ramshackle hootches were starting to bloat and pop their buttons. Clouds of black flies swarmed above them. The gooks would be getting ripe and splitting open before noon.

Both snipers were alert. Norman glassed the village. Dog had his patrol cap pulled low to shade his eyes. He watched the village through his rifle scope.

"I'm calling for our taxi," Norman whispered.

Dog did not stir. Norman had never seen such intensity in a man. Not even in Pablo Rhoades. He knew, he just *knew*, the kid would not leave until every dink in the village was dead.

Maybe he should just be thankful that he was still alive. He clicked the PRC-25 mike and requested a sitrep.

"No further sightings, Spartan Three," Lange's voice returned quickly. It sounded tired. *"But mama still thinks you'll have company for Sunday dinner. Over."*

Norman started to request their extraction code. He glanced at the kid. They were shielded behind a low upcropping of rock in a thorn thicket. Dog lay prone. He looked at Norman, then nodded at the village. Norman rolled away from the radio and scrambled to his spotting scope.

The gooks were up to something. One of them rushed from one hut to another. Dog let him go.

Minutes later, apparently in response to a signal, seven NVA soldiers sprang out of hiding and charged the tit of jungle nearest them. They fired their AKs in wild abandon as they rushed. Obviously they expected to find an American defensive position among the trees and lianas.

There was good shooting light, clear and sharp, and there was no wind.

Two NVA soldiers made it back to the village. Dog methodically picked the others off. He dropped them one after the other, like shooting off the little crows on a wire at a carnival. One fell and pounded his legs against the ground in agony until Dog came back and put him out of his misery with a second shot. He seemed disappointed that his first shot had not been a killing one.

"It's time to boogie," Norman said.

"Not yet."

Speechless, Norman glared. He crawled quickly to the radio. Facedown on the ground, he took the radio out of Dog's pack, slipped it into his own, and shrugged into the pack straps.

"I'm going home," he said to Dog. "You can come or you can stay and die."

Norman crawled into the jungle until he was out of sight of the village. He stood up and looked back. Dog hadn't budged. A band of sunlight streaked through an opening in the jungle canopy and fell next to the kid.

Norman felt like kicking things. He felt like ripping and tearing and clawing. He felt like shouting at the kid for being such an idiot.

He dropped to all fours again and crawled back. He let the radio in its pack down between himself and the kid and then, silently, grudgingly, resumed his vigil through the spotting scope.

The sun rose. It blasted the village with burning rays. It kicked up a hot intermittent wind that carried with it the growing stench of the rotting Vietnamese. Command helicopters for the operations that went on in the rest of the valley flew over several times. At 1100 hours Captain Lange came unexpectedly over the radio. His voice sounded urgent. He advised that one of the choppers had spotted the NVA rescue platoon. It was beyond the hills two klicks south of the village.

The snipers watched as Huey gunships swarmed the approaching enemy. The helicopters popped up and down from behind the hills like erratic pistons, working out on the jungle with rockets and machine guns. The hills muffled the *whump-whump* of the explosives.

Lange came back on, sounding even more urgent, and said an enemy *company* had been spotted one klick east heading toward Thieu Bien. The gooks were coming out to fight. Sparrow Hawk would be in the air in three-zero minutes. Colonel Steinke was attempting to muster up enough slicks to pull Horrible Hotel out and use the company to trap the North Vietnamese in a decisive battle.

The shit was coming down.

It was all going to fall on Thieu Bien.

It looked like the NVA would arrive first.

"Code Blue, Spartan Three," Lange urged. *"Code Blue."*

It was time to haul ass.

Dog looked hard at the village. "They're mine. They're confirmed," he said. "I'm going in there to get them."

Norman stared at him.

15

IT WAS COOL IN THE FRENCH FUCK WITH THE BIG CEILING FANS going. The fans were high and there was a skylight above them that let in enough sun to make rotating shadows below. Lange smoked his cigar down to a stub while telling of Dog's exploits at Thieu Bien. I took notes for another INS story. Maybe the kid *was* a psycho, but in war *psycho* was often spelled *hero.*

"Norman could have held his M Fourteen on the kid and I don't think that would have stopped him from going into that ville," Lange said. "The surviving gooks were scared shitless. They *di-di*'d out the back of the ville. Norman was pissed off, but of course he went with the kid. That sergeant'll never *di-di* on you in the field."

Lange puffed thoughtfully at his cigar stub. His eyes squinted.

"I don't know . . ." His voice trailed off.

He caught himself with a jerk.

"That kid is damned effective," he said. "I liked rubbing Steinke's nose in it."

He studied his cigar. He studied the high ceiling fan. His eyes shifted to mine.

"A company of gooks as mad as hornets were coming— and there that kid was going from dead gook to dead gook cutting off their ears. Mike, you gotta admire it, but at the same time . . ."

He left the thought unfinished.

"Norman refuses to go with the kid into the field again. I can't really blame him. Neither will anybody else. Norman says he has a death wish. He says he'll keep killing until some gook kills him."

It didn't concern Dog that the other snipers refused to spot for him. That was like the kid. I glanced up at Lange.

"Bill, are you sending him into the bush alone?"

"Pablo Rhoades went alone," he said. "They're a special breed."

"He's a kid," I protested.

Lange stared at me.

"On the inside," he said, "that boy's older'n both of us put together."

I shook my head. "Bill, what do you really know about him?"

"What do you know about a Buddhist monk? He never talks about himself. Even in his personnel file it's like he never existed before Vietnam."

A thought lifted one eyebrow.

"There is one thing," he said. "Word went around over in his old unit at the Three Nine—nobody knows where it came from, but it was strange—that the reason he enlisted in the Crotch was because of his girlfriend."

He shook his head slowly, as though in sympathy.

"From what I understand," he went on, "the girl was *murdered.*"

I stared at him.

"That's all I know about it," he said.

A minute later, while I was still digesting that, Brigette and Judy Wong entered the French Fuck—not *French Fuck,* for goo'ness sake. There were maybe a dozen men in the bar, mostly journalists and MilGroup people and American civilian advisers, and some classier good-time girls. The bar fell silent. All eyes turned toward the two beautiful Orientals in gorgeous traditional dresses with hems that swept the floor and big bows on the rears. Brigette's was a peach color with Vietnamese symbols and temples. Both women wore bone earrings. Their faces were made up like those of the little dolls vendors sold as souvenirs to GIs at Sin City.

Stunning wasn't quite the correct word for the pair of them. It didn't convey the right meaning. Brigette assumed this tiny aloof smile that she seemed to save for when she knew every man within sight desired her. The girls looked delicate, fragile, and at the same time entirely woman. Only an Oriental can look like that.

They passed among the tables toward us. Several men stood respectfully to let them pass. Brigette rewarded them with her aloof smile and a slight bowing motion of the head. Her long black hair was done up on top of her head and held by her rainbow-colored abalone shell comb. Her hair and eyes glistened.

I couldn't help smiling in proud acceptance that this lovely creature was mine.

Judy Wong walked with the slightest limp. In the little patent shoes she wore you didn't notice that her toes and part of her foot were missing. Brigette said she lost the foot when American helicopters shelled her village.

Bill Lange stood up.

"Mike . . ." he muttered.

That was all. He just stared, clearly mesmerized, through introductions and drinks. He still hadn't managed much more than a few schoolboy phrases when we rose to leave for lunch. The white-coated barman I suspected of being a VC spy whispered something into Judy Wong's ear. She sent him packing with an angry look. I figured it had something to do with the barman rebuking her for associating with Americans. Lange missed the exchange. He had been concentrating on Judy Wong's tiny doll features, missed the ashtray with his cigar, and was trying to put out a little flame he started on the table linen. Brigette kept smiling happily at the three of us. It was more of a smirk, except a smirk never quite fit her face.

"Tell me Judy Wong not win paramour," she murmured to me, aside, when we were seated at a table all four together at *Le Maison Faire* back from the windows with their steel mesh on them to keep out grenades. A guard armed with a Thompson stood at the door, screening customers, most of whom, like us, were Oriental women escorted by European men.

It wasn't necessary for Brigette to whisper. That old bulldog Lange was so engrossed with his Oriental doll that he wouldn't have heard a grenade go off underneath the table. Judy Wong spoke fair English, not as well as Brigette spoke it as Brigette was quick to point out, but she spoke enough that she and Lange were deeply involved in each other.

It was pleasant, their low shy laughter, like that of new lovers, and it was pleasant with the tinkle of silver and crystal in the background and the polite Vietnamese waiters in red livery and black cummerbunds whisking in and out among elegantly dressed diners. It was colonialism at its best.

Maybe it was a fucked-up world here, but I knew suddenly I would miss it. I felt a hollow somewhere.

"For goo'ness sake, Mike," Brigette scolded mildly. "You not hear thing Brigette say."

There was a sweet sadness in her face, as though she had read my thoughts.

Biness was *biness,* but I would miss her too.

"Mike, for goo'ness sake . . ."

I laughed and shrugged off the bad feeling. Enough time for that later.

16

MIKE KRAGEL DISPATCH (WITH PHOTOGRAPHS OF DA NANG street scenes—a restaurant window covered with heavy steel mesh, a fire-gutted discotheque, bloodstains on the street in front of a wall covered with blooming bougainvillea, a legless Vietnamese man sitting in a home-made wheelbarrow), 9 Oct 67:

Vietnam (INS)—Da Nang. South Vietnam's second largest city and site of the U.S. air base from which the war is conducted in I Corps.

What you see of Da Nang until you are there for a while is all surface. It is like standing on the sand at China Beach and looking at the gently lapping waves of the South China Sea. What you do not see unless you know where to look are the hordes of snakelike eels that the ships' lights attract to the Da Nang harbor when the ships unload munitions with which to feed the war. You do not see the leeches in the backwaters that crawl up your rectum and other private places. You do not see, unless you look, the garbage and human wastes that pollute the sea. Toilets are built on the docks and waterfronts. The excrement drops into the water, the fish feed on the excrement, and the people complete the circle by feeding on the fish.

Da Nang is like the South China Sea. It is all surface unless you know how to look beneath the surface.

From all outward appearances it could be any busy Oriental city. You do not see the war at first. Pretty women in traditional *ao dais;* peasants in cone hats and long poles across their shoulders from which they carry enormous weights; Orientals and Occidentals bustling about in dark business suits; rickshaws and pedicabs and Renault taxis and compact cars and Hondas all honking and brake-screeching; water buffalo led by peasants in black "pajamas"; vendors on the streets hawking their wares: "Souvenirs! Souvenirs!"

You can visit a museum, walk in the park and feed the geese, dine on splendid French cuisine at *Le Maison Faire* on Duc Phon Street, dance at *The Kansas City Lights* discotheque three blocks away, and sleep in air-conditioned luxury at *La Francais.*

You think there is no war in the cities. Then you look again. You see the eels.

On March 4, a bomb exploded in the lounge of *The Houston Hotel* in downtown Da Nang. The hotel housed U.S. military officers on R and R leave. The explosion killed three Marine officers and one army captain. It wounded seventeen others;

On April 18, a courier for the U.S. Embassy and his two-man escort were assassinated while delivering secret papers to top officials in Da Nang;

In June a sniper in Dog Patch, a Da Nang refugee shantytown filled with vice, black marketeers, illicit drugs, and Vietcong, picked off two American soldiers as they walked down the street. Dog Patch has been declared off-limits after dark to U.S. GIs.

"You never know who is the enemy and who is the friend," said Lt. Gen. Walt Towers, an adviser to the

ARVN (Army of the Republic of South Vietnam). "They all look alike. They all dress alike. They are all Vietnamese. Some of them are Vietcong. Here's a woman of nineteen or twenty. She's pregnant. She tells you her husband works in Da Nang and isn't a Vietcong. But she watches your men walk into a bar and get killed or wounded by a booby trap. She knows the booby trap is there, but she doesn't warn them. Maybe she helped plant it.

"That tells something about this war. The enemy is all around you. How can the enemy's troops, a thousand or more sometimes, wander around the countryside so close to Da Nang without being discovered? You can only beat the other guy if you isolate him from the population."

In Da Nang, heavy steel mesh covers the windows of most public places such as restaurants and bars, especially those frequented by Americans and Europeans. That is to keep terrorists from driving by and hurling grenades through the windows.

Steel mesh covers the windows of buses for the same reason.

Some buildings are burned down to blackened shells, the work of arsonists. It takes a long time for monsoon rains to wash the bloodstains off concrete, and even then there is always a faint rust left.

The presence of the war is imposed in other subtle ways. Vietnamese soldiers armed with automatic weapons man sandbagged checkpoints at intersections. Refugees occupy squalid shantytowns on the outskirts of every major city. It is estimated that one million people have fled the fighting in the countryside. Men, women, and children with arms, legs, and other body parts lost to bombs or machine guns beg on the streets and in the hotel lounges.

You do not sit near any window, not even if it is screened. You sit as far back as you can, with your back to a wall.

And then there are the spies and the Vietcong underground. "Loose lips sink ships," every new arrival is warned. Keep your mouth shut. Don't talk to bartenders, merchants, and especially not to bar girls and prostitutes.

"The VC have ears," said a CIA official. "Their ears pick up information about U.S. troop movements, morale, strength. They hear and pass on tips about sex preferences and personal habits of high-ranking diplomats and military officers. It is a strange kind of war. It is being fought in the bordellos and restaurants and streets of Da Nang and Saigon and Hue as well as in the jungles and rice paddies and villages. In this war you cannot trust anyone with a yellow skin. You may even be sleeping with your enemy."

17

WHO COULD FIGURE IT? IT WAS JUST LIKE BRIGETTE PREDICTED. Captain Lange got hung up bad on Judy Wong and you couldn't blame him; she was a gorgeous piece of tail. But she was still a slanteye and when you got back to the World you forgot about them. Not entirely, but mostly, until after a while they became some vague memory of an exotic past. It was like when you read Kipling's *The Road To Mandalay*. Years later you still remembered the *feeling* of it, but everything else was gone. There was just the feeling and it left you a little haunted.

Brigette and I saw a lot of Lange and Judy Wong. The captain made every excuse he could to get into Da Nang. At least once a week if his snipers weren't out on mission he caught a resupply chopper back in and stayed the night with Judy. Judy lived in a cottage six blocks from the Continental Palace with another Cinderella. She made sure her room-mate stayed away the night she knew her paramour was coming.

I looked forward to Lange's visits almost as much as Judy Wong did. Whenever he choppered into Da Nang we managed to have drinks together at the French Fuck and talk about the war while we waited for the girls. Afterward, with Brigette and Judy, we had dinner at *Le Maison Faire* or at one of the pseudo-American joints like The Dallas Steak-house. Sometimes we spent an afternoon together having pedicab races or strolling Duc Phon Street with the girls while they shopped or going to American movies with Vietnamese dubbed in. Lex Barker as Tarzan spoke in lisping Vietnamese that made him sound like a fairy. John Wayne speaking gook wasn't quite John Wayne. I had never laughed at John Wayne before.

"Not funny," Brigette scolded. "Very touching love scene."

Lange laughed a lot with Judy. She ironed out the lines etched deep into his features. You could see the strain start to dissipate whenever the girls floated into the French Fuck, Brigette with her tiny aloof smile that said she knew men were looking at her, Judy limping just a little while her eyes sought out her captain where we waited at our favorite table in back.

The white-coated waiter whom I suspected of being a VC spy got close to Judy Wong once more and whispered into her ear. His name I learned was Ngo Ton Hang. This time Judy blistered him with a burst of Vietnamese. Blushing furiously, he bowed himself away from her. His gaze kept darting back to our table. Lange started to rise. Judy reassured him with a smile. She gave Ngo a saucy snub of her nose. Something smoldered in Ngo's eyes. I saw it burning, but then the eyes were neutral again.

That was the last time Ngo attempted to speak to Judy Wong in our presence, although later I surprised them a few times talking together in the French Fuck and they seemed friendly, even familiar.

"Them from same village," Brigette explained later. "Judy Wong say Ngo most jealous of Judy Wong and Captain Lange. Him have fight with green monster inside him heart."

"If he's bothering you," Lange told Judy, "I'll have management get rid of him."

Judy clasped Bill's arm quickly. "No. Him nothing, Bill. *Dinky dow*. Him not worth we bother. Okay, Bill?"

"Don't even *look* at her," Lange warned Ngo when the Vietnamese brought fresh drinks.

Ngo bowed and bowed, his eyes and face as flat as the VC dusk.

"Mike, you not tell Captain Lange Judy Wong boom-boom?" Brigette asked one night, combing her hair with the rainbow-colored abalone comb while I watched from the bed.

She paused combing to fix my eyes in the mirror. The French kerosene lamp Brigette liked lent her eyes a tawny highlight.

"It not like Judy Wong cheap Dog Patch girl, for goo'ness sake," Brigette went on. "Judy Wong and Brigette Nguyen high stairs . . ."

"Upper class?"

"Yes, Big Shoot Mike. You unnerstand. Upper class. In Hue before come to Da Nang we both aide to nurses work in hospital. Judy Wong good girl same-same me. She boom-boom, but Judy Wong good Buddhist. She boom-boom, but she not chop-chop. Never put in her mouth, for goo'ness sake. Brigette neither . . ."

I laughed softly. Brigette blushed.

"It not count with you, Big Shoot. You famous paramour, for goo'ness sake. Good Vietnamese girl must please. Captain Lange important man too. If him know Judy Wong boom-boom, maybe him not want be paramour."

"I won't tell," I promised.

It was pleasant in the room. Like always. I came here and didn't have to think about Sharon and the divorce and going back to the World. All there was, was the room and the clean tantalizing scent of a pretty Oriental woman and the lizard outside the French doors on the balcony in the morning.

But nothing was forever.

Fuck it.

I stretched, naked beneath the clean sheets. Brigette changed the linen every day, and there were always fresh blooms of bougainvillea in vases when I came home.

Home?

When did I start thinking of this fucked-up place as home?

Brigette turned from the mirror toward me. The silk gown I'd bought her fell away from breasts that were small and firm and stood up. The rounded swell below pushed the nipples toward the top. Her lips were the same color as her nipples, and much the same shape.

Her hair hung in a black sheen to below her waist. Soft light from the French lamp touched the delicate scar across her nose. I thought it her only flaw. I asked her once how she got it.

"It not matter, for goo'ness sake," she said.

"From the war?" I asked.

"Mike, there be different kinds of war."

"Oh. You're a Schopenhauer," I said, teasing.

"Who?"

"He's a philosopher."

"I not know him."

"He's dead."

"Then why you make fun of Brigette, for goo'ness sake?" she flared. "You Big Shoot, Mike. You know important things poor Vietnamese girl not. Not fair you make fun of poor Vietnamese girl."

She was so serious that I couldn't help laughing.

"You are so goddamned adorable when you're pissed off," I shouted. I ran at her and grabbed the tiny body and whirled her around on the floor in my arms until she was

73

giggling and in good humor again. "Maybe that's why I love you," I said.

Brigette became serious again. She pushed back in my arms with her hands on my chest so she could look into my eyes. Brigette did that when she talked. She said you could see a person's heart through his eyes.

"You never say before you love me, Mike. We got biness or we got love? I not see biness and love in same temple."

I let her go. She was a slanteye. I wasn't going to be a squaw man. That was what the grunts called GIs who took up with Vietnamese women, even married them. Squaw men.

"It's business," I said. "Business."

I couldn't return her gaze. Maybe she really *could* see into your heart.

Now, she was looking at me with that same gaze. She hit a few more thoughtful strokes with her comb, running it out to the ends of her hair, and she watched me closely. I looked away, out the French windows and above the clicking fronds of the palm that topped out at a level with the floor of the balcony. I watched parachute flares exploding into tiny descending suns over the distant air base. Some GI on perimeter watch had caught movement outside the wire. The guards were always shooting at shadows, calling for illumination to drive back the night. Nights belonged to the Vietcong.

"Mike?" Brigette said, just above a whisper. "Mike, you have Schopenhauer things on your mind, no?"

Schopenhauer since that night about Brigette's scar had become a catchword that we used between us to describe moodiness or unhappiness. My moods always seemed to bleed over into Brigette. I shrugged casually in bed and changed the subject.

"Brigette, Captain Lange extended his tour in Vietnam for another year. Did Judy Wong say anything to you about it?"

"Captain Lange important man," Brigette said. "Him

commander of sharpshoot marines who kill boo-coo VC, make VC afraid. Very important man. Much prestige for Judy Wong have important U.S. captain for paramour. Him stay if him want to stay, for goo'ness sake."

I looked at her—the naked breasts through the opening in her wrap, the nipple-shaped mouth moist and parted just enough to show the white gleam of teeth. I felt myself desiring her.

Her eyes shifted to my desire. She dropped the gown with a whisper of silk and stood naked in the light. Her body was smooth except for the one triangular patch of silky hair dark against the yellow cast of her skin.

"Come here," I said.

She obeyed. She gently removed the sheet until I lay naked too, erect.

"For goo'ness sake," she whispered, giggling. And then she rolled over onto me and her heels hooked beneath my knees and she slowly settled down, drawing me into her, and she held my face between her hands and the lips that were like her nipples came down to mine.

18

BILL LANGE'S INFATUATION WITH HIS FLOWER OF THE ORIENT failed to consume his passion for snipers in general and his fascination in particular with the young sharpshooter who was quickly becoming a legend in I Corps. Dog intrigued the officer. Each time Lange caught the helicopter into the city he brought with him tales of the kid's most recent exploits, accounts of which I passed on through my INS "Top Stick" dispatches.

Lange was still stunned a week later by the incident of the so-called Lotus Bitch.

"I never want another nightmare like that," he said.

The Lotus Bitch was the leader of a VC squad that tortured captured gyrenes. She possessed a talent for prolonging her captives' agony. No one on Hill 55 slept when the Bitch went to work on some unfortunate American; his screeches and shrieks filled the entire hours between dusk and dawn. It sounded like someone had turned the Devil himself loose out there and he was tormenting lost souls. The Marines on the Hill listened in silent rage and fear while Lotus was busy at her work digging out a Marine's fingernails and teeth, gouging out his eyes, skinning him inch by inch. She was skillful enough to keep her victim alive and conscious while entirely removing the skin from his face. Marine patrols at dawn always found what was left of the victim hanging upside down in a tree like a butchered hog with his testicles cut off and jammed into his mouth. That was an old VC trick.

The Lotus Bitch made the men on Hill 55 dread the nights after someone became MIA. They knew where the MIA would turn up next.

"Sir, I'm going out there," Dog softly announced one night while men stood around in strained groups listening to the hellish screams beyond the wire.

The Boonierat Club was empty; Rafter closed it down and came out to the wire. Horrible Hotel's company clerk fled to his hootch and stuck his head underneath a sleeping bag to try to keep out the hellish sounds. Some men were blowing grass and drinking beer and getting meaner hour by hour. It was a trap to go out there, but the men were threatening to break out of the perimeter on their own anyhow to go to the tortured man's rescue.

"Don't you understand?" the MIA's buddy shouted. "That's Hamilton out there! God, I can't stand this! If we can't go get him, can't we at least call in mortar fire on him and put him out of his misery? Death's gotta be better than *this*. Maybe we'll get that bitch too."

"Sir," Dog repeated. "I'm going out there to end it."

Lange looked at him. Dog had his face blackened and his patrol cap pulled low. He wore his twin pistols and carried his rifle uncased. He was alone. Since the short siege at Thieu Bien, he always took to the field alone.

There was no moon.

"They want us to come out there," Lange warned. "They're waiting for us to try. It's suicide."

"Sir, in the short story 'The Most Dangerous Game,' the hunted becomes the hunter."

A new burst of wailing pierced the night and Lange's nerves. He looked away. He nodded his consent.

The kid simply melted into the darkness. When Colonel Steinke found out about it, he came to the first line of bunkers and sat down on the sandbags next to the captain. They looked out beyond the concertina and tanglefoot, across the grasslands to the dark fringe of jungle next to the river. That was where the screaming came from.

"He's *dinky dow*," Steinke said. "He was lucky the last time."

Lange kept his tongue. He already felt he had sent the kid to his death. He remained silently watching where the river lay in darkness, listening to sounds of torture scraping against the night breezes. Other Marines, hearing about Dog's mission, drifted over and took up vigil with the sniper commander.

"That kid's crazy," Steinke said. "Everyone knows it. The next sound we'll hear is *his* screams."

"Colonel, sir, with any due respect, I don't want to hear your shit. I have a man out there."

"So do I," Steinke retorted. "That's my man you hear screaming. It won't do anyone any good to have a duet out there singing to us. Captain, I'm holding you personally responsible for whatever happens."

Lange rose wearily and walked a short distance away. After a minute the other Marines crowded around him, their stares glued on the distant river. Steinke got up finally and returned alone to his headquarters.

An hour passed. It was an eternity. The wind picked up. It

carried Hamilton's cries to the waiting men with renewed clarity.

"What's taking so *long?*" someone muttered.

A rifle crack whipped into the base camp with the wind. Lange flinched. Hamilton's scream cut abruptly into silence. Sergeant Norman murmured, "I'll be goddamned. He did it. He shot Hamilton."

"It was necessary," Lange said.

"Yes. But God take pity on Dog's soul—*if* he has one."

They waited for Dog to return from his errand of mercy. Instead, fifteen minutes later, there was another shot, followed by two more. They waited. Lange's tautened nerves almost exploded when, a half hour after the final shot, the screaming started again. At first Lange thought it was the kid screaming. Then he understood.

The shrieks came from the throat of a *woman*.

Marines from the helicopter maintenance company, grunts on bunker or perimeter watch, the mess cooks in their tents scrubbing pots, the spectators at the wire—they vibrated Hill 55 with their wild cheering.

Revenge was sweet.

For an hour the wind brought to camp the screams of the Lotus Bitch in her dying agony. After a while, Lange walked away. The hilltop fell into silence. It was okay at first, but now everyone just wanted it to end.

There was a final shot from out there, this one from a .45. Soon, news came that Dog was back through the wire with the dead Marine's body. It was so horribly mutilated that doctors said Hamilton couldn't have lived even without the single bullet wound that pierced his heart. The Bitch had dissected the nerves from his arms and groin and clamped electrical charges to them; she sliced off his scrotum; both eyes and his tongue were gone; his knees were broken; a section of his intestine ballooned out through knife wounds in his belly.

Dog gently dumped the body in front of the battalion aid station. Then he turned. The crowd of awed Marines parted to let him pass. All you could hear was their breathing. The Marines stared after the kid; some noticed he had fresh ears on his parachute cord. He went to the Boonierat Club and Rafter followed him and brought him a beer.

"After what you did, man," he said, "it's on the house. It's on the house from now on."

The club filled, but the kid sat at the bar alone. After he finished his one beer, he got up and walked out. Everybody watched him go.

"I never asked him what happened out there," Lange said. "Maybe I didn't want to know the details. Maybe none of us did. But everyone on Hill fifty-five is rooting for him now. They don't want to go with him out there, but they all want him to get his hundred kills."

Lange paused.

"Fifty-eight to go," he said.

The kid had guts. Or something. It took something to shoot a fellow Marine to end his agony. Hank Baylor's eyes widened incredulously when I told him about it.

"You mean he tortured the cunt?" Baylor asked, twisting the tips of his handlebar mustache. It was a habit.

Tom Stoud was in the office too. We hadn't yet replaced Carl Can't. Stoud was wiry and balding on top. About fifty, with ten kids back home in San Marcos, Texas, he had somewhat the appearance and demeanor of a patient vulture. His wife's name was Luz. He picked her up in Mexico.

"It sounds to me like the Lotus Bitch deserved a little of her own medicine," Stoud observed. "But isn't it murder for him to shoot another Marine like that?"

"It was an act of mercy," I said. "Even Steinke wasn't chickenshit enough to ask any questions. Dog didn't say, but it appears that once he ended the Marine's suffering he saw his chance to get the Lotus Bitch. He took that chance. There's been no more torture outside the wire of Hill fifty-five since then—and there probably won't be."

"Write it up and get it on the wire," Baylor said. "It sounds like our little Top Stick is streaking for the finish line."

"I can't write all of it," I said. "They wouldn't understand back home."

"Hellfire!" Stoud snorted. "I'm not sure *I* understand it. Every time I read one of your pieces about that kid, it's like I can feel somebody walking on my grave. I can understand killing in combat. But what this kid does . . . What happened to turn him into such a cold-blooded killer?"

19

THE NEXT TIME I HAD A CHANCE I CAUGHT A SHIT HOOK, A Chinook helicopter, down to Plei Me where Col. Joe Watts's Three Nine was operating against the 33d North Vietnamese Army Regiment. Watts's battalion was set up in a temporary base camp on Chu Pong Hill overlooking the slow, muddy Ia Drang River flowing out of Cambodia. The terrain was scrubby and dry except along the river. Thick red dust covered the base camp's tents and vehicles and men.

"I'd offer you a beer," Colonel Watts said, "except I haven't seen a Budweiser in so long I probably wouldn't know whether to drink it or frag it."

The colonel was short and redheaded. Natural red, not red from the dust that caked his tired face. He watched intently as Huey gunships floated into the landing pad, kicking up more dust. One had a line of bullet holes in it that started forward at the plexiglass pilots' shield and chewed its way aft to the tail boom. Corpsmen ran out with stretchers to remove the door gunner.

"Goddamn!" the colonel said explosively. "We've seen

more action recently than since the big fight here in 'sixty-five. There's something heavy about to come down. They're swarming across the border like cockroaches."

The door gunner was dead. The corpsmen put him into a black body bag and zipped it up. The flight line crew stood and watched.

"We don't have beer," Colonel Watts said, "but we have Kool-Aid. Damned if we don't have Kool-Aid. Come on."

His command center was a GP large with the canvas sides rolled up to let the air circulate. Around the tent were sandbags stacked neck high. I took a gray folding chair and didn't bother to shake the dust off it before I sat down.

"*Stars & Stripes* printed a couple of your stories about Corporal Able," Watts said. "Sort of a local boy makes good, eh? I don't know what I can tell you about him, Mike. Most of the old-timers have rotated out or been evacuated with wounds. There's a lot of talk about him though. What is it now? Thirty-one kills?"

"Forty-two as of last week. He's busy."

Not counting Hamilton.

"Do you think he'll make his hundred?"

"Two months ago, I'd have had to say no. Now I have to say maybe."

Some more helicopters came buzzing in. The colonel watched them, squinting, until they settled. This time the corpsmen were not called.

"Able's determined," Watts recalled. "He looked so young when he first came in with the other replacements that we had him burning the shitters. The kid never complained. It was like he was waiting. He never had much to do with anyone. Some of the others tried to pal up with him. Oh, he was polite enough. You know how he is. He was polite, but it was like there was a vacuum inside. He'd take a book and go off by himself to read. Or fish. He liked to fish. I'm probably not telling you anything you don't already know."

"Dog was already Dog when he arrived in 'Nam," I mused.

"If you mean like an ice man, the answer is yes. He'll go back home in a year or so, if he survives, and hole up in a Texas tower or someplace and plink off twenty or thirty people and the police will blame it on Vietnam. But *him* you can't blame on Vietnam.

"There's some talk," the colonel went on, reflecting. He lit a cigarette. "I don't know how much of it is gospel and how much is bullshit," he said, "but I'll give you what I hear. I heard he murdered his girlfriend and got away with it before he came to Vietnam."

"He murdered her?"

I shook my head, refusing to believe it. Still, things started clicking. Whatever happened, it would have been in the Oklahoma newspapers. Maybe that was how Carl Can't recognized Dog. I had found out Vinita was only about fifty or sixty miles from Muskogee.

"The kid can run point though," Watts concluded. "They started calling him Bird Dog. Bird Dog. Huh."

I patched a telephone call through Japan to the United States, to a former INS wireman who quit and started writing copy for the San Francisco *Chronicle*.

"Marvin, I need a favor."

"Name it, Mike. You don't think I've forgotten how you pulled my ass off the beach at the Bay of Pigs, do you?"

"I was counting on that. Marv, this kid named Johnny Able. He's about twenty. From Muskogee, Oklahoma. See what you can find out about him, will you? His girlfriend might have died or been killed under mysterious circumstances."

"What's her name?"

"I'm afraid that's all I can tell you, Marv. Be a pal?"

"Can I get back through to you? It may take a few days. You're still in the shithole of the world, right? Mike, you'll die in one of these armpits."

* * *

The next time Bill Lange flew in to Da Nang I told him about the rumor that Dog's girlfriend hadn't just *been* murdered. Lange chewed his cigar.

"The kid's not *that* kind of a killer," he said. "I'd bet my pension on it."

Lange harbored almost a blind loyalty to his snipers.

"You're probably right," I said.

"Look, Mike. That's some bad talk against the kid. He doesn't need it, okay? He's doing a helluva job. Sure he's killing gooks, but isn't that why we're here? If I had a battalion of gook killers like him, we *would* be home for Christmas."

Lange fumbled in his utility pockets and produced a flyer printed on cheap yellow rice paper. He unfolded it and handed it to me. The first thing that caught my eye was the photograph. It was one of the pictures I took of Dog the first day on Hill 55. He peered down his rifle barrel into the camera. Even in the faded black-and-white copy, his eyes burned pale and deadly. The text on the flyer was in Vietnamese characters.

"The local VC have put out a reward on Dog's head," Lange explained. "Fifty thousand **P**. One of our patrols found this poster tacked to a village tree. Dog's hurting 'em bad, Mike. He's got the little yellow people scared shitless. Know what Charlie calls him now—*Cho Linh hon,* Ghost Dog."

Brigette and Judy Wong wanted to look at the poster.

"Him a baby-san, for goo'ness sake," Brigette cried, giggling. "Not look like Ghost Dog."

"I wonder how the VC got that photograph?" I mused.

Lange smoked and rubbed his fingertips across the back of Judy's hand.

"Maybe they picked it up from *Stars & Stripes.*"

I studied the poster.

"This particular photo was never published," I said. "It was among some Carl Can't printed for the wire before he got himself killed, but it was never used. The only other copies were at the hotel. God, Bill, I'm sorry as hell this happened. How is Dog taking it?"

"The kid just shrugged. 'Let 'em try,' he said. 'It makes the game more challenging. They can't get me.' Mike, that's the problem with this goddamn war. You never know who to trust."

20

I HITCHED A RIDE ON A SIX-BY OUT TO THE DA NANG AIR BASE. Sandbags covered the bed of the truck to keep any mines the truck might run over from blowing into the asses of the FNGs. The FNGs looked scared.

"It don't mean nothing," I assured them.

"What?"

I laughed.

At the air base I wrangled a flight on a UH-1D helicopter. We flew at three thousand feet in the clean morning air with Da Nang behind us and to our left and the South China Sea beyond that. The sun made the sea glimmer. The air was cool and fresh so high up with the doors open and the M-60 gunner leaning out over his gun. He was tethered to the ship so he wouldn't fall out. I watched with him the mosaic of rice fields and jungle and villages that passed slowly below in various shades of green and earth tones. There was a railroad, and the Tuy Loan River looked yellow from so high up as it meandered around and passed below the spiderlike hill off which Bill Lange's snipers operated with Col. Stick Steinke's Three Nine battalion and other elements of the 9th Brigade.

You never thought there was a war going on, looking at Vietnam from a height where you couldn't smell the cooking fires and the human shit fertilizing the rice, where you couldn't see the troops slogging endlessly back and forth looking for each other or looking to avoid each other. As many times as I had seen it, I still liked to look at Asia from the air. The sight of just one Buddhist temple always transported me back to a time before the Korean War and before I started covering wars for pay, to a time when Asia meant intrigue and romance and adventure.

You got disillusioned again, though, as soon as you settled back to earth.

The helicopter crew chief, hanging out over his gun, chattered into his helmet mike and gave the pilot thumbs-up. The tent city on Hill 55 resembled a huge Okie camp from dust bowl days. It reflected itself in the gunner's dark face shield as the chopper floated over it, nose tilted up, then settled out of the air like a bird.

Captain Lange waited for me on the ground, holding his cover on his head with one hand against the chopper's fierce blade wash.

"Dog's fishing," Lange said.

"Fishing?"

"He goes fishing when he's not on mission."

We stood on the crest of the hill, out at the edge of Maintenance. Lange pointed. There was the wide stretch of grasslands, then the jungle and the river beyond.

"That's where he killed the Lotus Bitch," the captain said. His finger shifted. "That's where you can find him. There's a canal that flows into the Tuy Loan. I keep telling him the gooks will be after the bounty on his head, but he says fishing relaxes him."

I shook my head. The kid was amazing.

"We can wait for him at the Boonierat," Lange suggested. "Rafter just got in a new supply of ice."

"Can't I find him at the river?"

"Only if he wants to be found. I'd advise against it, Mike. The kid's the only one who goes outside the wire alone."

"I'll go."

"I can't go with you, Mike. I'm expecting somebody. Duty, you know."

"I didn't ask you." I grinned at him.

"You know something, Mike? You and that kid—you got a lot in common."

A Marine guided me through the wire and the mines. Then I was on my own. I descended the hill along a gulley covered by an M-60 machine gun and claymore mines, then cut across the grasslands toward the canal. The knife grass grew taller than it looked from the hill. Once you were in it you couldn't see but a few feet in any direction. Although I knew sentries on the hill could spot anyone moving in the grass, I still paused frequently to listen for gooks sneaking up on me. I carried in my hand the .45 pistol Bill lent me, just in case. There was something unnerving about being alone and exposed to the enemy.

The sun beat down hard, leaching moisture from every pore. I wore cammies and a bush hat. The cammies turned black with sweat down my spine and at the armpits and underneath the camera bag that rode to the rear against my side.

I found the canal and followed it. It was narrow and shallow, growing progressively deeper and wider as it neared the river. In the shallows you could see the leeches like grass undulating in the current. I broke silently through the thickets and grass, going slowly and carefully. After Korea, after I recovered from wounds, I taught combat tactics at Fort Benning for a while before I took my discharge.

I parted the grass at the edge of a small clearing. There the kid sat on the canal bank with his shirt and hat off and the stubble of his hair bleached startlingly white against the tan of his face. He was fishing with a long green cane pole he had cut and a bobber made out of a dried cane chip. The water was darker here, and deeper, and the current rippled around cattails and other aqua plants protruding above the surface.

The kid stared into the water. He seemed preoccupied, his mind drifting back, perhaps, to his Oklahoma creeks. He looked pensive, relaxed, alone but liking it. He looked vulnerable. He looked like some farm kid catching catfish in a neighbor's pond. There was something poignant about the scene, something touching.

I found it difficult to imagine the kid murdering anyone.

"You can join me if you like, sir," the kid said, startling me. He was still watching his bobber. He was getting a bite.

"You're good in the bush," he said. "I didn't pick you up until you were already off the hill."

I stepped into the clearing, feeling a little chagrined because he caught me.

"The time you spend hunting and fishing is not subtracted from your allotted time on earth," he said, glancing my way.

"Does that include hunting men?"

Again he turned those eyes on me for one heartbeat. His eyes were not those of a farm kid. His rifle and pistols lay on the grass next to him, within reach. He returned to his fishing to yank a big silver-looking perch out of the water. It flopped desperately in the grass. The kid flowed smoothly to his feet, wet his hands in the canal, and then removed the fish from his hook.

"If you don't wet your hands first," he explained, "you take the protective covering off the fish's scales. It gets diseased and dies."

He placed the fish gently in the water and freed it.

"You don't keep them?" I asked.

"No need killing something without a reason, sir," he replied. "Besides, they have worms. The Vietnamese eat them, but they survive with pests and parasites in their systems that would kill an American."

He threaded another hopper on his hook from a jar full of them and sat back down on the grass with his cane pole. I came and sat on the grass near him.

"Take off your shirt, sir," he invited. "The sun feels wonderful."

I removed my utility jacket. The kid's torso was tanned, like he spent a lot of time here with his shirt off. My arms and face were brown, but my chest and belly were the color of a fish's belly. A fish didn't have all that black hair though.

The kid fished in silence. I felt like an intruder.

"About the wanted posters," I ventured.

"What about them, Mr. Kragel?"

"I don't understand how the gooks got those pictures I took of you. I checked and I still have all the prints."

He almost smiled. "It don't mean nothing. Isn't that what they say?"

"The only thing I can figure is the VC somehow got copies from Carl Can't."

I watched the kid.

"You remember Carl Can't?" I asked. "From the road?"

"The ARVN aircraft shot him," Dog said. "Friendly fire. It's the worst kind."

"He died, you know, before I got him to Saigon."

"I knew he was going to die. You can see it in them when they're dying."

I pressed on.

"Carl recognized you," I said. "He knew you."

"Is that what he said?"

"Not exactly."

"I don't see how he could know me."

"He's from Oklahoma too. Isn't that a coincidence? He was from Vinita."

I thought it might get some reaction. It didn't. Dog caught another fish and went through the ritual of releasing it.

"People are always *from* Oklahoma, sir," Dog said. "It started during the Great Depression. Most of them are like the migrants who went to California: they never return."

"How about you? Will you return?"

He shrugged slightly.

"What about your folks? Your girlfriend? You do have a girl, don't you?"

There *was* a reaction this time. I knew I saw something in his eyes before they bleached out again.

"Sir," he said, "there is no one."

He swept his hand around him. "This is home," he said.

Exasperated and not hiding it, I said, "Talking to you is like pulling teeth."

"I'm sorry, sir. I try to be honest."

"Then *be* honest, but, goddamnit, stop calling me sir. I'm not that old yet. My name's Mike."

"Mike," he said, trying it. "Mike, like Shakespeare said, the world's a stage and we're all actors upon that stage. Actors exist only as long as they're upon the stage. There is nothing before or after. All you can ever know about that actor is his role. Vietnam is my stage. What you see right now is all there is of ol' Dog."

No. There was more. There was depth to this kid. And mystery. No wonder he intrigued Bill Lange.

"What we are before we go on stage determines how we play our roles," I shot back.

Dog looked at me. He wore his smile that was not a smile.

"Kid, nothing exists in a vacuum. My readers want to know more about you. Goddamnit, kid, what's behind those eyes, what is there inside you that compels you to go out there alone day after day to collect your fucking ears? What drives you? Who are you? That's what my readers want to know. *Who* are you?"

"I'm a Marine, sir . . . Mike."

"What else? Goddamnit, what else?"

He caught another fish and released it before he replied.

"I can't tell you," he said. I thought he was being honest.

"Just answer my questions," I suggested. "That'll be a start."

"People can lie," he said.

He looked at me for a long moment. He looked amused. Maybe he wasn't totally without humor.

"Maybe there is a way you can find out," he said.

He waited for me to ask.

"How's that?"

He placed his fishing pole on the grass and stood up. I stood up with him. I followed him to where we could see the line of jungle that curved along the river. He swept his hand toward the jungle and faced me. He almost smiled.

"The real Dog exists only out there," he said.

I looked at him.

He returned to his fishing.

"No one goes into the bush with me," he said. "They think I have a death wish."

He laughed. I had never heard him laugh before. It was not entirely unpleasant.

"I want to live long enough to collect my ears," he said, like he was trying it for shock effect.

This kid couldn't shock me, not after all the shit I'd seen. His eyes challenged me.

"When do we go?" I asked.

His brows rose slightly. "I heard you weren't like other journalists," he said.

"I'm not as smart as they are. When?"

"There's a price on my head."

"I helped them put it there."

He hesitated.

"Okay," he said. "The Two Nine's going back out early next week. The snipers are going too. We're going into the Hai Van. Marines call it The Valley of the Shadow of Death. *'Yea, though I walk through the shadows of the Valley of Death, I shall fear no evil . . .'"*

I finished it for him: *"'. . . for I'm the meanest motherfucker in the valley.'"*

He laughed more easily this time.

I left the blond kid there fishing on the canal. I had glimpsed something in him that was as yet undefinable but that was nonetheless human and made him seem somehow vulnerable. It appealed to something in me.

"Are you certain you want to do this?" Lange asked. "Going into the bush with Dog guarantees you'll see action."

"Somebody has to record the event when the Top Stick falls," I replied.

Lange pushed the Boonierat Club again, but only half-heartedly. "I'm meeting an ARVN officer in an hour," he said.

I had already checked with the operations sergeant. A Huey was flying out from Da Nang with Lange's ARVN, then flying directly back. I had to meet a deadline on a couple of wire pieces I hadn't finished. Lange walked me to the flight line. He seemed nervous. He chewed on his cigar.

There was something familiar about the young Vietnamese army officer who got off the chopper and came scurrying bent over away from the rotor wash. He ran with a slight limp. It wasn't just that he looked effeminate. A lot of the Vietnamese looked effeminate with their slight builds and the way even the men went around holding hands with each other.

I looked hard at Lange. Dink civilians weren't supposed to come behind the wire.

"Mike . . . ?" Lange said.

"I don't want to hear it, Bill," I replied quickly. "It's your fucking career."

I ran past the ARVN officer and buckled myself into the chopper against the firewall. Lange stood and watched as the helicopter pulled pitch, drifted off to one side, then nosed down and began picking up speed and altitude. The two figures on the flight line grew smaller—Bill Lange the bulldog and his paramour Judy Wong disguised as an ARVN officer.

Men did stupid goddamned things when their dicks took over.

21

THE HAI VAN PENINSULA WAS ONE SPOOKY GODDAMNED PLACE even before the drums started thudding. The jungle, where it hadn't been killed by herbicides, was double and triple canopy. Where the jungle died from the sprayings it was brown turning to gray. You could smell the chemicals from a klick downwind. They smelled sweetish like soured milk and heavy enough to collect in your throat. Dog avoided the dead zones after we broke off from Horrible Hotel and were on our own. But even where the jungle remained green and dense we saw no birds or animals. Insects didn't even burr. There was just the dripping from last night's rain and heat wriggles steaming from the foliage.

It was like walking through an abandoned cathedral, or a graveyard.

I kept looking back over my shoulder. Civilians weren't supposed to go armed, but it was a comfort having the new M16 Lange slipped me just before Three Nine started boarding helicopters at dawn.

"Thirty round clips and capable of fully automatic fire," Lange said, still looking self-conscious because I knew his little secret about Judy Wong.

"It has a maximum effective range of only four hundred sixty meters," Dog interjected. "Sir, we don't let Charlie get that close to us."

"Charlie's thick out there," Lange said, his voice rising above the whumping of the choppers dropping in for the troop airlift.

With my camera case and the M16, I scrambled with Dog onto the metal floor of one of Hotel's allotted ships. Dog's Winchester remained in its case. He wore his holstered .45s and his string of ears. I looked around. The grunts were young and they were all looking at me. I was forty years old. Some of the grunts sat on their flak jackets. I didn't have a flak jacket. Neither did Dog. Sitting on your flak jacket might keep you from getting your balls shot off if some gook in a rice paddy opted for a little skeet shooting.

I didn't need this shit. I had had my war. This war belonged to *this* generation. Let this generation fight it.

My heart started pounding when we took off. Dog stared calmly out the open door.

It don't mean nothing.

"Brigette," I said before I left, "it don't mean nothing. I'll be back before you miss me."

"I miss you already, Mike."

"Brigette, are you Schopenhauer?"

"Yes. Schopenhauer. Hai Van most dangerous place. Beaucoup VC, Mike. Dog Ghost number sixty-nine ten t'ousand *din cai dao."*

"Ghost Dog," I said.

"No correct me now, Mike. Maybe *Cho Linh hon* not come back. Maybe you not come back too."

Tears flooded her dark eyes.

"I always come back," I said.

"This time different."

"Why is it different?"

"It different, for goo'ness sake. Brigette not want you same-same Captain Lange's other shooters."

After nearly six months without a single casualty, Captain Lange had lost two snipers in as many weeks. Sgt. Roger Norman was the first. He was short and on his last mission as spotter for a trainee named Colson when a VC sniper turned the tables on them. A single 7.62 round from a Russian Mosin-Nagant nailed Norman dead center. He said, "Uh! Goddamn . . . !" The heavy bullet slammed him to the ground and he died.

The trainee Colson was a Clydesdale horse of a man. He called in his emergency extraction code, hoisted Norman's body onto his shoulders, and carried the dead sniper out to the chopper pickup point.

Dog came to look at the body. It lay inside a black bag on a gurney in a tent at the Battalion Aid Station waiting with three other corpses for a chopper ride back to Da Nang, and then home. Dog unzipped the bag and looked at the congealed grayish face. Norman spotted for him at first when none of the others would. Then Norman wouldn't do it anymore either.

"If he'd stayed with me, sir," Dog remarked to Lange, "he'd still be alive."

The second sniper, Cpl. Ron Dougherty, went down less than an hour after he and his spotter broke off from their patrol after insertion. The spotter stayed with Dougherty's body all night, hiding in thorn thickets and dragging his dead partner from hiding place to hiding place while the VC searched for them with lanterns. A story went around that the spotter's hair turned solid white overnight. He had been evacuated back to a psychiatrist at Da Nang.

"Just like Collins," Lange said. "Mike, you remember me telling you about him? This one is catatonic too. Goddamn, Mike. Goddamn."

We were drinking in the French Fuck with Brigette and Judy Wong when Lange told me about his dead snipers. Lange drank much more than normally. His face looked flushed, eroded by new lines. Neither he nor I had mentioned Judy Wong on Hill 55, but Judy told Brigette she had flown the helicopter twice more since then to be with her paramour. Lange was taking a chance, but maybe he needed her.

"Bill, don't lay guilt on yourself about them," I said. "It's a war. Men die. You can't be responsible."

"But I am responsible, Mike. I take these kids and I teach 'em how to kill, but I can't teach 'em how to deal with the killing. And I can't teach 'em how to deal with the dying. Some of 'em get to like the killing, and maybe that's the worst thing of all."

Ngo was on bartender duty in his white coat. Lange glared at him.

"Norman and Colson were going to set up a hide in a place we call the Thirteenth Valley," Lange said, chewing on it like it was a cigar. "We had never operated in there before. Dougherty was careful in the bush, the most cautious in the platoon. Goddamnit, Mike, these were seasoned snipers. You just don't pick 'em off like you would a regular GI grunt. The VC have got smart or something. I can call it coincidence one time. But *twice*. Mike, the goddamned gooks *knew* my men were in there."

I thought of that when the drums started beating in the Hai Van. I had heard of the jungle telegraph before—great logs hollowed out to make drums whose sounds spoke for miles—but this was the first time I had experienced it. It was like suddenly your heart started thudding and it magnified until its beating became a part of everything around you. I knew now how the tiger felt when the beaters started and it couldn't tell where they were or from which direction they were coming. I empathized with Stanley and Livingstone making their first explorations of darkest Africa.

The drums meant the VC knew the enemy was loose among them.

Dog dropped to one knee, listening. I dropped with him. The drumming came from everywhere.

Drums? *Drums?*

What kind of war was this?

22

I FOLLOWED DOG QUICKLY ALONG THE VALLEY FLOOR TO WHERE the terrain rose into the escarpment. My heartbeats matched the heavy pounding of the drums. Once or twice Dog doubled back on our trail and we cut sign for trackers. Dog humped the radio in his jungle pack; I carried rations and camera gear and the spotting scope in mine. We sweated and drank Kool-Aid from one-quart canteens, emptying one at a time so the partially empty ones would not slosh. Old tricks of the bush were coming back. We found a thin stream trickling from the side of the valley and filled the empty canteens and put in more Kool-Aid and iodine tabs.

The drums kept beating. Dog listened and nodded slightly to himself.

Spooky shit this. I had almost forgotten what it was like to pit your life against an enemy. Every nerve ending in my body sprang alive. I felt Dog watching me from time to time, as though trying to judge my reactions. I returned his gaze.

The kid was enjoying himself.

The climbing out of the valley grew demanding. We emptied our canteens again. The sun rose high, but most of the time we couldn't tell where it was because of the thickness of the forest. Sometimes the drumming paused, but it always started up again. We struggled halfway up the valley wall and then started cutting around it to our right. We stayed well below where the mountains crested in swirls of mist; the mist would burn off as the day progressed. The kid was bushwise. The only way the gooks could approach was from below us.

When the drums stopped in the early afternoon, we knew trackers had picked up our trail. Taking a brief break on a narrow ledge that overlooked the Hai Van Valley, I saw that we were inside a wide bowl about two miles across. It bulged off another valley where Colonel Steinke's Two Nine was operating. From this distance Steinke's command chopper and the circling gunships looked like motes in the air.

We had ventured into solid VC country, and the VC were going to a lot of trouble to catch us. It occurred to me that maybe the VC somehow knew we weren't just a couple of lost Marines. The reward on Dog's head was certainly worth the trouble. It was almost a year's pay for an NVA private.

We kept moving. The drums remained silent. There were no sounds in the valley. The VC were on our spoor.

You could tell Dog ahead of me had spent a lot of time in the woods. He moved almost without sound; nothing escaped his scrutiny.

He fell suddenly to his knees in a particularly thick swatch of jungle that cascaded off the mountain into a small valley within a valley. He was alert, his eyes darting. I covered our backtrail with my M16. Dog caught my eye. He drew his hand knifelike across his throat. Danger.

Parting a growth of elephant ears and pushing aside some thorns, he revealed a road less than an arm's length ahead.

The Red Ball was well tracked—sandal prints, cart and bicycle tracks, ruts made from smaller trucks. The live thatched roofing that grew over the trail turned the road into a dimly lighted tube through the forest. The road was invisible from the air.

The NVA could move a lot of troops and material south on it.

After waiting, looking and listening, we crossed the trail in a rush and burrowed into the brush on the other side. We left our footprints on the road. I motioned to Dog that we should cover them. Dog shook his head and led the way up and along a ridge thick with thornbushes.

He kept looking for something. I kept looking behind us.

For a while we followed a faint pathway, leaving more clean trail for the trackers to follow. Dog paused periodically to listen, but he made no attempt to disguise our trail. He kept looking for something.

The jungle became so thick we had to force a pathway. We emerged from the jungle eventually into a kind of clearing against a rocky outcropping. A downed Huey rested lodged in stunted bush next to the wall of the natural bowl we were traversing. The helicopter was broken and corroded. Its glassless eyes peered down on us like those of a giant mantis. Green tendrils of vine and liana were pulling it back into the restless earth.

A skeleton sat strapped at the controls. Warrior ants and other insects had stripped the bones clean, polished them. The skeleton grinned into the awful silence. From its appearance, he had gone down about the time Special Forces advisers started their Vietnam buildup. The U.S. star on the chopper's tail boom had almost faded.

Dog approached the wreck cautiously while I framed him with my Canon SLR. I took pictures of him removing the skeleton's dog tag chain from around its neck. He showed the dog tags to me: *CW02 Fred B. Fulbright, U.S. Army.* I took more shots of him as he stood by the helicopter in a bank of sunlight and looked uphill at an outcropping of rock about six hundred yards away. I took pictures while Dog wasted precious seconds looking and the VC trackers closed in on us.

"Let's *di-di* the fuck outa here," I suggested, whispering. I didn't need a story badly enough to get shot for it.

Dog was all business. I might not have even existed. Seeming satisfied with whatever decision he had made, he scrambled through jungle and across a rock slide and up a fissure in the valley wall that soon widened and deposited us on the ledge above the crash site. I dropped fatigued and breathing heavily behind a boulder; the rock was so hot from the sun that it scorched my hands. I edged around to the side of the boulder and looked down. I didn't need the spotter scope to pick out the different-colored green that marked the clearing where the crashed helicopter rested. I realized then what Dog had in mind.

Dog touched my shoulder. "Wait." It was not a sound; his lips simply formed the word.

He disappeared along the side of the valley. We were high and just below the crest. I broke out the spotting scope and adjusted it on its short-legged tripod in the shade of some thornbushes so the sun would not reflect on the lenses and give our position away. The helicopter and the clearing jumped out at me.

Dog returned as noiselessly as he departed. He dropped alongside me.

"Afterward," he whispered, "we can move under cover along the ridge."

Prone, getting ready, he dug his elbows into the rocky soil. He wrapped the Winchester carrying strap once around his left arm and brought the rifle barrel down twice until the stock fitted snug against his shoulder and the Unertl scope was about two inches from his eye. Too near and the recoil drove the scope into his eye, too far back and the sight picture was unclear and diminished and he wasted time getting back on target.

He was ready. We waited.

"I'm going to pick off Tailend Charlie first," he whispered. He wasn't looking at me. His eyes remained intent on the clearing by the helicopter in that singleness of purpose Lange talked about. "I read this book one time," Dog went on, "about a WW Two sniper who practiced picking off drag with his first shot. By the time his other targets heard the first rifle shot he had two or three more down. I tried it. It works."

"You read about snipers *before* you came to Vietnam?"

The kid chanced a glance at me, then returned to his scope.

"Watch for me through the spotting scope when they come into the clearing," he said. "Help me adjust *if* I should miss."

I scanned the sides of the bowl above us.

"What if they get foxy and circle up high?"

"They won't. They think we're on the run."

I flinched involuntarily when the drums started again. This time there was just one of them thudding from somewhere on the opposite slope of the bowl. It filled the stagnant air with its slow, rhythmic beat.

"They're trying to keep us moving," Dog murmured, waiting, watching, his eyes sharp and piercing like those of a bird of prey.

His intensity unnerved me. I thought he wasn't quite normal.

But then, *here,* like this, how could you be normal?

Brigette asked me once what it was like to be normal.

"In your world, how normal people live?" she asked.

It had been a long time since I had had to think about it. I laughed to cover my discomfort.

"We work," I said.

"We work here, for goo'ness sake."

"Then it isn't work we do," I said. "In Vietnam, most of your people live outside the cities. They still build things with their hands and grow things. They plant their rice and they work it and they actually see what they produce. They harvest what they grow and they use it to satisfy their needs or they trade it for something else they need. It can be hard, I know, and brutish, but it still must be a satisfying thing to have that kind of control, to be the cause and effect of your daily life."

"You not grow rice in 'Nited States?"

"Only a small percentage of us grow or produce *anything*. Most of us are in the service industry."

"You are *servants?*" she asked in surprise. "Who do you serve?"

I laughed. "Each other. We do things to make the lives of other people easier."

"Like what, for goo'ness sake?"

"Like waiters and clerks and government workers. More and more of us are on welfare and do nothing."

"That seem easier," Brigette agreed. "Is easier mean better, Mike?"

"It is less satisfying in the long run. It's even pointless. You have time to fill and maybe you don't know how to fill it. You go to work at some job the results of which you seldom see. You come home to a Budweiser beer and football on the tube. You never see or understand where you fit into the scheme of things. You do not see the cause and effect. Most of us don't even care. That's what's frightening. We don't give a fuck. We die watching 'I Love Lucy' reruns and Walter Cronkite on the news while we have dinner. There's a war here killing our sons but we don't give a fuck as long as it isn't *our* son who is being killed."

Brigette looked long into my eyes the way she did. Her hair was drawn back and kept in a long ponytail by the abalone shell comb and a rubber band. I was getting ready to go to the office. The lizard watching from the balcony looked pink in the glow of the rising sun.

"Mike, you famous writer journalist, for goo'ness sake. You tell 'Nited States about war and other things."

"Brigette, you're an innocent," I said. "Don't you understand? Nobody really gives a fuck as long as it doesn't touch them personally."

"I hear on radio where college children and—what you call . . . hippies?—yes, hippies . . . they change 'Nited States, Mike."

I scoffed. "They're the most screwed-up of all. All they

want to do is trip out on acid and fornicate in public
fountains. They're a spoiled generation throwing a public
tantrum. They'll end up popping beer tops and watching
Johnny Carson on TV."

"Mike," Brigette said, "you most bitter man in your own
country. You not normal."

"God, I hope not."

"Brigette not think I like live in 'Nited States of Amelica."

In the United States of America she would be just another
gook getting Americanized into the Giant Melting Pot of
Westinghouse and GE, Chevrolet and Sears Roebuck. Fuck
all that. Maybe I'd never go back home. Fuck Sharon and
her divorce and my pension, too, and the little retirement
plot of land on the Kankakee.

And fuck Budweiser beer and Sunday afternoon football
on TV.

I looked at Dog where he waited like a predator. Nearly
one hundred ears on his belt. Double that and he would
have his all-American quota—one hundred kills. What kind
of goal was that?

And I was recording his kills for him, for the world to see
and appreciate.

What kind of goal was *that?*

I almost laughed aloud.

Normal? What was that?

Fuck it. It don't mean nothing.

I was watching through the spotting scope and I gave a
little start when the gooks appeared by the crashed helicopter. First they weren't there, then they were. VC in cone hats
and black pajamas and tire-tread sandals, not NVA regulars
in khaki uniforms and pith helmets. I counted four of them
armed with Chicom AKs, short brutal little weapons with
the banana clips curving toward the muzzles. They trotted
slowly into the clearing, all in a row like ducks. The point
man had his nose to the ground like a hound on trail. He
stopped and they all stopped.

The others regarded the chopper curiously, but the point

man kept alert. He studied the terrain ahead of and below him, as though he suspected our clear trail might be leading him into a trap. Then his head swiveled up toward us. The sun shone on his face. When his eyes came out from the shade of the cone hat, it was just like Bill Lange said.

His eyes leaped out at me. I knew he couldn't see us, but still it was like he and I were eye to eye.

The drum stopped beating.

I had killed North Koreans and Chicoms before. I don't know how many. They attacked in human waves, mostly in the poor light of dawn. You kept shooting into them until they were scattered like bloody rags all over the landscape. You didn't have time to look into their eyes. It was impersonal killing, if killing can be impersonal, and it can.

I looked into this man's eyes and wondered what it would be like to drop the hammer on him. *I will kill you, you personally,* and then you kill him.

My trigger finger automatically tensed on the barrel of the spotting scope. I wished for a hunting rifle instead of the short-ranged assault M16 that lay beside me.

Crack!

For a mad instant I thought the spotting scope had turned into a rifle and I squeezed the trigger. I recoiled from it, as from a viper, but then was back on it in time to see the VC soldier in the rear crumple to the ground.

Before the others could react, indeed before they even heard the first rifle report, Dog dropped the next one in line.

His third shot crippled the leader. It smashed him to the ground. He spun around on the grass like his left leg was pegged. The surviving VC grabbed him by the back of his shirt and half-dragged, half-carried him in a stumbling run toward the dark safety of the jungle. He looked back over his shoulder as he ran, terror written on his face in large script.

It was downhill shooting, and difficult. Dog's fourth shot missed clean. I saw it kick up a geyser of dirt and jungle debris.

"Low and right!" I barked, overcome by the excitement.

I quickly shifted positions to keep the scope bearing on the running VC.

Get those motherfuckers!

The *fifth* shot . . .

It was not Dog's.

Something pinged the back of my right thigh. It was like the heavy strike of a snake. It stung me and then I heard the shot. It came from a distance and high up on the same side of the bowl with us.

23

INSTANTLY, WHILE THE SOUND OF THE ENEMY SNIPER'S RIFLE SHOT was still reverberating across the bowl, Dog sprang to all fours, like a cat. Rock splinters exploded from the granite two inches from his head as the sniper fired again. Dog jerked me to cover behind the sun-warmed boulder.

Then we were down and low. Specks of blood dotted Dog's face from the rock splinters. He blinked his eyes rapidly to clear them and make sure they were all right. I was breathing heavily and reaching for my wound. It was warm and wet and sticky. It was starting to burn, but I didn't dare move to check it until we knew where the gook sniper was.

I had shifted positions almost the instant the sniper fired the shot that got me in the leg. If I hadn't moved when I did . . .

War was full of *ifs*.

Dog's eyes were searching.

"Goddamnit, I told you they'd circle," I grated out through clenched teeth, fighting to regain control, frantic at the thought of being wounded and not knowing how bad it was.

I could be bleeding to death.

"Flesh wound," Dog said, looking. He sounded apologetic for having let the other sniper surprise us. "It's going to hurt, but you can still use it."

His eyes returned to their searching. He seemed to be measuring, calculating.

"I've found him," he said at last. "Now I'm going to go get his ears."

I looked at him. Our faces were inches apart.

I said, "I'm going with you."

Those bleached-out eyes. There was nothing behind them except animal cunning.

"Let's go," he said.

Since the enemy sniper blocked the direct route, Dog led the way in a low crawl off the back side of the rocky ledge. So far, there was little pain from my wound. The flesh and muscles started to stiffen, but there was little pain. I realized as we crawled that my M16 was as useless as a primitive throwing spear in this contest. This battle would be carried out at long distance, sniper against sniper. I was along only to record it.

I wondered if the gook sniper cut off *his* victims' ears as trophies.

We worked our way on our bellies along a shallow gulley that cut upward toward the rim of the bowl, then wormed ourselves into a thicket of fern and decaying logs on a narrow shelf. Dog fished in his pack and handed me a pair of binoculars; the spotting scope remained below by the boulder where I had been shot. I inched forward with the binoculars and slowly, carefully, parted the ferns. Dog came forward, too, with his deadly Winchester.

I glassed the terrain, moving across it in sectors, starting with our former position below and scanning along the face of the escarpment. I gave particular attention to where a hogback thrust up out of the jungle and rode upward on the escarpment like the scaly back armor of some prehistoric monster. Spotting no movement, I inched on for another five hundred yards to where a sheer cliff blocked off movement in that direction.

The sniper had two choices: Either he scrambled down into the jungle, joined the surviving trackers, and called in reinforcements; or, he climbed through the dense cover of the hogback to the rim of the bowl where the high ground gave him command.

I figured him for the last choice. Snipers were a peculiar breed. Even gook snipers. How often did a sniper face sniper with the opportunity to prove himself Top Stick?

Dog scanned with his rifle scope. He didn't say, but I knew he had also homed in on the enemy's options.

We glassed the terrain for another precious quarter hour, knowing more enemy might be on the way. Then we dropped off the shelf and cut up through jungle at the bottom of a draw, climbing heavily in the midafternoon heat. The wound in my thigh burned like it had fire ants stuffed in it, but it stopped bleeding. My muscles trembled from fatigue and loss of fluids. We paused and drank our last canteen of water. The Kool-Aid tasted metallic like iodine.

It took nearly an hour of toiling to find our way out of the draw to the upper rise of the hogback. I panted like an old racehorse on a fast track. My utilities turned black from sweat. Dog took a deep breath and seemed refreshed. His eyes darted constantly. He'd leave me behind if I faltered. Now I knew how Carl Can't must have felt when I took him with me on the road to Bien Hoa.

We began climbing our side of the hogback. Occasionally, I glimpsed the top of the rim through breaks in the foliage. Another half hour at most, moving carefully the way we were, and we'd be in command.

Dog increased his pace. Whoever reached the top first had the advantage. I realized we were in a race with high stakes. The next shot fired in this deadly contest meant death for someone.

I could see the lead for Hank Baylor's next INS dispatch:

Veteran journalist Michael W. Kragel has been declared missing and presumed dead in combat action on the Hai Van Peninsula. Kragel, forty, has been covering the Vietnam War since the first Marine landing at Da Nang in 1965. He landed with the Expeditionary Brigade. In 1966 he won a Pulitzer for his series on combat medevac flights. Listed as missing in The Valley of the Shadow of Death, Kragel was accompanying Marine sniper Lance Cpl. Johnny Able about whom the journalist has been writing a series. Able had made a vow to kill one hundred enemy soldiers. Able, twenty, is also missing and presumed dead. . . .

"I'm not dead yet," I muttered through pained breathing. Fuck it. *Fuck* it. Fuckit fuckit fuckit fuckit . . .

The rim loomed ahead. As the hogback steepened to grab at the summit, it became more rounded, wider, and less thickly vegetated.

On the side of the hogback opposite us the other sniper must have lost his footing in the scree and rubble. He slipped noisily. Rock went bowling downhill, crashing through the jungle. I whirled with my finger on the trigger of the M16, but all I heard afterward was the furtive sound of the Viet sniper scrambling uphill. He was throwing caution to the rockslide and bounding through the jungle, determined to reach the top first.

Dog glanced back at me. Then he started to sprint uphill. Our lives depended on crossing the finish line ahead of the gook marksman. I scurried after the kid, using saplings and other growth to help propel myself forward and up. Wind whistled through my teeth. I gasped for breath. God, I was getting too old for this shit. My vision was a red blur. I vaguely saw the top of the hill. The finish line.

I expected a yellow grinning face to appear behind a scoped rifle.

Thirty yards.

Twenty.

Ten.

Where was the sonofabitch?

Dog's lanky frame scooted low over the crest and I heard him fall behind cover. I was right behind him, exhausted, sweating, staggering, in pain, reaching for the last reservoir of strength, but I made it.

We were at the top first. We won. Dog cast me that unsmile of his and his blue eyes sparked once to life, but he did not let himself celebrate beyond that. His eyes once again paled to the white heat of the sky as he tunneled through growth to the very lip of the mountain.

We commanded the high ground. We saw both sides of the hogback as it ski-sloped down toward the thick fur of the valley jungle. We were at the highest point around.

Nothing stirred below, although the enemy sniper was down there somewhere, waiting for a target now that he had lost the race.

It was a standoff. We slowly settled into it. A deadly game of patience. Whoever blinked first lost. Dog and I took turns on the binoculars. We watched for the sniper and we watched for enemy reinforcements. Neither appeared.

The sun's fierce rays beat down through the trees to reach us. My leg stiffened as the sun descended. It was behind us now, shining downhill into the gook's eyes, an advantage that would not last. Already the valley floor was in shadow. Minute by minute the darkness crept up the sides of the bowl, like a pool filling with ink. In less than an hour The Valley of the Shadow of Death would consume itself. The advantage shifted from us to the gook sniper as soon as the darkness reached him while we remained in sunlight.

I looked around for a way out.

Dog remained unmoving. Patient.

The kid had no nerves.

We waited.

It was my turn on the binoculars. Slowly I scanned a wooded draw about three hundred yards below us. It led off to the right of the hogback and appeared to dead-end farther back against a wall of rubble.

"What's that?" I whispered.

Dog's Winchester shifted toward the draw.

"There it is again," I muttered. "Something reflecting like a mirror."

Dog uttered a muffled sound, and then he fired. There was an answering shot, but it turned out to be a reflexive action and the gook's bullet flew wild. The twin rifle reports echoed off the valley walls and careened across the black valley below.

A man shot in the brain reacts like a chicken off the chopping block. The body flops and flails violently about as though charged with electricity. It was horrible. I had never seen anything like it. Leaping and kicking, the body wallowed out a large bloody hollow in the undergrowth. When the gruesome spectacle finally ended, we scrambled down to have a look.

The corpse was dressed in NVA khaki; the enemy was sending his best to deal with the American snipers. Dog turned the fresh corpse over. There was a large ragged hole where the sniper's face used to be. Dog picked up the enemy's Mosin-Nagant sniper rifle with its short thick-barreled scope. His bullet had smashed against the outer barrel of the scope, destroying the scope before it destroyed the gook's face and brain.

That meant the gook was aiming at us when Dog squeezed off his round. If his scope lens hadn't caught sunlight when it did . . .

Another *if* in war.

Dog shook his head. Then he unsheathed his Kabar and with two deft strokes sliced off the dead man's ears. He poked little holes in the gristle with the point of his knife and strung them on his parachute cord with the others. His eyes met mine. They were like that first time through the camera lens. There was no cruelty in them, however. No malice. They were simply without depth.

"This one doesn't collect the bounty," Dog said, looking at the dead man.

When the kid touched his grisly string of trophies it *was* almost like he was fingering a rosary.

"Are you Catholic?" I asked him on impulse.

The kid looked at me. "There is no God," he said. "How's your leg, Mike?"

"It's still attached."

"Mike," he said, "it's getting dark. We can't be extracted until daylight. How do you feel about spending the night under the stars?"

"It's not the Muskogee Hilton."

"Muskogee doesn't have a Hilton."

He paused. "Mike," he said, "you did well. Wait here."

He slipped off down the hogback to cut the ears off the two corpses by the helicopter.

24

DOG ACCOMPANIED MY LITTER OFF THE CHOPPER WHEN THE medevac reached the Battalion Aid Station on Hill 55. A surgeon removed the old first aid bandage. It was crusty with dried blood and a night burrowed into the thickest and nastiest piece of jungle we could find. The doc said the bullet made a clean hole through muscle, without complications. He swabbed it out and shot me full of antibiotics.

Mostly I just wanted to sleep.

"It's going to be as tender as the insides of a fat lady's thighs," the doc said, "but you, sir, are a very lucky man."

He glanced at Dog loosely collected in the open flap of the tent.

"You are more than just lucky," he amended.

Dog's pale eyes raked across him. Dog still carried his Winchester and wore his double pistols. He remained baby-cheeked through his tan; I had a heavy dark shadow of beard. The kid moved over to the operating table.

"Was it worth it?" he asked, his voice soft and polite in spite of the fringe of sarcasm.

"Ask me next week," I said.

It had been a long night in a wet hide. It was nearing the monsoon season. Rain clouds swept in as soon as the sun went down. By midnight we were shivering like starved and abandoned curs in a cold downpour. I was burning with fever and freezing from the soaking.

But I found something in the kid, a depth. He seldom permitted anyone to see it, but it was there and there were times during the night when I was sure I saw more than he intended. It was unsettling, but at the same time strangely compelling, as though I peered through him back into my own life.

I didn't want to look back on my life. Like I said, I hadn't left anything back there.

"Mike," the kid said while the surgeon finished with my wound.

His expression did not change.

I said, "Johnny."

He reached out. He gripped my hand briefly. Then he was gone.

A bonding often occurs between men who face death together. They share an understanding beyond words.

The surgeon watched Dog go. "I'll be damned for a lost sinner," he said. "Did I actually see something human in that kid?"

I ignored him. I swung my bandaged leg off the table. I was trying my weight on it, against the doctor's protests, when Captain Lange ducked through the tent opening. His ever-present cigar puffed fitfully. It was stuck square in the middle of his face. There were deep lines in his face. Our last radio contact with him had been before the clearing and the crashed helicopter. It must have been a long night for him too, with nothing to do but wait in the Ops Center, pacing back and forth before the bank of radios.

"Try to raise Spartan One again," he kept saying.

"Captain, it's no use. Their radio has either gone out, they're behind a mountain, or—"

"Or nothing!" he snapped. "Raise them."

"Sir . . . We'll keep trying."

Dog and I weren't the only ones who made enemy contact

in the valley. Captain Lange had had to extract two of his sniper teams because of excessive enemy activity. While Dog and I were eluding trackers, Echo Company and Horrible Hotel logged three enemy KIA and destroyed a cache containing rice and munitions. The companies withdrew into perimeters for an overnight. Colonel Steinke anticipated kicking them out at first light to pincher in on a suspected enemy command post in an old French fort high on the southern tip of the peninsula.

"What's *your* body count, Captain?" Steinke asked with a smirk.

Lange stifled a retort. The night and Steinke had worn on him.

Now, you could see the relief in his eyes. He jerked the cigar from his face and looked at me standing gingerly on my bad leg.

"Civilians don't get Purple Hearts," he said.

"Lend me a hand," I said. "I need to get back to Da Nang."

He quickly gave me his shoulder to lean on.

"I sent word to Brigette that you're back and okay," he said.

That meant Judy Wong had been on the hill again. I looked at him. He glanced away. In the old days when Pablo Rhoades was here, he wouldn't have even thought of bringing a cunt out while his snipers were in the field.

"Fuck Brigette," I said. "The war and the cunts are separate things."

Using Lange as a crutch, I hobbled toward the flight line on the other side of Operations. The surgeon shrugged as though to say combat correspondents were as crazy as snipers. Lange remained silent until we came to the line of Hueys waiting on the grass.

Then he said, "Mike, she keeps me sane."

"Did I say anything?"

"Everybody's not like Dog and you," he said.

I stopped. We looked at each other. My hand resting on his shoulder kept him at arm's length.

"Mike, I don't neglect my men. I was inside that Ops Center all night."

I switched my gaze to the choppers. A puff of smoke popped from the one on the end as its blades slowly began rotating, sending droplets from last night's rain flying through the air like jewels. The crew chief watched outside with a fire extinguisher in his hands. The red morning sun glinted off it.

"Is that my ride?" I asked.

Lange nodded.

"Bill," I said, suddenly grinning. "It don't mean nothing."

And it didn't. So what if the bastard was bringing out a piece of ass once in a while. He deserved it.

"Mike?" Lange ventured. He waited. "Mike, you ought to tell Brigette you're leaving Nam."

"You never tell cunts anything."

The bulldog was acting like a fucking poodle.

"You and Dog," he said. "Islands."

He waited another long moment.

"Aren't you going to tell me what happened out there?" he asked.

It wasn't the first time I'd been wounded. It don't mean nothing. I shrugged my camera bag underneath my free arm and started hobbling on my own toward the helicopter whose blades were now noisily thrumming the air. I shouted back over my shoulder.

"Dog'll give you the After Action."

I waved wearily at Lange as the helicopter wheels broke free of ground. The ship climbed, floating sideways, nose down. I scanned for Dog below and located him inside the sandbagged sniper compound. The hootches of the rifle companies and their support elements surrounded the snipers in rows of red mud-stained GP tents or Quonsets or prefabs. Hill 55 had five fingers and a thumb. At the tip of each, like a fingernail, was a 106mm recoilless rifle. Wire and concertina in layers and ploughed mine fields wove a pattern around the sprawling hill. Just behind all that, along the crest of the hill, were sandbagged fighting emplacements clumped down every few meters.

The hill looked impregnable.

In the midst of it all sat Dog crosslegged in the door of his hootch, alone, cleaning his Winchester. The rifle always came first. He looked up at the rising helicopter. The fine morning sun gleamed silver on his short-cropped hair. He lifted a hand and held the pose until I could no longer make him out. He watched me go, and he was alone down there.

He looked vulnerable.

25

I REMEMBERED WHEN MY PARENTS DIVORCED. I MUST HAVE BEEN about ten. I remembered when Dad left. He didn't know it, but I ran into the woods behind the house and I watched him leave. He drove down the long narrow road through the hardwoods to the main county road by the mailboxes. When I could no longer see the Plymouth, I cut across the pasture from the woods in a shortcut that put me in the sumac thickets by the side of the county road. I watched Dad go by again. I could tell he was crying. Unseen, I lifted my hand to my dad and held it like that until he disappeared, and held it some more after that.

Sharon wanted kids. She threatened to get pregnant whether I approved or not. I told her I'd leave her if she got pregnant. I meant it.

The helicopter crew chief touched my shoulder. His head was a bubble of helmet and dark visor. I saw myself in the visor. It gave me a start. I looked old and tired and worn. I looked like my dad the day he left home.

The crew chief slipped up his visor so I could see his face instead of mine.

"Are you okay, sir?"

I couldn't hear him above the rush of wind and the whumping drone of the engine, but his lips mouthed the words. I nodded and looked out at Vietnam below, past the dark snout of the M-60 machine gun mounted in the doorway. I fumbled in a pocket of my filthy jungle utility blouse and brought out a copy of the VC wanted poster with Dog's picture on it. I gazed at the picture. Then I carefully refolded it.

Fuck this shit. I didn't need it. I hadn't left anything back *anywhere*. When I left again I still wasn't leaving anything behind. You traveled faster without baggage.

"Cap'n Lange say you tough bastard, for goo'ness sake," Brigette had said.

She smiled wisely and touched her fingertips to her head. "You tough bastard in here," she said, "but you soft bastard here." Her fingertips moved to her heart.

"You not let nobody see. But Brigette see, for goo'ness sake. Big Shoot Mike got heart for Brigette Nguyen. Big Shoot Mike got real heart."

I scoffed. "We come into life alone, we go through it alone, and we leave it alone. The grunts know. It don't mean a fucking thing."

"Tough guy," Brigette said.

"Yes."

"No," said Brigette. And she smiled impishly the way she did.

"What do you know about it?" I snapped.

She was just a gook cunt.

I didn't need all this shit. The wound, the night in the woods, the NVA sniper flopping around like a wrung-neck chicken, Brigette, Lange and Judy Wong, Carl Can't, Sharon, the divorce, and the kid.

You collected baggage whether you wanted it or not.

But you could always leave it behind.

My bandaged leg stuck out in the helicopter in front of

me. I slammed my fist into it. The pain was good. It kept my mind focused.

The crew chief turned his bubble toward me. I saw my face again and quickly looked away.

"They told me my father was in prison," Dog whispered last night.

After the sniper was dead and Dog collected his trophies, we traveled hard up and out of the basin and around toward the west until it was dark. The drums did not start again. Clouds imprisoned the moon and the stars, and the rain starting ensured we would not be tracked. Dog burrowed into a thicket of thorns and ferns and vines. I followed the sound of his slithering in mud until I bumped into him.

There was a big tree in the middle of the thicket. I felt it with my hands. I felt Dog propped with his back against it. I pulled my leg along and huddled next to him so that our shoulders touched. He withdrew at first, but then as the rain continued in a blackness as deep as space I felt his shoulder touch mine again. He did not withdraw this time. We moved closer to each other.

After a while we began to talk, whispering. Talking, like touching, helped drive back the void. It was raining hard and the drumming of rain on foliage kept our voices confined between us.

"I never knew them," Dog whispered. "My parents. I always told everybody they were dead."

I was so hot with fever I thought I heard the rainwater hissing like on a hot stove when it struck me.

"How do you feel?" Dog asked.

"Relative to what?"

We listened to the rain. I tried to keep us talking.

"Who raised you then, kid, if your parents didn't?"

"I did," he replied.

I waited to see if he would go on. Finally he did.

"There were a few foster homes," he said, "but I took off on my own when I was fourteen. I was living in Muskogee with the Lawsons. They were older and the only reason they kept me was because they needed the money the welfare department gave them. 'You're an odd boy,' old Lawson told me. 'I don't know how you got like that, but you won't ever fit in anywhere.' I was fourteen and that's what he told me. He was right though. I never fit in. I suppose I'm like my father in that respect. He must not have fit in either. That's why he was in prison."

Darkness makes for intimacy, even between misfits.

"So what did you do?" I prompted.

"One night I waited until they were asleep. I slipped out of bed and put everything I owned into a flour sack. That wasn't much. I had two pairs of jeans, some T-shirts and underwear, and a winter mackinaw. I took my clothes and a loaf of bread, some cheese, and a few books I owned— Hemingway's *The Old Man and the Sea* and *For Whom the Bell Tolls;* John Steinbeck's *The Grapes of Wrath; Gulliver's Travels;* and *Robinson Crusoe.* I took my Boy Scout knife, a hatchet from the shed, and a bolt-action twenty-two rifle.

"If you walk east out of Muskogee and cross the Arkansas River and go across the farmland you come to a mountain and the woods. There's an abandoned WW Two army post on top of the mountain where they used to keep German POWs. Camp Gruber. It's thousands of acres. The only time it's used is on weekends by the National Guard for training. I found an old bunker there and lived in it until I was eighteen."

"With your books and your rifle?"

"Sometimes I sneaked into Muskogee or down to the lakes and broke into houses. I stole food and clothes when I needed them and ammunition for the rifle. Mostly though I stole books. With books, I had all I needed. I seldom went hungry. With a twenty-two rifle I could pick off a deer at two hundred yards or more."

He paused.

"A man is a much easier target than a deer or a duck or a squirrel," he said.

I felt him start to shiver. I moved closer to him to share our warmth, so we could leech it from each other. I tasted the cold rain. I tasted the night. The night was colder.

"I never tell these things about myself," Dog said from faraway, as though he already regretted it. "Do you remember Jim the Preacher from *The Grapes of Wrath?* That's who I feel like sometimes."

"Why?"

"There is one place in the book where he says he feels like an ol' graveyard ghost. That's how I feel sometimes. Like an ol' graveyard ghost in a big graveyard where everybody's dead."

He fell silent after that.

I felt compelled to talk too, whispering, telling this kid about Sharon and our marriage and the divorce. I talked about things so far back I hadn't thought about them in years. I was a forty-year-old man telling things to a kid young enough to be my son. I told him about when Dad went away and about the times afterward when I ran away from home too.

"The cops always found me and brought me home," I said.

"That's because you had somebody who cared enough to want you home," Dog said.

Mom died when I was in Guatemala before the Bay of Pigs fuckup. I didn't want to tell the kid she was dead. I hadn't even told Brigette about that.

"Maw died," I said softly to the rain.

And she was dead and I knew it.

"See?" said Dog. "Life's a graveyard."

I waited, blinking back the darkness.

"There must have been *somebody* for you?" I probed presently.

I thought I had lost the kid, such a length of time passed. Then he whispered into the rain.

"Margie."

It sounded like he had not said the name in a long time.

"Nothing is forever," he continued. "War teaches you that."

"Life teaches you that," I said. "What happened?" I asked.

Rain hammered on the foliage.

"An ol' graveyard ghost," the kid murmured. I felt him shivering hard now, and it was more than the cold and the wet soaking through to the bone.

Impulsively, I put my arms around the boy and drew him toward me. He was so skinny. He stiffened, and then he relaxed. Each of us in our own way, I guess, held the son and father we had lost or never known. We held each other like that through the night and the rain while the fever in me burned fiercely. We drew apart when the rain stopped and the jungle gradually emerged into gray form. The kid looked at me. Those eyes were like the first time I saw them through my lens. I wondered if they had been like that even when it was dark and no one could see.

26

I HAD MANAGED TO HOLD THE WAR AT BAY THROUGH THE READY lenses of my cameras. But then in The Valley of the Shadow of Death the war started to seep through. I felt it. I felt it again like in Korea, and like I hadn't felt it at the Bay of Pigs and the Hungarian uprising and in French Indochina and at all the other little brushfire wars I had covered. I *wasn't* the meanest motherfucker in the valley. Sometimes in bed with Brigette the night closed in thick and wet on my dreams and I tasted the fear and the aloneness of the rainy jungle hide in which I had held the kid in my arms.

Things about that night carried me back. Once, in Korea where our main line of resistance overlooked Old Baldy, I held the platoon leader like that. I was a sergeant and I held the lieutenant like I held Dog because the lieutenant had a sucking chest wound. Pink froth bubbled from the hole through his lungs. I slapped a piece of plastic over the hole and tied it down with a sleeve torn from my jacket. The lieutenant was dying. It was dark and we could hear whistles where the Chicoms were regrouping for another attack. The lieutenant and I, we were just kids, not much older than Dog, and I held him because it was dark and we were afraid and he was dying.

"I don't want to die by myself," he kept saying.

I *felt* the war.

I erupted straight in bed. For a moment I thought the sweat running off my body was the jungle rain and the ceiling fan was the sound of the night breezes in dark foliage. Brigette grabbed me and I grabbed her back and held on.

"Baby-san, my baby-san," she cooed, and her hands were all over me, checking me, making sure.

Brigette watched me constantly since I returned wounded. She appeared at the INS office during the day, something she had never done before. The phone started ringing at the office if I was as much as ten minutes late. She waited for me in the lobby of the Continental Palace.

She wept all night the first night. I slept fitfully. Whenever I opened my eyes she was there sitting on the edge of the bed touching me with one tiny hand, watching me intently, as though afraid I might vanish if she averted her eyes.

She kept crying until her eyes were red and swollen and her hair escaped from the abalone shell comb.

"Biness is biness," I mocked her in the morning light when the dreads of the night dissolved.

"Don't tease Brigette, for goo'ness sake, Mike. Promise never you go with *Cho Linh hon* no more. Mike, promise Brigette, for goo'ness sake."

Hank Baylor was almost as adamant about it as Brigette. "What's with you and that kid?" he demanded.

"It's a story. You said we needed a hero."

"But not if you have to follow him to hell. Mike, you're getting ready to transfer out of this shitbag country. Don't go home in a body bag. Carl Can't's obit was enough for one season."

What the fuck was wrong with me? I couldn't get enough of Brigette. I was okay until the streets became purple with the advance of night and the parachute flares started popping over the distant air base. Then I wanted to be with the girl, holding her, and being held like I had never let another woman hold me.

I was getting as *dinky dow* as Bill Lange over Judy Wong. You couldn't get hung up over a gook cunt. You couldn't take a slanteye home and you couldn't stay here with her.

But Brigette was so good when the nights came as they always must. Every once in a while a man happened upon a woman who seemed to fit him naturally, like a good pair of shoes or a Hong Kong tailor-made suit. Brigette *fit*.

"I paramour of famous writer," Brigette said. "Famous writer must not die, for goo'ness sake."

The French kerosene lamp brought out softly the scar across her nose. It highlighted her hair. I stroked her hair in bed.

"I won't die," I promised.

"You die if you write more story about sniper soldiers. No more go with them, Mike. You must promise Brigette that."

She knew not to interfere with my work. Tonight, however, I felt mellow.

"Why are you so Schopenhauer about the snipers?" I asked her.

"Sniper soldiers will die. You not go there again, Mike. Them take you from me."

"You could always find another famous paramour," I teased.

Brigette tossed her head. "Biness is biness," she agreed.

"Business."

"Mike, maybe you not go away ever to wife in 'Nited States. Stay with Brigette, for goo'ness sake. I take care of you good when you old man in bed. Brigette stay young and pretty, have nice ass for long long time. Brigette have nice ass when wife's ass sag like river mud. It good biness have nice ass. You think Brigette have nice ass?"

I laughed. "It'll do."

She looked horrified. She jumped out of bed naked and turned her back to me and looked back over her shoulder, studying herself.

"You think Brigette sag?" she cried.

I reached for her. "You have a wonderful ass," I said.

"Better same-same Jane Fonda?"

"You have a big screen movie star ass of all asses."

"Better ass than wife?"

"Hers is an ugly stepsister to yours."

"See? Brigette stay paramour of famous writer for long long time, for goo'ness sake."

We made love. Then we made love again and afterward she lay with her legs wrapped around my waist and her triangle of moist hair flattened against my ribs.

"You stay with Brigette long time?" she asked plaintively. I had never heard that tone in her voice before.

I kissed her lips that reminded me of nipples and did not answer.

"Mike?"

I still did not answer.

27

DENNIS FRY, THE LAWYER FRIEND IN CHICAGO, KEPT WARNING ME that I should come home if I expected to save anything from the divorce. It was difficult sometimes to patch a telephone call through, but he got through.

"If you don't come to Chicago, Mike, you'll be lucky to

escape with your B.V.D.s. Sharon's asking for an uncontested divorce, claiming you abandoned the marriage. She wants all real property accumulated during the marriage and a share of your pension."

"I'm coming," I said.

"When?"

"When I can."

"Maybe I can stall things if you'll give me a commitment."

I said, "Soon."

"That's not a commitment."

"That's the only one I can give you."

"Mike, what's keeping you in Vietnam? We're talking about your future here."

"That's what I'm paying you to take care of."

"There's a hearing next Thursday. I have to tell the judge something."

"Tell him he may as well screw me too."

"Goddamnit, Mike. I need to tell the judge when you'll be here, *if* you'll be here."

"Dennis, I'll call you back."

"I have to know, Mike."

"I'll call."

Baylor was trying to pin me down too. "Bernie Bernstein is retiring from the Chicago office," he said. "You can take over as Chicago Bureau Chief and handle the divorce at the same time."

"I have some things to do yet."

"Brigette?" he asked. "Have you told her you're transferring?"

"Why the hell is everybody so concerned about Brigette?"

"You're not?"

"Just fuck it, Hank. Fuck it all."

Baylor twisted out his mustache to ends so sharp he could have tacked dispatches to the bulletin board with it.

"Mike," he said, "Horton's still bugging me to pay for that jeep you and Carl Can't got shot up. Anyhow, you know that Korean broad of his?"

"Kim Kimshi."

"Whatever. Horton hasn't been back to the States in nearly fifteen years. The AP assigned him permanently to Asia. He divorced his wife and took up with the slanteye. They tell me he eats fish heads and rice and once shaved his head like a Buddhist monk."

"What's the point, Hank? I'm no squaw man," I protested. "I'm a patriotic U.S. citizen who believes in LBJ, the Great Society, and round-eyed women. In that order, amen."

"The point is, Mike, you can ask INS to extend you in Vietnam for another year. Until you make up your mind about things."

"Why would I want to do that? I'm not crazy like Horton. You wouldn't see me lending *him* a jeep."

It was time to go when a war started getting to you. At least a dozen times I attempted to break the news to Brigette. I looked at her in the morning when she was still sleepy-eyed and warm and smelled good like a woman does whom you have made love to and who has lain curled up next to you all night.

"Brigette . . . ?"

"Yes, baby-san. Mmmmm."

Nuzzling me.

"Brigette . . . I . . ."

"For goo'ness sake, Big Shoot."

"Big Shot."

"For goo'ness sake, what you say?"

Dark round pools of eyes you could fall into. But biness was biness, for goo'ness sake. She was just a gook cunt.

But, still, even Dog had certain loyalties. I owed Brigette *something*. She had always been there for me from the day I picked her up at the French Fuck.

"Mike, Brigette not never want 'nother man, for goo'ness sake. Not Vietnamese man, not GI, not for so long as you want me. You not have to say you love Brigette. All must do is look in Brigette's eyes and say you want me. I stay. Brigette know when you not want no more. You hide soul from everybody, but you no can hide soul from Brigette Nguyen."

If I couldn't tell her in the light of day that I was leaving, then I certainly couldn't tell her at night when the worst thing that could happen to a man who was feeling war was to sleep alone. It was okay maybe to be alone when you were twenty like Dog, but it was not okay when you were forty and getting your first glimpses of your mortality.

"Is Dog the reason you're staying?" Hank Baylor asked.

"Maybe there's a curiosity to see if he makes his goal."

"Is that all there is?"

"The kid saved my life in the Hai Van. If he hadn't pulled me behind the rock . . ."

"And if some VC collects the bounty on his head?"

"America will have its dead hero."

Tom Stoud listened from his desk, peeping baldly up over the framed snapshots of his ten half-breed Mexican kids.

"Somehow hero isn't the picture I get of a man who wears a string of human ears on his belt," he said.

"The war did that to him," I said.

Stoud's brows shot into question marks. Baylor scratched his head and fiddled with his mustache.

Marvin, the former AP man working for the San Francisco *Chronicle,* finally managed to get a call through to Da Nang.

"Mike, I asked for Da Nang and got Istanbul. Some Jap operator couldn't understand a word of English. I'm billing these calls to you, bud."

"What did you find out about Dog?"

"Who?"

"Corporal Johnny Able."

"You know how to pick 'em, Mike. He was some kind of jungle boy raised by the wolves or something. There was a reporter at the Muskogee *Phoenix* recalled a girl being found raped and murdered outside Muskogee near some deserted army post two or three years ago. The reporter said she thought that was how the police found your Tarzan living in the woods. The police kept it all pretty hush-hush, but my contact said she thought Wolf Boy was questioned about the killing."

"Did you get the victim's name?"

"I have it jotted down somewhere. Yeah. Her name was Margie Crowe."

Margie. The name Dog muttered in the rain.

"Marvin, tell me. Did the cops ever make an arrest?"

"The case is still unsolved."

"Thanks, Marv. I owe you one."

"You owe me eighty-three dollars and change on long-distance calls. When you coming home, buddy?"

"You never know."

"Bullshit. You'll never come back. Not to stay."

I finally made a much-delayed sympathy call to Carl Can't's parents in Vinita, Oklahoma. Carl Can't was a shithead who got himself killed because of a gook cunt in the road, but somehow I felt vaguely guilty over it. I should never have taken him with me.

I expressed condolences, then edged around to the real purpose of my call.

"Mr. Dubose . . . ?"

"Call me Frank. You were Carl's friend and with him when it . . . happened."

"Frank," I said. "Carl knew a boy from Muskogee, a blond kid named Johnny Able. Does the name mean anything to you?"

"Should it?"

"It was about two or three years ago. It might have had something to do with a girl named Margie Crowe."

Silence.

"Frank?"

"Mr. Kragel . . ."

It was no longer *Mike* and *Frank*.

"Mr. Kragel, my son is dead and I'm not sure I appreciate you trying to smear his name."

"I don't understand what—"

"My son had nothing to do with that mess. Let the dead lie in what peace they can find."

There was a loud click and the receiver buzzed in my ear.

What the fuck *happened* back there in Oklahoma?

I kept thinking about it.

"Mike, for goo'ness sake, you Schopenhauer."

"Yes. Schopenhauer."

28

CURIOSITY WAS A POWERFUL THING IN A JOURNALIST. IT DROVE you to delve around in people's lives, even—or maybe *especially*—in parts they wanted to keep hidden. My mind kept clicking. I knew that sooner or later I had to find out what happened involving Dog and Carl Can't and a dead girl named Margie Crowe.

I was still limping around, nursing my wound and trying to make up my mind about what to do and when to do it, when Horton from AP came pounding at the hotel door. It was so early even the goddamned lizard on the balcony wasn't awake. The garlic *kimshi* odor on Horton's beard and breath drove me back from the door.

"Go away, Horton. We'll pay for the goddamned jeep."

"INS is too rinky-dink to pay for paper staples. Mike, I just got the word and thought you'd want to know. Hill Fifty-five was hit this morning. They're medevacking a shitpot full of Marines to the air base. I understand Lange's sniper compound was hardest hit."

"Let me get on my pants. I'll hitch a ride with you."

"There goes another jeep."

Brigette jumped out of bed looking wide-eyed and frightened.

"Mike, I tol' you, for goo'ness sake. *I tol' you!*"

"What the hell is the matter with you, girl? Get back in bed. I got work to do."

The air base had gone on full alert. The MPs at the gate checked our credentials for a change before waving the jeep through. Huey medevac birds slicked in and out of the pad behind the Quonsets of the brigade hospital. Sparrow Hawk waited in full combat gear at the assault chopper line. Double guards manned the towers, and dogs patrolled the wire with air force APs.

Horton screeched our vehicle to a halt in front of the hospital. I slipped on my Press brassard to avoid being questioned by the excited knot of Marine brass gathered outside in the first sunlight. I was relieved to find Bill Lange alive and unharmed, although he wore a helmet and his utilities were smeared with mud and blood. He looked as haggard as Winston Churchill during the London blitzes. The cigar clenched in his teeth was burned down to a stub.

"Dog?" I asked him.

"The kid's okay. But Deke the Geek is dead. So is Johnston. Willie B, Kansas City, and C.C. Coltrane are inside in surgery. God, Mike . . . God . . ."

He chewed the cold cigar and shook his head and looked haggard. His eyes burned feverishly deep in his face. Dried blood crusted one worn cheek stubbled with grayish beard. We walked off from the others where we could talk.

"Mike, sappers broke through the wire about two hours before dawn. They were on us before we knew it. They blew up the big GP and tossed grenades into the sniper hootches. It would have been a lot worse except Coltrane had made his first kill and most of the guys were on an all-niter at the Boonierat Club.

"Dog was the only one who heard them coming. He slipped out the back of his hootch and took up a position in the corner bunker. The attack was concentrated on the sniper compound. I knew my snipers were hurting the gooks, Mike, but Jesus God . . .

"It looks like the gooks came to destroy my snipers. Mike, the motherfuckers *knew* how to get through the wire."

He looked at me. He turned and walked away. I watched him attempt to relight his cigar. His hands trembled. I took the lighter from his hands. Inscribed on the side of the Zippo was the Marine Corps emblem and the phrase ONE SHOT-ONE KILL. I touched the flame to his cigar while he puffed smoke.

"Mike, I killed those men," he said. His voice sounded hollow, agonized.

"What are you talking about?"

"Didn't you hear what I said? The gooks knew how to get through the wire and where the snipers were. Mike, somebody from the *inside* sketched out our defenses for the VC."

Then I understood.

"Mike, I know Judy better than I've ever known another human being. She just *wouldn't,* Mike. Would she?"

Goddamn her.

"Somehow Steinke found out about her, Mike. You should have seen Dog's eyes when Steinke threatened to bring me up on charges for bringing a civilian aboard. That kid respected me. Now, I've betrayed my own men. I might as well have put a thirty-aught-six to their heads and squeezed the trigger. Steinke's a bastard, but I don't blame him. It'll ruin my career, but I'd do the same thing to an officer who did what I did."

His cigar went out. He grabbed it from his lips and stared at it. Slowly, his fingers wrapped around the brown stub and he crushed it. He let the shreds sift through his fingers.

"I trusted her," he said. "God save that slant-eyed bitch's soul."

29

MIKE KRAGEL DISPATCH, 22 OCT 67:

Vietnam (INS)—The sniper war of Capt. Bill Lange, sniper platoon leader and sniper instructor commander of the 9th U.S. Marine Division, has accounted for more than fourteen hundred enemy casualties since Lange founded his school a year ago on Hill 55 in the Da Nang enclave.

Formerly, enemy soldiers stood in plain sight at ranges of seven hundred to one thousand yards and directed mortar fire onto Marine base camps, knowing they were safe from retaliatory fire.

No longer are they safe. No longer do they stand in plain view.

"My trained snipers consistently hit and kill at one thousand yards," said Lange.

While the longest recorded one shot-one kill was made by former Marine sniper Sgt. Pablo Rhoades with a mounted 50-caliber machine gun fired single-action, the longest scoring rifle shot was made by the 9th MarDiv's current Top Stick, Lance Cpl. Johnny Able, a soft-spoken marksman from the hills of Oklahoma.

In support of a Marine infantry assault on a suspected North Vietnamese Army sanctuary north of the ancient capital of Hue, Corporal Able crawled on his belly in short grass through heavily occupied enemy territory for more than two miles in order to set up on a hillside overlooking the enemy's command post.

According to MACV command, NVA troops have been infiltrating south in large numbers for the past several months, presumedly to launch a major offensive before arrival of Tet, the Vietnamese New Year.

Shortly after dawn, Corporal Able shot and killed the NVA commander as the commander inspected his troops. The 272-grain boat-tailed bullet from Able's Winchester 30.06 Model 70 traveled fourteen hundred yards, over two thirds of a mile. It rose twenty feet in the air in a three-second loop before striking the enemy general in the heart.

Advancing Marines later found the body hidden in a bunker complex.

"It was the most incredible shot," said Able's commander, Captain Lange. "There is no one else in the world who could have made that shot."

It was Corporal Able's fifty-ninth confirmed kill. He has vowed to exceed by seven Sergeant Rhoades's record ninety-three kills.

So great is the enemy's dread and fear of Marine snipers that the North Vietnamese command and its Vietcong auxiliary have set up countersniper operations of their own.

Bounties have been offered on the lives of several of Lange's snipers who have consistently hurt the enemy. The enemy has printed up wanted posters on the snipers and distributed them to their troops and among the villages from the city of Quinhon to Khe Sanh on the DMZ. The price on the head of Cpl. Johnny Able, known to the Vietcong as *Cho Linh hon,* Ghost Dog, exceeds the yearly wages of the average North Vietnamese Army soldier.

"Time after time Corporal Able has sneaked into Indian Territory to hit the enemy in his own front yard," Lange said. "He has hit NVA generals in their command posts and VC guerrilla soldiers sneaking through the jungle. We have heard rumors that the enemy so dreads American snipers that troop movements that once took two or three days now take a week or more. They never know when or where the next deadly shot will come from. It is said Corporal Able is the most feared man in all of South Vietnam."

Two weeks ago, an estimated company-size element of Vietcong attacked Hill 55, where Captain Lange's sniper platoon is stationed. After Action reports indicate the enemy mission was to destroy the sniper platoon, against which the attack was concentrated. Two Marine snipers died in the assault and three others were wounded. One of the wounded later died.

Cpl. Johnny Able was not injured. He killed two enemy soldiers during the battle with his .45 pistols.

The NVA has dispatched specially trained sniper teams of its own. Corporal Able shot and killed one of these expert snipers during a mission into the Hai Van Peninsula. A week ago, Col. Clarence "Stick" Steinke, commander of 2nd Battalion, 9th Marines, was shot and killed by a single bullet from an enemy sniper as the colonel prepared to board a helicopter to oversee search and destroy operations.

"The sniper who killed him was good, really good," said Steinke's executive officer, Maj. Floyd Grebner. "It took an expert woodsman and marksman to, in broad daylight, slip undetected to within rifle range of Hill 55, get off one accurate shot, and then escape undetected. Our most expert Marine sniper could have done no better."

30

JUDY WONG LIMPED INTO OUR ROOM AT THE CONTINENTAL PAL-
ace and wiped her eyes with the backs of her hands, like a
little girl who has fallen off a bicycle and skinned her knees.
She even looked like a little girl in the traditional *ao dai* she
wore with pants. She gave up tight jeans and short Cinderella skirts when Lange took up with her.

Brigette ran and hugged her; they held onto each other
and blubbered and chattered in Vietnamese. I couldn't
understand much Vietnamese, hated it when Brigette spoke
it around me, but I understood enough to know that Judy
Wong's heart was breaking because she hadn't seen Lange or
heard from him since the sapper attack on Hill 55.

She put on a good act for a spy.

Brigette shot me a warning glance not to say anything. She
helped Judy Wong to the bed, where they sat on the edge,
and Brigette rocked her grieving friend back and forth,
cooing to sooth her. The French kerosene lamp reflected
itself in Brigette's eyes looking up at me over Judy's bowed
head.

I turned away and slid open the French doors and closed
them behind me, cutting off the sound the crying girls made.
I stood on the balcony three stories above dimly lighted Duc
Phon Street and wished I hadn't quit smoking. The palm
fronds clicked in the top of the tree on a level with me. I
looked down into the street, attracted by the raucous cackle
of some boom-boom girl.

Korea, I remembered, smelled like soured cabbage *kimshi*
and burning cooking oil. Cuba had its smells too—fried
bananas and the sea. Every country had its distinctive odors

that smelled like that country and which you always associated with that country.

Vietnam smelled like dead fish, rot, and human shit.

I realized I hated this goddamned place. Things were getting too complicated. A journalist was supposed to be an *observer*, not a participant. Your camera lens kept everything at bay. It was like a movie you watched and then reported on for the critic's section of the morning paper. That was how it was supposed to be.

The actors weren't supposed to try to kill you. The leading lady had a nice ass and a good pair of jugs, but you looked at them and went home and didn't worry about her demanding anything from you. You didn't get personally involved in any of it. You were a part of it while it was happening, but you were also outside of it and apart from it.

This goddamned country smelled like dead fish, rot, and human shit.

"'Every bondsman in his own hand bears the power to cancel his captivity,'" quoted Dog when I choppered out to the Hill after the gook sniper killed Colonel Steinke.

"Shakespeare," I said.

"It's from *Julius Caesar*. Ol' Dog reads, sir," he said with his unsmile.

We walked between the sandbagged hootches of Maintenance Company, past battalion headquarters with its stars and stripes flying disconsolately at half-mast in honor of the fallen commander. I was still limping a little from my bullet wound. Dog wore his string of ears and his .45s. He wore his pistols all the time since the sapper attack. Captain Lange would join us later at the Boonierat Club.

"Is it that goddamned obvious—my captivity?" I asked.

"You have to know when to make the break."

I started to pay Rafter in military scrip when he brought us two beers, cold, and chunked them down in front of us, but he shook his head.

"Corporal Dog doesn't pay at the Boonierat Club," he explained.

I looked around. Three Marines with their shirts off were

dealing Five Card Stud in one corner. Otherwise, the hum of insects in the heat outside the screens was the only sound. Rafter smiled obsequiously at Dog and leaned on his elbows across the top of his homemade bar. Nothing in the club hootch seemed to have changed, except Rafter had added a bulletin board upon which he displayed all the published news clippings I wrote about Dog's exploits. In the center of the display, as though in mockery of the VC efforts to stop *Cho Linh hon,* hung one of the Vietnamese wanted posters with Dog's picture on it.

"Kid, how about you?" I asked Dog. "Will you know when to make the break?"

"Forty-one to go," he said.

"And when you get your hundredth kill?"

He shrugged.

"When you climb a mountain," he said, "do you think about what you will do *after* you reach the peak—or do you simply concentrate on the summit? There may be nothing after the summit."

"There's always something else."

He shrugged.

The kid was back to his old self with the bleached-out eyes and smile that was really not a smile. We were comfortable with each other, but there was no mistaking that the night in the jungle rain was in the past and not to be spoken of.

"You and I—we can handle it," Dog decided presently. "It's the skipper who needs to make the break."

"He extended for another year," I pointed out.

Lange didn't say so, but Judy Wong was the reason he extended.

"The skipper hasn't been himself," Dog said with a trace of genuine concern in his voice. "He took it hard. About the girl, I mean."

I glanced up. "You knew about her?"

He nodded. "The skipper is having a hard time handling it."

"We don't know for sure it was her," I said.

"We know. She almost caused Colonel Steinke to court-martial the best man on this hill."

I glanced up sharply. Something in his voice.

"How convenient of Steinke to get himself killed," I said. Nothing in the kid's demeanor changed.

"Yes," he said. "How convenient."

"There's another quote from *Julius Caesar* I like," I said. "Ol' Dog isn't the only one who reads. It goes something like this: 'He reads much and is a great observer. He looks quite through the deeds of men.'"

Dog sipped his beer dispassionately while he thought about it. He returned my gaze, peering unblinking into my eyes the way he had through his telescopic sight the first time I took his picture.

"No one is that good an observer," he decided.

Lange replaced Dog at the table after Dog drank his limit of one beer and left.

"I can't say I'm sorry about Steinke," Lange said over his second or third beer. "Steinke was a gold-plated asshole. Not many people were sorry to see him get it."

Lange's bulldog face was still lined and tired, but it looked better than it had the morning after the sappers broke through the wire.

"Where were you when it happened, Bill?" I asked, unable to resist.

He looked up quickly.

"Mike, I know what you're thinking," he cried, looking horrified. "You're a journalist and you train to be skeptical. But, goddamnit, Mike, you have to believe me when I say I don't know anything about Steinke getting shot except that a gook sneaked up the canal and across the field to make the shot."

"Where was Dog?" I asked pointedly.

"Mike, the kid was out on a mission. He was out all night until noon."

"Steinke was shot when? Midmorning? Did Dog bring back gook ears?"

Lange hesitated. "You don't get a kill every time you go out," he said. "Mike, how can you even think what you're thinking?"

"Journalists are cynics."

I let it drop. This was a war. Men got killed in a war. Some of them were assholes and deserved it.

I wasn't a part of this war anymore. The baggage was getting too heavy for me.

"It don't mean nothing," I said.

Lange looked worried.

"What are you going to do, Mike?"

"I'm going to write my war stories. Then I'm going to say 'Fuck it all.'"

"It was a gook," Lange insisted. "That's the truth. A gook sniper."

Truth was subjective. It was what you said it was at any given time. What did it matter anyhow? No one gave a damn for the truth in Vietnam.

It don't mean nothing.

I wasn't a part of the war anymore.

The boom-boom girl below on Duc Phon Street cackled again. Then I saw her clinging to the arm of a U.S. Army officer in khakis. I knew he was an officer, because enlisted men weren't allowed in Da Nang after dark. The officer staggered and almost fell in front of a passing pedicab. The scantily clad whore grabbed him. He held onto her and slobbered and giggled drunkenly. He grabbed her and kissed her and then fell flat on his ass. She helped him up and I watched them staggering away together with the officer's arm thrown around the girl's tiny shoulders.

Brigette used to do that, would probably still be doing it if I hadn't picked her up at the French Fuck.

"Biness is biness, for goo'ness sake."

"What kind of business is that—fucking for hire?"

"Mike, you not unnerstan'. You not unnerstan'."

"Then enlighten me so I will understand."

"Life hard for Vietnamese girl, for goo'ness sake. Life happen, and girl must do what she can."

"What happened? Didn't you tell me once you were a nurse's aide? That's better than fucking for pay. That's all I know about you. I don't even know how you got that scar on your nose."

She looked long and seriously at me. "Big Shoot Mike, Brigette's life start with you. There no Brigette before Mike, for goo'ness sake."

"Bullshit," I said.

"No bullshit, Mike. No water buffalo shit neither."

I didn't like the thought, but I had to accept it. Brigette was a boom-boom girl. She was a whore. As soon as I left, Brigette would be back in *biness*. At least until she found another paramour. She'd be like the cackling Cinderella below on the street hustling the drunken army officer.

Biness was *biness.*

I wished I hadn't quit smoking.

I heard the door close when Judy Wong left. A minute later the balcony doors slid open and I felt Brigette standing next to me on the balcony. I scented her hair that hung long down the low back of the slit-sided dress I bought for her in Hong Kong. I bought it because I read James Mason's *The World of Suzie Wong* and I always imagined Brigette being a little like that—a mysterious good-time girl with a big heart and a past.

She was a whore. Whores were baggage. You left them behind when you were ready to move on. It was easy to leave a whore behind.

I always put my arm around Brigette when we stood on the balcony with the palm fronds clicking and the night breezes cool. This time I didn't. Brigette took my arm and hugged it sadly to her breast and snuggled close to my side.

"Judy Wong very unhappy," she announced presently.

Parachute flares started to pop like miniature suns over the distant air base. Like the old saying went, the more things changed, the more they stayed the same.

"Mike, you Schopenhauer?"

I waited for a minute.

"Brigette, I want to know something."

"I cold, Mike. Put arms around me."

"No, Brigette. Judy Wong is a Vietcong spy?"

I felt Brigette stiffen against me.

You didn't have to be a genius to figure it out. Bill Lange's

troubles started when he met Judy Wong. His snipers had
been plagued ever since then. Sergeant Norman and the
other one got it first, when they shouldn't have, and then
there was the sapper attack on Hill 55 that eliminated five
more. It even explained Dog's picture on the wanted poster.
Judy Wong was always coming to the hotel with Brigette.
She could easily have taken one of the photos I kept there,
copied it, and returned it before I knew it was missing. Judy
Wong was probably the reason trackers picked up Dog and
me so quickly on the Hai Van. They were expecting us.

Men led by their dicks were fools.

I glared at Brigette. A tear formed and streamed off her
cheek. I glared down into the dark canyon of the street
instead.

"Judy Wong was always wanting you to fix her up with an
American," I persisted. "Now I understand why."

"For goo'ness sake, Mike. How you say that? Judy Wong
heart break like you drop little porcelain Buddha. Her love
very much Cap'n Lange."

"Prostitutes don't love. It's business, remember?"

"Mike, you so very foolish."

"I suspected Ngo in the French Fuck was a VC. Now I
understand what the connection was between him and Judy
Wong. He was her contact."

I turned on Brigette. "Maybe *you're* a VC spy too."

Her eyes snapped wide in surprise and horror. Tears
gushed. I grabbed her shoulders. She felt so tiny and frail,
like I could have crushed her between my hands. I let her go
and turned away. She wept, but she let the gap stand
between us.

"Judy Wong not VC, Mike. Brigette not VC."

"I feel responsible," I said. "Because I let it happen,
there's a colonel dead out there. And I don't think the
enemy did it."

"Mike, Brigette so unhappy you same-same unhappy,"
Brigette whispered through her tears.

I couldn't look at her.

"Mike, what you do now?"

"Why does everyone keep asking that? I'm a journalist.

Journalists observe and write what they observe. We don't get directly involved in the blood and guts and gore. Journalists are spectators. You don't jump out of the stands and grab the ball for the touchdown. Let somebody else make the touchdown, if there's going to be one. I'll record it. Fuck it."

"Mike . . . ?"

"Go away, Brigette. Just get the fuck away from me."

She wept. Then she turned away.

Fucking baggage.

After a few minutes of being alone on the balcony, and feeling the aloneness, I looked through the glass doors where the French light shined in the room. I watched Brigette sitting at the little dresser combing her hair in the mirror. She was crying. She always combed her hair when she was upset. The soft light turned the abalone shell comb into a piece of rainbow in her hand. The reflected colors swept down her cheek with the movement of the comb.

She felt me watching and turned on the low stool to face me.

I didn't like the sadness in her. I turned away. When I looked back, Brigette still faced me across the room and through the glass doors. Her eyes pleaded.

She looked so beautiful sitting there. I remembered the first time I saw her. She was such a beautiful child with her clear golden skin and her black hair and her eyes delicately slanted like dark almonds. "For goo'ness sake," she said, and the way she said it made me laugh. "For goo'ness sake." I would always remember that about her. That and the way she looked the first time I saw her. And I would remember now.

I went into the room silently. The lizard was in front of the door waiting for insects. I shoved him gently out of the way with my foot. I closed the doors and pulled the drapes. Brigette rose slowly from her stool. The slit in her dress exposed one smooth thigh. With a little hushed cry she flung herself across the room and into my arms. I picked her up in the middle of a long kiss and carried her to the bed and started to undress her. She held her hands up alongside her head like a little girl does getting ready to go to sleep.

"Mike," she asked, "you not really think Brigette VC too?"

31

NGO TON HANG VANISHED FROM THE FRENCH FUCK. ONE DAY HE was there. I watched him. I could tell he was nervous. The next day he was gone with his little white waiter's coat. Like, somehow, he knew I was on to him.

"How I know where him go, for goo'ness sake?" Brigette demanded.

"You told Judy Wong I knew about them," I accused.

Bill Lange remained agonized over what had happened. "How could I have been so *dinky-dow?*" he said.

The two of us were having drinks in the French Fuck.

"The waiter running out proves it," Lange said. "Remember that time we were here and they had something between them? They were in this together."

He drew viciously on his cigar.

"I must have been *dinky-dow.*"

He walked out of the lounge with his head bowed. Poor bastard.

I saw Judy Wong once more after that. I occupied my table in the French Fuck with my back to the wall when Judy limped in on her half-foot and made her way toward me. I was sitting and brooding and trying not to think of all the things I knew I had to think about. Brigette was upstairs getting dressed. Judy Wong stood in front of me, wiping her eyes. They were swollen from crying.

"I not same-same VC!" she cried. "VC numba ten t'ousand."

"VC numba ten thousand ten," I agreed. "Tell it to Brigette, Judy Wong. I don't want to hear it."

Two days later, Judy Wong's Cinderella roommate pounded frantically on our door. She flung arms and tears all over the room when Brigette let her in. She brayed with grief and terror. She rattled Vietnamese. Then Brigette burst into tears and threw herself at me to hold.

"Judy Wong! Judy Wong!" she cried.

"What about Judy Wong?"

"Judy Wong dead, Mike. Kim Lee come home and Judy Wong dead. Who shoot Judy Wong?"

I asked the White Mice that at their headquarters. They didn't know, and they didn't care. The National Police didn't get too excited over a murdered hooker.

"Somebody blow out boom-boom girl's brains," said a tee-wee, a lieutenant. He wore a white bill-cap and his face really did look like a mouse's.

"A GI?" I asked.

He shrugged. "Somebody."

"Aren't you going to investigate?"

He assumed a patient, long-suffering look. "War," he said.

"War?"

"VC, GI, ARVN, police, politics, newspaper—them all boom-boom." He laughed and cocked an imaginary pistol. "Sometimes them bang-bang boom-boom girls. Boom-boom girl die all time. Many Vietnamese die in war. Boom-boom girl part of war. Who care about one boom-boom girl?"

"Business is business," I said.

He smiled as though he had never thought of it that way before. "Yes," he said. "Business is business."

This goddamned country smelled like dead fish, rot, and human shit.

32

MIKE KRAGEL DISPATCH (WITH PHOTOGRAPHS OF WOUNDED GIs and black body bags being loaded into the belly of a C-141 aircraft), 28 Dec 67:

Vietnam (INS)—The grunts who fight this war say there are three ways to leave Vietnam: By rotation after you've survived your year; strapped to a litter; or in a body bag.

All three ways go out on the same "Freedom Bird." GIs who still have time to serve in-country roll out the black body bags stacked like cocoons on a baggage cart. They load the cargo first so the other homeward-bound GIs won't have to see it.

The wounded come next. They are on litters with IV bags attached. Some of them are missing arms or legs. Some are unconscious. Some are smiling. Others are apprehensive about how they will be received at home. They have heard about campus protestors calling them "baby killers."

"If one of those hairy hippie crudballs gets in my face when I get off in San Francisco," says a decorated veteran of the 101st Airborne, "I swear I'll waste him."

GIs on rotation board the air force jet last. They wear new greens and khakis that have been stored in barracks bags for the past year. They look uncomfortable out of their dirty jungle utilities and boots worn white. They board silently and wait, as though knowing *something* will happen at the last minute to prevent their going home.

"Charlie won't let us leave," a 3rd Division Marine murmurs. "Watch. Something will happen. Charlie will keep us here. Watch."

You can see them relaxing, however, moment by moment, as the big bird takes off from Da Nang Air Base and the outline of Vietnam fades behind them.

The pilot comes over the intercom as soon as the airplane passes into international waters over the South China Sea.

"Gentlemen, welcome aboard the Freedom Bird. Congratulations, soldiers. You have done your duty. You're going home. Next stop—Clark Air Force Base, Philippine Islands."

A wounded trooper from the 173d Airborne cheers so much he pulls the IV needle from his arm.

Part Two

Part
Two

33

SHARON AND I HADN'T SEEN EACH OTHER IN OVER A YEAR, AND then we met like strangers at the divorce hearing. She came breezing into the courtroom on point with her lawyer Avarice running slack and Greed and Sloth bringing up rear security. They were all so goddamned solemn, like this shit really meant something.

I stared. I couldn't believe the starched broad in the mannish businesswoman's suit and tie was the same one I slept with for a dozen years. She had never really been much in bed, but she looked like sex was even more alien to her now. She looked matriarchal. She looked middle-aged, but successfully middle-aged, like a man does who has struggled up the corporate ladder and got a little thick around the middle, a little stooped in the shoulders, a little haggard from the pressure.

You have a tendency to romanticize about a woman whom you haven't seen for a long time and who once meant something to you. It is always a disappointment when you see her again.

"She looks like she gets more pussy than you do," I

whispered to Dennis Fry as he stood to represent me. After two continuances, Fry had been ecstatic that I finally arrived.

"Vulgar as always," Fry commented, whispering back. "You're not in a war zone now, pal. A lot of things have changed since you've been gone. Haven't you heard of Women's Liberation?"

"Women's lip? Women are trying to grow balls and beards."

"That's a sexist remark. A good lawyer could make a civil case against you on that."

"Fry, there are no good lawyers."

"Tell me that after I save your pension and your ranch."

"It's not a ranch. It's five acres."

"Shhhh," Fry said.

It was a ridiculous thought, but I tried to picture Brigette Nguyen dressed like Sharon, with her hair in a fashionable beehive and her shoulders squared in a suit. I grinned. Sharon stared angrily. I started to chuckle. Dennis nudged me hard with his elbow. Sharon glowered.

I felt absolutely shabby in comparison to my wife. I wore faded safari trousers, roughout hiking boots, and a khaki shirt with military epaulets. I had lost weight, too, and the shirt hung slack on me. I hadn't had time to go Stateside shopping, but I wished I had at least gotten a haircut and trimmed my mustache.

"We don't have time," Fry said when he met me at O'Hare. "We're due in court in two hours. Look how tanned and lean you are. You look so young and fit that Sharon'll be absolutely furious with jealousy. Her fag lawyers will probably make a play for you. The judge'll look with favor upon a returning Vietnam vet. Are you limping, Mike?"

"I'm not a vet," I said. "At least not from this war. Besides, we heard in Nam the hippies and professors burn returning vets at the stake."

"There's more truth than fiction in that. It seems something's always burning in the U.S. lately. If it isn't

Columbia University, it's Newark or Detroit. It's either the SDS or the Black Panthers. The ACLU and Timothy Leary defend everyone's right to burn or smoke whatever he pleases."

"I think I'll get on that plane and go back to Nam where it's safe."

"Mike, the U.S. is where the real war's happening. It's the Time of Rages: the young against the old, black against white, hawks against doves, peace lovers against you warmongers, men against women. Mike, the homosexuals are even coming out of the closets and demanding the right to burn something too."

"I already miss Vietnam."

Fry laughed. "Maybe I'll go back with you. You know, Mike, I really didn't expect you to come home. I thought you didn't care one way or the other about the divorce."

"I don't."

He looked surprised.

When we were together at INS, Dennis was a lean, hard man, almost as tall as I, with a curly shock of dark hair and drooping mustaches. Mustaches went with the territory. Now, he was pale and soft from air-conditioning, and he smelled of musty law libraries.

"Why did you come back then?" he asked.

We were on our way downtown from the airport in the backseat of a Checker cab. I gazed out the side window. Coming back was almost like a cultural shock. Rice paddies and grass hootches and a pastel colonial city replaced by all that glass and concrete. Chicago looked *unlived in, antiseptic,* like somebody scrubbed it after every use. It looked like there wasn't a lot of living going on.

"You got to know when to let go," I told Fry, and he accepted that. We rode for another while in silence while I gazed out the window and collected my thoughts.

"Things have really changed," Fry said presently to renew the conversation.

"From here it looks the same," I replied.

"Mike, we need to talk about Sharon."

"You talk about her."

"If you want my opinion, the only reason she filed for everything was to force you to return to Chicago."

"She couldn't live without me, right?"

"She's been living very well without you, as a matter of fact. No, I don't think it has anything to do with hormones or old love letters. Sorry, Mike, but those are the facts. Beneath Sharon's trappings of success—and she's done very well for herself—dwells a woman scorned. It sounds silly, but I think she wants you to see just how angry and hurt you've left her. I think when it comes down to the nut cutting, she'll drop her claims and consider the divorce revenge enough."

I watched Chicago pass by.

"It don't mean nothing," I murmured.

"What?"

"It's a phrase the grunts use all the time. It can mean lots of things, really, but mostly it means that if you're still alive *that's* the only thing that's important."

"Mike, have I ever told you that even back in college I didn't understand you?"

"I understood *you.* Every skirt in Phi Beta understood *you.*"

He chuckled.

"We gave 'em hell, didn't we? Want to stop for chicken on rye at Sane Sol's first?" he asked. "You remember Sol, don't you?"

"I remember he doesn't serve fish heads and rice and the toilet flushes every time."

Sane Sol reminded me of a fat old leprechaun, only Jewish. He pumped my hand vigorously and said how sorry he was that I'd been away fighting in the war.

"I'm a journalist, Sol. I don't fight 'em. I write 'em."

"Oh. You still get shot at, don't you, eh?"

"He's limping," Dennis said. "You don't notice it much, but it wasn't there before."

Sol beamed. "A wounded hero you are, lad. Let me tell you, of the antiwar demonstrations I don't approve. Uncle

150

Sam must stand up in the world or death camps will happen here in Chicago."

I sat with my back against the wall. Habit. Fry grinned. He noticed.

As we ate, Fry said, "I heard Bernie Bernstein was retiring as bureau chief of INS and you were taking over the Chicago office. That'll settle you down, Mike. It's about time. That's always been Sharon's complaint—that if you even heard a rumor of war somewhere you were ready to pack your old Ranger parachute bag and take off. You still have that bag, Mike?"

"I have it at least until she divorces me and takes it."

He laughed, but then he said, "Neither of us is twenty-five anymore, Mike. I feel that if Sharon knew you were going to head the Chicago office she might take you back. Twelve years is a long time to flush down the drain."

"It's already gone down the drain."

"You can never go home again, huh, Mike?"

"Maybe you can if you know where it is."

He lit a Marlboro cigarette and looked thoughtful. He smoked for a minute and looked even more thoughtful.

"Mike, if we give Sharon some more time once she sees you, I think she'll drop her claims. The judge'll shit, but I'm going to ask him for one more continuance. Maybe he'll give me a week or two so you and Sharon can get together and talk. But be honest with her, Mike."

"I'll tell her she's a bitch."

"Is there any chance of you two getting back together?"

He saw the answer in my face. I just wanted to get it over with.

Around us in the restaurant the lunch crowd of downtown businessmen and secretaries were pushing and shoving as they noisily vied for tables. They might not be so god-damned self-centered if they had Charlie around to toss in an occasional grenade. That'd keep them on their toes. Teach them that *it don't mean nothing*.

"Mike, there's another woman?" Fry asked. "You can tell me it's none of my business."

"It's none of your business."

"An Oriental?"

My jaw tightened. "It's nothing, Dennis. Just a gook—"

I started to say *whore,* but it just didn't feel right. For goo'ness sake.

"You know how it is," I said.

His brows lifted, but he said, "Yeah, I know how it is. Mike, it's awful good to see you again, hoss."

Lawyers Greed, Sloth, and Avarice whispered a lot together at their table when Dennis asked for another continuance.

"Judge, my client has just returned wounded from Vietnam," Fry argued. "We ask for some time for him to become readjusted to society outside a combat zone."

Greed stood up. He couldn't see his shiny pointed shoes for his belly.

"We object to the defendant passing himself off as a war veteran," he sniped. "Your honor, the defendant is a news writer."

"A journalist," I corrected.

"A war correspondent," Fry quickly amended. "Nevertheless, your honor, he was wounded in action. A combat correspondent suffers hardships and dangers along with the GIs. All we're asking is enough time for Mr. Kragel to settle in."

It was Sloth's turn. Sloth was tall and skinny, like a hungry hound.

"We should like to bring to the court's attention that the defendant has for twelve long years repeatedly abandoned his wife, home, and responsibilities in order to run off to one foreign affair or another."

"Two weeks?" Fry pleaded.

Avarice jumped up. "Your honor, Mrs. Kragel points out to the court that she has dutifully performed as a wife to her husband and that, now, as always, he expects her to wait at his whim and call."

The judge banged his gavel. "Gentlemen. Gentlemen. The court is quite familiar with the circumstances surrounding this case. Nevertheless, the defendant has finally presented himself. I'm inclined to give him the benefit of the doubt.

Mr. Fry, this case *will* proceed two weeks from today. Vietnam or hell and high water, I *will* hear this case at precisely ten A.M. Is that clear to your client, Mr. Fry?"

I caught up with Sharon in the crowded hallway outside the courtroom. Her face froze into a sheet of ice; she became Ice Woman. Greed and Avarice stepped forward. I asked them politely, "Do you gentlemen want to wear your asshole around your neck like a collar?"

They stepped back.

"Mike, you'll never change!" Sharon cried.

I was face-to-face with her and I didn't know what to say. I was always better with a typewriter.

"Sharon . . . ? Sharon, I'm sorry."

That was it. Like I might have stepped on a stranger's toe in the elevator.

Sharon looked sad. I couldn't tell if she really was, but she looked it.

"Is that what Dennis told you to say?" she asked softly.

"I mean it, Sharon."

"Mike, have you seen the new bumper sticker: *Shit Happens?* Well, it does."

"When did you start talking like that?"

"I'm the broad who was crazy enough to stay married to you for twelve years, remember?"

I grinned lamely. "Oh, yeah. You must be Sharon."

"But not the same Sharon. There was a time, Mike, when I lived my life through yours. You were the glamorous war correspondent dashing off to find adventure. I lived life in your shadow, Mike. I always told our friends that some day you'd write the Great American War Novel and I'd stand by your side when you received the Pulitzer."

She paused to light a cigarette. I wondered when she'd started smoking.

"You'll never write your novel, Mike. You're too busy. Even when you received your Pulitzer for newspaper journalism, you celebrated with some other woman while I waited at home like the dutiful little housewife. You didn't think I knew that, did you, Mike?"

It wasn't sadness I saw in her; it was anger and bitterness.

"Sharon, I guess I never realized. I—"

"Mike, you never realized. You're self-centered and you're going to live your life exactly the way you want, no matter who it destroys."

People were bustling and shoving each other in the hallway around us, queueing up at the elevators, their faces stony and masked. The smells that distinguished this country were cigarette smoke and Brut and Chanel No. 5.

I looked back at Sharon. Her eyes were blue and there was a fine network of wrinkles around them. Age was always so much kinder to men than to women.

"Sharon, I've been offered bureau chief of the Chicago office."

She gave a little snort. She knew how to humble me without saying a word.

Defensively: "I'm considering accepting it."

Sharon glanced at her watch. It was a gold one.

"You won't," she said. "There are always your wars."

She drew on her cigarette, studying me.

"Tell me, Mike, did you just pack up and walk out on her like you walked out on me?"

The look of surprise that flashed across my face made her snort again.

"Don't look so shocked, Mike," she said with a wry smile. "I still have friends. Brigette? Isn't that the Kewpie doll's name?"

"You can be a cruel woman when you set your mind to it."

"I had the best teacher—you. Look, I've accepted the inevitable outcome of our relationship. In fact, divorce is the way I want it. I face things, Mike; you don't. But you'll have to, sooner or later. You're a middle-aged man, Mike. One of these days you're going to have to stop running."

"I've never run from anything—"

I felt like she had me backed against the wall.

"Big strong macho man, right? Mike, the way I hear it, this Brigette might have been a good thing for you if you had more guts for her than you had for me."

The bitch.

She glanced at her watch again. "Mike, I have an appointment—"

She started to walk off with her lawyers in attendance. She paused. She was still a striking-looking woman if you saw her from other than the standpoint of a soon-to-be ex-husband.

"About the divorce, Sharon," I said. "I want to get it over with as quickly as possible."

She smiled. "I deserve everything," she said, "just for putting up with you."

"Maybe you do, Sharon."

She hesitated a moment longer. Her voice softened.

"Mike, I was scared to death when I heard you'd been wounded."

34

DENNIS FRY INVITED ME TO STAY WITH HIS WIFE, MARY, AND HIM in Barrington Hills until I could get settled in. Instead, I rented a furnished room not far from the Greyhound bus station, near the INS office. The room had a daybed in it, a chair like you find in motels, a lamp with a stand made out of a cypress root that was starting to split, and a chest of drawers with a mounted mirror.

The single window looked down from the third floor onto Roosevelt Boulevard. You looked down into a canyon of stone and glass and metal. You couldn't see much of the street, the window was so small, but what you saw was like an elaborate anthill where the people were frantic like ants and all looked alike.

I looked out the window at night, and there were no distant parachute flares bursting over the airport. Here, you'd never be awakened by some whore in the street cackling with a GI, or by a lizard playing voyeur through the window.

I counted the steps across the room. Six one way, five the other. I sat on the side of the bed and looked at my hands, my feet. I tried to read a *Life* and thumbed through the last two issues of *Time*. The "International" section had a progress report on the war in Vietnam. President Johnson and his advisers were debating on whether or not to bomb North Vietnam to stop the infiltrations. Richard Nixon warned that the U.S. should not trust the communists enough to relax vigilance during the coming Tet cease-fire.

I threw the magazine on the floor and got up and jerked on my coat. Snow outside drifted down from the blackness into the city canyons. I found a corner bar. An aging barfly with her face masked in makeup glanced away after apparently deciding I wasn't a likely prospect for the night. She gazed out the window and watched it snow. The neon signs outside blinking on and off made her face glow like a Halloween mask.

There was also a man in a black overcoat drinking alone. The bartender had a DEATH BEFORE DISHONOR tattoo on his meaty forearm. I started to sit with my back against the wall, but then shrugged and perched on a stool at the bar.

"Draw," I ordered.

The bartender brought the glass of beer. I glanced at his tattoo.

"Marine Corps?" I asked him.

"WW Two," he said. "That was when Marines were really Marines and a war was a *war*. Vietnam ain't no war. The Marines today are like Boy Scouts."

"Yeah," I said.

Fuck him. I got up and took my beer to one of the tables by the window. I watched it snowing.

Let the motherfucker with his "death before dishonor" follow Dog into the bush. Dog'd show his ass *war*.

The bartender brought me another beer.

"It's from her," he said, indicating the sad bitch with the Halloween mask.

Apparently, she had had second thoughts. She was looking like she thought I might be responsible for throwing her out in the snow when the time came. I started not to accept the beer. But, then, what the fuck. I saluted her with the glass by way of thanks, and then I didn't look at her again although I felt her watching me.

"Semper fi," the bartender said.

"Yeah. *Semper fi."*

"You in the Crotch?" he asked.

"No."

"Then why'd you say *Semper fi?* That's only for Marines."

"I knew a Marine once."

"Buddy, you trying to be a wise ass?"

I looked at him. "I have the Christmas spirit," I said.

"Christmas was three weeks ago."

"I missed it."

He blinked. "Buddy, where you been? On the moon?"

"Vietnam."

That caught him by surprise.

"Ain't you a little old? What are you? Some old gunny or something?"

"Something," I said.

He looked at me, shook his head, and walked off.

"We get 'em in here," he muttered.

I watched it snow.

35

IN DA NANG I LIKED TO WAKE UP AND HOLD BRIGETTE FOR A FEW minutes in the mornings. Sometimes we made love. Mostly, though, she just snuggled her butt against me and took my hand and placed it on her breast so I could feel her breathing. I felt her tiny and warm and secure against me.

"I feel most alive in morning with you, Mike, for goo'ness sake."

For goo'ness sake. For goo'ness sake.

There was no warm Asian sun in Chicago. It was cold and dreary and sterile. When I awoke in my closet that rented for a room, I automatically reached for Brigette and opened my eyes expecting the lizard on the balcony and the morning tropical sunlight streaming through the glass French doors.

"Girl must be practical, for goo'ness sake," Brigette said slowly the day I left Vietnam. I continued packing clothing into my old Ranger parachute bag.

Everything I owned was piled up on the bed in our room above the French Fuck. It wasn't much. Like Baylor said, we gypsy types didn't collect much on our way through.

I expected more protest than that from her. I straightened up to look at her when the silence continued to build. The bed was between us, but it wasn't the only thing suddenly between us. Her pretty face wore that inscrutable Oriental mask Asians donned when they confronted outsiders.

"Don't do that," I said.

"Not do what?"

"You know what. Put on your Vietnamese face."

"Brigette *is* Vietnamese," she said. "Brigette have Vietnamese face. If Brigette have 'Nited States face, you not leave so quick, for goo'ness sake."

"That has nothing to do with it."

"Yes," Brigette said stubbornly. "Brigette have ugly Vietnamese face with slant eye, yellow skin. Okay for American boom-boom Vietnamese girl, have short-time with her, but then good-bye, so long. No more slanteye girl, no more gook whore. Go back to America, go back to faithful wife."

"We both knew this day was going to come."

I had put it off as long as I could. I could go into the bush and face physical hardships, but when it came to things like this I had just as soon skirt around the flanks and leave it alone. I even thought of sending Brigette out shopping and then packing and leaving before she returned. But I couldn't do it. You had to have some loyalty.

"Biness is biness," Brigette insisted, squaring her shoulders and tilting her chin a little higher.

I paused in my packing. I looked out the French doors. The lizard was watching us from the balcony.

"It's been more than business," I admitted.

I came around the bed to her. She fended me off.

"Mike, not touch, for goo'ness sake. Shake hands."

She took my hand and shook it.

"That how biness people say good-bye," she said.

"Stop it, Brigette."

She looked long into my eyes, the way she did. "Brigette know," she said. "Mike still want Brigette."

I turned sharply away. It was true.

"You don't understand, Brigette," I said. "I don't want to be a part of this war anymore. I'm losing my objectivity. Things are happening. It's getting to me. It's getting too confusing."

I had to make the break. It was time to go.

"Will you go back to Hue?" I asked Brigette.

"Brigette biness girl, for goo'ness sake. Brigette practical."

"You're going back to the streets!"

"What concern that to you, Big Shoot?"

"Big Shot."

"Brigette not Schopenhauer over Mike. Who Mike Kragel, for goo'ness sake? Oh, yes. Brigette remember now. Mr. Kragel famous writer, one time paramour of Miss Brigette Nguyen. He not such Big Shoot. Miss Brigette Nguyen have even more famous paramour now. New paramour want to marry Miss Nguyen, for goo'ness sake."

"Drop it, Brigette."

She shrugged. She turned away. I watched her walk out onto the balcony with her head up. She closed the glass doors between us.

I hurriedly finished packing. She stood by the balcony railing with her back to me. She wore the slit-skirted dress I bought her in Hong Kong. It outlined her perfect tiny curves. Her black hair hung down her back almost to her hips.

I wasn't a goddamned squaw man.

I shouldered my canvas camera bag and picked up the Ranger bag. I started to the door. Then I turned in time to catch Brigette looking at me. Her wet face glistened in the morning sunlight. She was crying her heart out, but she snapped her head away again so I wouldn't see.

"Oh, Jesus God!"

I had to get out of there. I stumbled over the threshold. I almost ran to the elevator. I didn't look back again.

"Everything same-same okay, Mr. Kragel-san?" the Vietnamese bellboy asked.

"Why shouldn't it be?"

"You cry, Mr. Kragel-san."

"Fuck you, Tal Li!" I cried angrily. "And fuck this ratbag country. It fucking *stinks.*"

It wasn't so easy to leave the war behind after all. Fry was more on target than he thought when he told the judge I had some adjustments to make. For one thing, I continued to reach for Brigette in the mornings and she wasn't there.

"Take all the time you want," Bureau Chief Bernie Bernstein told me. "I know how it is when you first get back. You're used to running on adrenaline. It takes time to slow things back to the real world."

"Is *this* the real world?"

Bernie laughed. "I'm afraid it is, son."

"I don't even watch Sunday afternoon football."

"There are other things."

"Yeah? Johnny Carson is a wimp."

"So's Dick Clark, and Jane Fonda is a pinko. You sound like what you need to do is get laid or something."

"What does an old fart like you know about getting laid?"

"Inside this bent, gray, seventy-year-old body throbs the blue veiner of a twenty-year-old. I'm going to start using it too as soon as you take over the office."

Everyone in INS knew stories about Bernie Bernstein's exploits as a correspondent. He hit the beach at Anzio and was in on the D day invasions. Word had it that he sneaked into Berlin ahead of the Russians and fucked Eva Braun while Hitler was out somewhere screwing his dog Blondi. Now he was just an old Jew telling stories. There had to be a better way to end up than that.

"Tell me about Ernest Hemingway," I said.

"He shot himself."

"Weren't you with him at the liberation of Paris? Is it true he was impotent at fifty?"

"Maybe that's why he shot himself."

"I'd shoot myself," I said.

"That reminds me," the old journalist said. "Baylor sent you a teletype last night. He says Dog is still alive and now has seventy-three kills."

How much would 146 ears weigh—about three pounds?

Bernie rummaged in the litter on his desk and handed me a strip of yellow teletype paper.

"Do you always read other people's mail?" I asked, just to keep the bantering going.

"Only if it's worth reading. I don't read yours going out."

He grinned, toothless.

Kragel, INS Chicago:

Dog MIA 5 days. Back now. 73 conf kills include 2 VC snipers, 1 French collaborator. Enemy activity increasing. Dog average 2 kills day. Intel reports Tet buildup. 5 O'Clock Follies claim Tet truce lead truce talks. Brigette last heard back Hue working hospital.

Baylor, INS Da Nang

When I couldn't stand the city or hanging out at the VFW, I rented a car and motored out to my retirement plot on the Kankakee. The river was high and brown from the fall and winter rains. It reminded me somehow of the river that ran beyond the field at the base of Hill 55. It reminded me of the day Dog was fishing in the canal.

I walked in the brown grass. There were some naked willows along the riverbank, and, farther away, the leafless spires of birch. Icicles hung from the willows. Frozen earth crunched underneath my feet. It was threatening to snow again. Traffic on IS 53 growled by on the flats, through the farmland. Other people were already building houses on their little retirement plots. I heard hammering in the distance. I heard the traffic. I heard a siren.

There had to be a better way to end up than this.

I got to thinking of Dog and the mystery surrounding his past in Oklahoma. The more I thought of it, the more I realized I couldn't just drop it. I was a muckraker. I had to know the full story. Vietnam followed me.

Finally, I drove back to the city and booked a flight to Tulsa, Oklahoma, for the following Monday. Eastern Airlines said they had no flights into either Vinita or Muskogee.

"Vinita, sir? You're the first passenger I ever heard of who wanted to go to Vinita."

36

A WILDERNESS OF SCRUB OAK AND ELM AND PERSIMMON THICKETS and briar patches furred the Oklahoma hills. I stopped the rented black Chevrolet for a moment at the huge stone pillars that marked the entrance to abandoned Camp Gruber east of Muskogee. I heard the wind dragging through the forest's dead leaves, like someone rattling old bones.

I drove another mile or two and got out again. You could see the foundations of buildings constructed by German POWs during WW Two. They were weed clogged. There was nothing else I could see on the other side of the fence except some old roads leading back into hundreds of acres of what was now a wildlife sanctuary.

A cold north wind bit at my cheeks as I stood by the side of the road and gazed at the brown-wooded hills. I liked the feeling of standing there in the cold wind looking at Oklahoma. I had to suppress the urge to strike out on foot. I understood suddenly why a kid named Johnny Able who became Dog in a war half a globe away might have preferred the freedom of these hills over foster homes in the city. The kid was like Peter Pan.

Except there was no Never Never Land.

A beat-up red pickup truck went by on the road. Two men in it wore cowboy hats. The pickup slowed and the men looked me over. They went on. There was a rifle rack in the back window cradling a shotgun and a hunting rifle.

On around the road from Camp Gruber lay the tiny settlement of Braggs. It was a gas station, a Country Kettle cafe, a thrift store, and another deserted gas station where several old men in farmer overalls huddled inside around a wood-burning stove playing dominoes and watching the nine A.M. KATY whistle by on the railroad track across the road.

"Why, yeah, sir, I *could* tell ya how to find ol' Delbert Crowe's place," one of the old men said. "There was lots of news fellas 'round two or three year ago quizzin' 'bout Delbert's girl. The one Chick Macabee found dead out at the camp."

He rummaged out a twist of chewing tobacco and sliced off a plug with his pocketknife. He leaned back in his chair and stuffed the tobacco chunk into his cheek. He resembled a beady-eyed old squirrel with a nut in its pouch. Tobacco juice oozed out the corners of his lips and seeped into the network of wrinkles on his chin. He spat at a tin can on the floor. It looked like the old men missed the can more than they hit it.

The other four domino players watched as though the fate of the world hinged on what happened next.

"You a news fella?" the ancient hillbilly demanded.

Someone snickered and said, "Either that or a bill collector."

"Gentlemen, I asked a simple question," I said. "I'm looking for the Crowe residence."

"Yep. You're lookin' all right," said the spokesman for the bunch. They returned to their dominoes.

I shrugged.

"Fella," said the hillbilly, "we ain't meanin' to be uncivil. Folks is friendly hereabouts, but you be a news fella or my name ain't Angus Walkabout. Ol' Delbert's been pestered 'nuff. He an' all the folks in Muskogee County knows who kilt his daughter."

"And who do you think did it?"

"We 'uns don't just *think*, friend. We *know*. All them stories in the Muskogee *Phoenix* about the Wild Boy bein' a Vietnam hero don't change nothin'. It just proves he's a born killer. It's tearin' ol' Delbert up inside seein' all them news stories about him. The boy's a dog all right, an' if'n he live long enough to come back to these parts then ol' Delbert'll shoot him down like a dog."

I looked at the drooling, scratching old men playing dominoes.

"I wouldn't have thought you gentlemen could read," I said.

Clippings from the Tulsa *Tribune* news morgue had mentioned no arrests, no names of suspects. There had been only four or five headlines and one photo of lawmen in boots and cowboy hats gathered around a gully in the woods and another close-up school picture of the victim. The copy described how a 'coon hunter out with his hounds in the woods stumbled upon the nude body of seventeen-year-old Margie Lou Crowe near a road on the military reservation where local teenagers went to drink homebrew and party. The state medical examiner said the girl had been sexually assaulted and beaten so badly that one of her ears had been ripped off. She died from manual strangulation, garrotelike. A strand of hay baling wire had been left twisted around her neck.

The investigation turned up one suspect—a runaway teenager living at the abandoned reservation.

"He's not a Wild Boy or anything like the rumors," the Muskogee County sheriff told reporters. "He's just a runaway. We're questioning him about it, but there is no evidence he did it."

The last published piece about the homicide was a short plea for anyone who had information concerning the crime to please come forward.

"We have no viable suspects, no leads," the sheriff admitted.

A farmer at the Country Kettle where I stopped for coffee gave me directions to where the Crowes lived across the railroad tracks and on out a road to a dead end at the edge of the village. The farmer looked me over, but he didn't ask any questions.

Two rusted junk cars—one an Edsel, the other a VW bug—sat stripped down to the axles in the Crowe front yard. The hoods and doors were missing, but they might have been lying in the dead weeds that grew up to the sandstone door stoop of the sprawling old house.

The house was scabbed with peeling white paint. One end of the porch had caved in on top of a disabled washing machine. The woods came up almost to the back door. I saw tire swings hanging from an oak limb out back and other signs that Margie Crowe had had brothers and sisters.

I did a second take on the teenaged girl who burst out the front door and came running across the yard toward me, waving and smiling. Long light brown hair rippled behind her. She wore tight jeans and a man's plaid work shirt with the tails flapping. She was putting on her coat as she ran.

She looked exactly like the photograph of Margie Crowe in the newspaper. She was even about the same age.

She halted abruptly when she reached the yard fence and I got out of the Chevrolet. Her smile vanished. A yellow cur dog came loping around the side of the house wagging its tail.

"Oh," said the girl. "I wasn't paying attention. I thought you were Jamie come to pick me up for school. We're late."

"Sorry."

The girl grinned suddenly. Margie had been grinning in her picture.

"I was in such a hurry," she said. "I guess you came to look at the ol' cow we got up for sale."

"Not the cow," I said. "I'm looking for Delbert Crowe."

"You came to the right place as long as you don't have to live here. I'm one of his daughters. I'm Shirley."

I walked over to the fence. It was sagging in most places and the wooden gate was wired together with hay wire. The yellow dog found a hole and trotted out to water my tires.

"How many daughters are there?" I asked.

"There used to be four, but there's just three now. And Jamie. Jamie's my brother. He went down to fix a flat. He's supposed to be right back. I saw the black car and I thought . . . Jamie's car is old though. You ain't from around here, are you?"

Shirley looked me over. She looked at the rented Chevrolet.

"I'll go get Papa. He's waiting on Cecil to take him to work in Gore, but he ain't left yet."

She went back into the house, walking loose-jointed and easy and pretty. Dog knew how to pick his girlfriends if Margie Crowe had been anything like her younger sister, which it seemed she had been.

Shirley returned a minute later with a burly man dressed in iron gray work clothes. He hadn't shaved or combed his hair and there were egg stains on his shirt. Dirty long-handle underwear stuck out from his shirt at the wrists and neck.

His appearance reminded me that this was redneck and good ol' boy country.

"You ain't here 'bout the cow?" the man asked gruffly, walking out and standing on the other side of the fence from me.

The man looked stubborn.

"My name is Mike Kragel," I said, trying the friendly approach. I stuck out my hand to shake.

Delbert Crowe advanced cautiously and shook my hand limply across the fence.

"You ain't here 'bout the cow?"

Fuck the cow.

Shirley wandered into the street to wait for her brother. I saw someone watching us from a front window of the house, parting a tattered curtain.

"I do like this country," I said, grinning. "It sure is pretty land."

Crowe's expression remained sour. "What was your name again, friend?" he asked.

"Mike Kragel."

"Kragel. That name sounds familiar. What can I do for you, Kragel?"

Right to the point.

"Mr. Crowe, I'm a journalist with the International News Service. Look, I know it's painful for you, but I'd like to ask some questions about your daughter Margie."

Shirley Crowe heard and returned, watching, frowning. A wary look entered her father's eye.

"I thought I knew the name," he said. "You the fella that's

been writin' all that horseshit 'bout that Able kid in Vietnam."

"I've been writing about a Marine sniper who's been recommended for the Silver Star," I replied.

Crowe flared. "The Marine Corps might call the sneaky little bastard a hero. Back here he's the sonofabitch who murdered my oldest girl. That's the kinda thing folks in these parts don't forget easy. Margie wasn't much and she was odd, but she was still my girl."

"Mr. Crowe, from what I can determine you and your neighbors are the only ones who've convicted Johnny Able."

"The law just can't prove it. But it was him always sneakin' around here sniffin' up to Margie like a boar 'coon in heat. My girl was found right out there at the camp where Able was livin' in a hole in the ground. That's proof enough for me an' anybody else with a lick of sense."

The man was already starting to grate on my nerves.

"Maybe I don't have a lick of sense," I said, "but I always assumed a man was considered innocent until proved otherwise. That's why I came. I want to find out the truth of what happened."

"You fellas wouldn't know the truth if it slipped up an' bit you on the ass. Now why don't you get in that fancy new car an' haul your city slicker butt back to Vietnam or wherever you came from. Me an' my family ain't got nothin' to say to somebody who goes around makin' somethin' special out of a murderer."

I looked at him until he blinked.

"It must be very satisfying to be so self-righteous," I said.

"What? What'd you say?"

I didn't come out for a fight. Fuck this redneck. Maybe I'd even feel the same way if I thought I knew who killed my daughter. Providing, of course, that I had a daughter.

I got into the black Chevrolet and turned around at the dead end. I had the windows rolled up and couldn't hear what Crowe was saying, but his lips were flapping angrily when I drove by him again. Shirley had already gone into the house to get out of the cold.

Everyone seemed convinced Dog killed the girl.

A flash of movement caught my eye as I slowed to cross the railroad tracks back onto State 10 that ran through Braggs. The girl Shirley was running toward me down the railroad right-of-way, waving frantically. I stopped and waited for her, reaching to roll down the passenger side window. She was flushed from the morning cold and the run. Her breath made miniature clouds. Hoar frost still tipped the dead grass on the leeward side of the rail bed.

Shirley stuck her head inside through the open car window.

"Mom sent me," she gasped. "I ran out the back door soon's I could, but I thought I was gonna miss you. Mister, my dad's about to leave for work. Mom asks if you can come back in an hour. She wants to talk to you about Johnny and . . . and my sister."

It occurred to me that Shirley Crowe, even more so than her mother, might have the answers to my questions.

"You knew Johnny Able too?" I said.

Shirley glanced uneasily up the road. "Come back in an hour."

She was gone then, back down the railroad. She left tracks in the hoar frost. I watched until she cut through the woods that grew behind her house. I shook my head, wondering. Something was happening in that family.

37

MARYANN CROWE REMINDED ME OF A PICTURE I HAD SEEN ONE time of a sodbuster's lanky wife caught in a dust bowl storm. Her house was dark, even with the window curtains drawn open. Down a hallway I saw an unmade bed in the last room. Breakfast dishes remained on the table in the kitchen to my right. Shirley got up and poked another stick of firewood into the potbellied wood-burner. The stove breathed and the lid clanged, emitting a little puff of smoke.

"Turn the damper down," Maryann told her daughter.

"But it's *cold* in here."

"This old house has always been cold," Maryann said. "It just keeps getting colder."

The other children went on to school, Maryann said, but Shirley stayed home because she could tell me more about Johnny and Margie than anyone else.

"That poor little blond orphan," Maryann said. "Living out there in the dark woods all by hisself."

I sipped strong black coffee and thought of Dog in Vietnam—*living out there in the dark woods all by hisself.*

Margie Lou Crowe, her mother said, had been the odd one in the family, what with her nose always stuck in a book and what with her always wandering off to be alone with her thoughts and her books. Although in appearance she could have been Shirley's twin, with less than two years' difference in ages between them, in temperament the two girls were as different as night and day, as sunshine and clouds.

Margie was the gentle one, the calm one. Maryann smiled.

She remembered that almost no one could raise a wild cottontail rabbit, but Margie had. The dogs carried in the baby bunny from its nest. It was as small and hairless as a newborn mouse. Margie took it and mixed a formula of warm cow's milk and Karo syrup and fed it every two hours, even at night. She got up and held the little creature and talked to it and fed it its formula.

Everyone knew you couldn't keep a baby cottontail alive; they always died. This one didn't though. Not with Margie tending it. Jasper grew up and would stand on his strong hind legs and beg for cake. Jasper loved cake.

Margie had a way with wild things.

"Margie Lou is touched in the head," Delbert Crowe always said. "That girl ain't normal. You ain't normal, Marge, hear? All that readin' is makin' you goofy. Get in there an' do the dishes, Margie Lou. We ain't havin' nobody in this house that ain't earnin' their beans. If you don't like it, you know where you can go as soon's you're old enough. You can go an' be a slut on First Street in Muskogee. You so lazy an' got so many big idees from readin' them books, that's where you gonna end up. Get in there at them dishes, Margie Lou, before I take a switch to your legs."

"She ain't hurtin' nothin' by readin', Papa," Shirley said, always quick to defend her sister.

Shirley was defiant, spirited. She stood up to her dad's bullying, even when it meant she took the switching instead of Margie Lou.

"You don't have to do that for me," Margie sometimes said in her soft voice. "Sissy, Papa can't hurt me."

"He switched you till your legs was all bloody."

"But don't you see, Sissy? Papa is the way he is because he knows he can't touch me, not in here where it counts."

She touched her forehead. Then she gently laid her hand on her sister's head.

"What's in there belongs to you. No one can ever take it away from you if you don't let them. What's in your head belongs to you and to no one else in the world. That's what makes you *you*. The whole world exists right there inside your head, Sissy. You can do anything, go anywhere, be anyone—right inside your own head."

Margie stroked her sister's long hair. Shirley was twelve at the time, Margie fourteen. Shirley frowned. Sometimes Margie was hard to understand.

"Don't fight Papa so hard, Sissy," Margie counseled. "He'll break you like he has Mom. The reason he hates me so much is because he can switch me until he breaks my back, but he can never touch me or break me where it counts. Papa is a bitter, unhappy man, Sissy."

"He's a mean man."

"Yes. But he's mean because he doesn't know the secret."

"The secret?"

"Yes, yes. The secret I've just told you—that you can be anything you want to be right inside your own head."

At first, Shirley thought the Wild Boy was someone Margie created inside her head.

Margie often went to Camp Gruber to play. She said she could feel all the soldiers who had been there before. She said it was not an unhappy place.

"The Wild Boy lives there," Margie confided to Shirley one night. They were in bed. Julie Lee and Wynona were asleep in the other bed and Jamie had turned in early. Papa down the hallway was snoring. Shirley and Margie sometimes stayed awake to lie in bed at night and whisper.

"Who's the Wild Boy?" Shirley asked. "Is he part of your secret?"

"No, no. The Wild Boy is *real*. He lives in a big hole in the ground that the soldiers left."

The two little girls lay in the dark with their cheeks touching, whispering.

"Don't he have a mother and father?" Shirley asked.

"He said his papa went to jail and died. He never had a mother."

"Everybody has a mother."

"I don't know. He's very shy."

"Don't he have a name?"

"He says it gives people power over you if you tell them your name. He said he had been watching me and that no one could see him unless he wanted to be seen. He said he was invisible."

"Is he *really?*"

"I guess so. I didn't see him at all until one day he was sitting on a tree stump watching me. He was so dirty and filthy and his hair was long and matted up until he looked like he'd been in a cocklebur patch."

The little girls tittered.

"Did he talk to you, Margie Lou?"

"I started walking toward him. He got off the stump and I guess he went invisible."

"You mean—like a ghost?"

"He ain't a ghost, Sissy. He's a real boy."

"Don't he get lonesome? Ain't he afraid to be in the woods by himself?"

"The Wild Boy ain't afraid. He's the Wild Boy, Sissy."

Shirley lay silent a moment, thinking about it.

"Margie Lou, the Wild Boy is part of your secret, ain't he? It's okay if he is. I won't tell. He's just in your head?"

"He is not! I'll prove it to you."

Margie took her sister to the camp the next day and they waited inside the woods by the big stump where Margie always met the Wild Boy. Once, they heard a twig snap, but it was nothing except a deer. Margie called for the Wild Boy. Tears came to her eyes because he did not come and prove that he was real. Shirley patted Margie on the back.

"It's okay, Margie Lou," she said. "He don't have to be real."

Margie came alone to the stump the next time.

"I can't let anyone else know I'm here," the Wild Boy said. "They'd try to catch me and send me back to those people."

"Sissy thinks I made you up in my head."

"Why would she think that?"

"She said everybody real has a name."

"I have a name. I just can't tell it to you. It belonged to me when I was someone else, and I don't want to be that someone else anymore."

"I don't like calling you Wild Boy. You ain't wild."

"I am wild," he said. "I'm wild and able to take care of myself, like the deer and the squirrels. I don't need anybody else."

"You are able," Margie agreed. "Hey, that can be your name. I can call you *Able.*"

They laughed.

"Will you always come back if I have a name?" he asked.

"Yes. I'll come back anyhow, but I want you to have a name."

"I'll have a name for you then. It's . . . Have you read *Johnny Appleseed?*"

"That's your name?"

He didn't laugh much, but he laughed again.

"No. I mean yes. It's Johnny."

"Johnny Able," Margie said. "Johnny Able, I'll come back every day to see you. Can I tell Sissy though? Sissy and I won't never tell anybody. Johnny Able will be our secret. I can bring you more books to read, and when spring comes and it's warm we can have picnics. Johnny, we'll have such fun! No one will ever know."

Rumors spread about the Wild Boy over the next several years. Every now and then someone reported to Happy McClure, the game warden, that he had seen a slender kid with long tangled blond hair carrying a dead deer out of season, but Happy had never been able to prove anything. Sometimes, though, he came across fire rings and matted bedding grass over by Greenleaf or Tenkiller Lake, and some of the summer cabins were burglarized.

All the burglar took though was food and sometimes a pair of jeans and .22 caliber ammunition if there was any around. And books. Nothing else was ever touched. Once, an astounded cabin owner reported that someone broke into his cabin to *return* books that had been taken in a previous burglary two weeks before.

Otherwise, Johnny Able's only touch with the outside world came through Margie Crowe and her sister. During school hours, Margie met the boy in the woods south of the school. They found a private place underneath an old oak whose heavy boughs drooped and touched the ground all around. Margie slipped food to him from the school cafeteria, and she brought her textbooks to the oak to tutor Johnny. He was eager to learn. She tutored him again afternoons when she sneaked away from home and made her way to Camp Gruber.

"Margie Lou was never like the other kids," Maryann Crowe explained. "She always acted so much older than she was. Like she knew things. I think she made her daddy nervous, being like that."

The school principal, Mr. Higbe, summoned the Crowe parents to his office during Margie's sophomore year.

"I'm concerned about your daughter," he said.

"Margie Lou makes straight A's," Maryann pointed out.

"Yes, yes. She's on the honor roll every semester. She's the brightest sophomore at Braggs High."

"Then whatsa matter?" Delbert demanded. "She causin' a ruckus or somethin'? You just tell us an' I'll make her behave."

Mr. Higbe was tall and lanky with black eyes, a prominent Adam's apple, a thin mustache, and no hair on top of his head. Margie referred to him as Ichabod Crane. He seemed nervous in Delbert Crowe's presence. He couldn't keep his eyes from the food stains on the man's shirt.

"It's socialization," he blurted out, beginning to sweat.

"It's *what?*" Delbert asked, blinking.

"Socialization."

Mr. Higbe later confided to some of the other teachers that talking to Mr. Crowe was about like teaching algebra to Angus Walkabout's team of mules.

"Mr. Higgie," said Delbert Crowe, "the missus an' me'll have a sit down with Margie Lou tonight an' tell her she'll either study an' learn it an' make A's like she does on everything else or I'll switch her till she does."

Mr. Higbe blinked.

"I'm talking about the way she relates to other people in a social environment," he explained, continuing to sweat.

"Then she ain't behavin'? That's what you're sayin'?"

"He's sayin' . . ." Maryann tried to interject.

"Shut up, Maryann. Can't you see me an' Mr. Higgie—"

"Higbe. *Higbe.*"

". . . are tryin' to get to the bottom of this?"

"Folks," said Mr. Higbe, "I think I might have been overreacting . . ."

"No," Delbert persisted. "You said our girl has been actin' up an' we her parents. What she been doin'?"

Mr. Higbe looked to the door, as for rescue. He tried again.

"She doesn't socialize with the other children," he said. "I've noticed, for example, that she hurries out of the cafeteria to be by herself. She always takes something with her—an apple, a sandwich, a carton of milk . . ."

"She's *stealin'!*"

"No. No. Please. It's okay. What I'm trying to say is that I followed her to see where she goes every day at noon. I lost her in the woods for a few minutes. Then I heard voices. But when I found her and approached, she was alone up underneath a tree."

"What was she doin'?"

"She said she went there to study," Mr. Higbe said.

Delbert Crowe's neck settled into his shoulders. He mulled over things. Then he exclaimed, "She's meetin' some boy there. I'm holdin' the school responsible."

"I didn't say that."

"But that's what she's doin'. What else could it be?"

"Delbert, we don't know she's meeting anybody," Maryann reasoned, trying to calm her husband. "You know how Margie Lou is."

"Well . . . she's always been real odd, Mr. Higgie."

"It's not Higgie. It's—never mind."

That was the last time Mr. Higbe summoned the Crowes to his office. Margie Lou continued to slip off during school lunch break. No one ever followed her again.

However, Mr. Higbe told the sheriff after the tragedy that he still thought the girl was meeting someone.

"I think it was the runaway and truant who's been hiding out on the old army post," he told the sheriff, who in turn asked Margie's parents about it.

"Everybody around Braggs has heard about the Wild Boy," Maryann said. "We've all caught a glimpse of him now and then."

"I caught more'n a glimpse," Delbert exclaimed. "I *seen* that little sonofabitch sniffin' around her."

It had been on Margie's sixteenth birthday. Maryann gave her daughter a party of sorts, the first one ever. The Crowe kids were there after school around the big oak with the tire swings. So were the Peatree kids whose father used to drive the cotton truck hauling hands to the picking fields. Lois and Dot, the Tweedy girls, came too.

Delbert was supposed to be at work, but he came home fired again and started drinking homebrew from a quart fruit jar he bought from the bootlegger Hedge Edgeman.

Maryann baked a cake for her daughter and used some of her cream money to buy candles and a present. A few minutes after the cake was cut, Margie Lou disappeared. By this time Maryann knew her daughter was secretly meeting the runaway boy, but she didn't say anything. Margie Lou was the poor boy's only friend.

Delbert Crowe's long suit, however, was not tolerance. He happened to be watching from the kitchen window when Margie slipped into the woods out back with a piece of cake for Johnny Able, the Wild Boy.

"Where's she sneakin' off to this time?" he demanded of his wife.

"Delbert, you know how peculiar Margie Lou's been."

"By God, I'll kill her if she's out screwin' some young billy goat."

"Delbert!"

Crowe went out the front door and hurried around the cow shed and the pigpen and kicked the dog to run it back home. But when he caught up to Margie Lou the cake was gone and she was by herself, standing in a maple grove yellow-and-red-leafed from autumn. She was waiting for her father.

Delbert flew into a rage. He sputtered and shouted.

"Where is he?" he roared.

"Where is who, Papa?"

"Whoever you meetin' out here like a bitch in heat. Don't you lie to me, you prissy little slut."

"I've never lied to you, Papa. I'm just not going to tell you."

Her father was like a spring bear emerged from hibernation—mean and tearing about in the woods. He ripped off a switch from the nearest tree. With a menacing gaze fixed on his daughter, he plucked the leaves off the switch one by one until he had a long, thin rod with strips of bark still hanging from it. He slashed the air with it, like with a rapier. He advanced on Margie.

"You tell," he threatened. "By God, you tell or I'll beat you into next Monday."

Margie's eyes widened. They were gray and clear and wise for her age. She seemed to shrink, resigning herself to another switching. She waited.

Delbert lifted the switch high above his head. He was already starting to swing when a voice made the switch freeze in midair.

"The next thing after you touch her, your dead face touches the ground," the voice said calmly.

Delbert slowly turned toward the voice. He later described for the sheriff the boy standing in the forest shadows.

The kid was slender, almost skinny, but he was tanned and stood erect so that he looked bigger than he was. His hair hung to his shoulders and was bleached almost white from the sun. Delbert didn't even notice the .22 rifle resting in the crook of the kid's elbow, for the boy's eyes were what caught and held him. Delbert didn't tell the sheriff that part, but Margie Lou told her sister Shirley. Delbert stood hypnotized by the pale blue eyes like a field mouse fixed by a rattler's gaze. He could not wrench his eyes free of the Wild Boy's cold blue hypnotic stare.

"I will kill anyone who touches a friend," the boy said.

Then, Margie Lou told Shirley late at night when they talked in bed, Johnny Able became invisible.

Delbert Crowe did not switch his daughter that day—nor for many days afterward. It didn't stop him from it altogether, but he never seemed quite comfortable doing it. Sometimes after he switched Margie and it was over, he went outside and looked around.

"That boy kilt my daughter," Delbert insisted to the sheriff after Chick Macabee found Margie dead.

"How do you know that?"

"If you saw him you'd know why."

Shirley wouldn't believe it. She told the sheriff that when her dad wasn't around.

"I'm going to have to question him, Shirley," the sheriff said.

"Nobody can find him unless he wants to be found. He didn't hurt my sister, I know it. They were in love. They were going to get married as soon as Johnny turned eighteen so he was legal and could come out of the woods."

"Ask him to come talk to me—just me and him," the sheriff persisted. "He has nothing to worry about if he's innocent. Tell him I won't bring him in just because he's a runaway."

"I don't know if he will. I've been out there every day since it . . . you know. He won't come out of the woods. Maybe whoever killed Margie Lou killed him too."

The sheriff said Margie Lou put up a good fight before she succumbed. There was skin and hair underneath her fingernails.

Shirley continued to go to Camp Gruber every day. Margie Lou was the only person Johnny Able ever took to his bunker, so Shirley didn't know where to look to find him. All she could do was go to the old stump and wait.

One day over a week after the murder Johnny Able finally

appeared out of the forest. Shirley gasped at the sight of him. He had lost weight he couldn't afford to lose and his eyes were black rimmed and sunk deep into his skull. Worse yet, he appeared to have been in a fight. Old bruises turning green marred his face. There was an ugly, open wound seeping pus on his cheek. He moved slowly, absently.

"Yes," he said when Shirley informed him she had been waiting.

"Sheriff Cantrell wants to talk to you," Shirley said. "He promised he wouldn't take you back."

"I don't trust any of them," Johnny said. "This is something I can handle."

"Johnny, do you know who did it?" Shirley asked.

The kid looked at her. He looked away.

"Johnny, talk to the sheriff, please?"

The kid agreed to meet the sheriff, but only alone and in the forest.

Maryann Crowe cried softly in the dark living room with the firewood in the stove popping and crackling. She looked away. Shirley sat on the sofa next to her mother and placed an arm consolingly around the woman's bony shoulders. Maryann fiddled with a hole worn in the arm of the sofa. She poked her fingers into it. She ripped it bigger and didn't notice.

"I have got to know who killed my daughter!" Maryann cried suddenly, looking straight at me.

"What does the sheriff think?" I asked.

"Sheriff E.W. Cantrell ain't the smartest man in the world."

Shirley hugged her mother while her mother continued to weep and tear at the hole in the sofa.

"Margie Lou was the only important person in Johnny's life," Shirley said quietly. "He didn't do this to Margie. I don't care what people think. You know him, Mr. Kragel. You know he wouldn't, don't you?"

I thought of the ears on Dog's belt, the Lotus Bitch screaming from the jungle when he tortured her, of Hamilton and the single shot that ended his suffering. I thought of the mysterious death of Col. Stick Steinke, and of Judy Wong.

I thought of those blue eyes the first time I saw them.

"They never found out who killed my sister," Shirley said. "I keep remembering how Johnny looked that day when he came out of the woods, that weird look in his eyes. You know how you look when you have a high fever? Johnny Able was all skinny and beat-up and in his eyes . . . in his eyes he had a fever. I thought he hated me. I thought he hated everybody."

38

THE ARVN AIRCRAFT WERE STRAFING THE ROAD. IMMEDIATELY, Carl Can't was dying, and I was on the back of the truck with Dog's .45 in my fist and Carl's head in my lap. The Vietnamese refugees on the truck stared at me, but the horde on the road didn't even notice me.

Then my thigh was burning from where the gook sniper shot me. It kept burning until I wanted to scream. Dog's face loomed in front of me. I wanted to scream into Dog's face. I saw his eyes. They were writhing somehow, like snakes. Dog was trying to tell me that every bondsman in his own hand bore the power to cancel his captivity.

"Every bondsman," he said, and there were hideous gurglings and cacklings in the background and Dog's eyes writhed like snakes. "Every bondsman . . . Every bondsman . . ."

I bolted upright in bed.

It was still dark and I started to reach for Brigette to hold me. For an instant I thought I was back home. Why did I keep thinking of the Continental Palace and Brigette as home?

I blinked. It was dark, but lights were shining through the thin drapes. After a moment I recognized the motel room. It was a pillow beside me in bed, not Brigette.

I felt sweat streaking from my armpits.

It don't mean nothing.

The war was over for me.

I got up and padded barefoot to the bathroom and came back and pulled the drapes. I looked out onto an empty parking lot in front of a shopping center. I saw a Sears and a TG&Y and a pizza place at the far end next to the Shawnee Bypass that skirted Muskogee. It would be getting daylight in another hour or so. I wished I hadn't quit smoking.

The thought that Dog was dead wouldn't quit nagging me. It started yesterday afternoon when I returned from Braggs and checked in on the telephone with Dennis Fry.

"Everyone's looking for you, partner," Fry said. "Where the hell are you?"

"Jump starting the world. Who's looking for me? Movie starlets? Heads of state? The Nobel nominating committee?"

"Me, for one."

"Oh. Lawyers and ex-wives."

"I was right about Sharon," Fry said with a triumphant rise to his voice. "Mike, we're going to save your pension and your ranch."

"It's not a ranch."

"We're still going to save it. Sharon is signing over any claims she has against you. It's a no-fault divorce, Mike. Each of you takes out of the marriage what you put into it."

"I didn't put much into it."

"Nevertheless, it's over. You can at least try to sound grateful."

"I'm grateful."

It don't mean nothing.

"Mike, Bernie Bernstein has also been trying to find you. He sounded pissed. He has no idea where you disappeared to."

"Tell him I'm in Muskogee."

"What's a Muskogee?"

"As in Oklahoma."

"What are you doing there?"

"Looking. What did Bernie want?"

"He said if by chance I talked to you for you to get in touch with Hank Baylor in Da Nang. He said it was urgent."

I didn't want Dog to be dead yet. I put off calling Baylor. A rule in journalism was that something wasn't so until you saw it firsthand or until someone who saw it firsthand told you. What I was looking for wouldn't mean anything if I found out first that Dog was dead.

I stared unseeing out the window at the shopping center parking lot. Dog was alive until *I* said he was dead. You ain't dead till you're dead.

I found I was crushing a handful of drapery in my fist.

"I've been reading your stuff on the sniper," Dennis Fry had said my first day home from Vietnam, before the divorce hearing. "What's with it?"

"What do you mean?"

"Mike, we've known each other since college. We were journalists together. It's more than a professional interest when you write that much copy on a subject."

"It's high drama," I replied. "When will he get it, where, how, and will he get his hundred kills first? It's life as we know it boiled down to bare bones. What are you doing, Fry? Trying to play shrink?"

"I'd be afraid of what I'd find out."

"Fry, fuck off."

It was still dark but beginning to be pink in the sky above the Arkansas River when I checked out of the motel. I found an all-night diner on York Street—the only all-niter in town—where a beefy man with an alcoholic's red-veined nose dished out eggs and sausage and biscuits and gravy for ninety-nine cents. You sat at a counter covered in linoleum. A policeman trying to stay awake over coffee until the end of his shift glanced at me. The only other customer was a skinny young woman who left her dog tied outside to a fire hydrant.

The policeman yawned, the skinny young woman yawned, I yawned.

I had to sit with my back to the door. Wire mesh screens covered the front windows.

"Vandals drive by and throw Coke bottles through the windows," the alkie fry cook explained.

"In Vietnam it's grenades," I said.

"You been to Vietnam?"

"I didn't leave a thing in Vietnam."

The fry cook chuckled. "That's what I said when I got back from Korea. I ain't left nothing there worth going back for."

"I hear that," I said.

I didn't leave a thing in Muskogee either. I drove north through Wagoner and Chouteau and Pryor. A sign said twenty-five miles to Vinita. It got daylight, but the light was wintery, weak. The country was mostly open winter-brown fields where cows grazed shaggy in their winter coats.

It wasn't Vietnam. Vietnam was always green.

I got to remembering one spectacular sunset when Brigette and I were in the countryside to visit a village where her aunt lived. It was the nearest I ever came to Brigette's past. Watching the sunset was like viewing an Oriental painting. Gorgeous colors backlighted a Buddhist pagoda and, farther back, a kid setting a water buffalo in a rice paddy. The colors shifted and changed, merging, growing from brilliant to pastel. The boy on the buffalo did not move. Brigette stood breathless next to me, her lips—the color and shape of her nipples—parted a little in appreciation.

She was very beautiful in the sunset. Looking at her was even better than looking at the sunset. I wondered about the scar across her nose that she would never tell me about.

At last she shifted her gaze and looked long into my eyes the way she did. She touched my face gently, like a blind person will who is trying to memorize the features of someone dear.

She took my arm. We walked together across the rice paddies on a raised dike trail. A rooster crowed in the hamlet of grass-thatched hootches beyond the palms and bamboo. The water buffalo with the boy on its back plodded slowly toward the village, as though reluctant to turn the day over to the night.

I told Brigette we had to get back to Da Nang. Nights belonged to the Vietcong.

"Them not harm us *here,* Mike, for goo'ness sake," Brigette said.

"You don't know that."

"Brigette know. You safe with Brigette, Mike. Brigette Vietnamese girl, for goo'ness sake."

"My saviour," I said, teasing. "My protector."

We slept on a rice straw mat in a grass-thatched hut. We made love, and no one came to disturb us. The sun returned warm and friendly. I brushed aside the beaded drape that served as a door and looked out upon a fresh morning.

Naked kids played with scroungy village dogs, one of which had been caught and was being butchered by a toothless old man and his granddaughter. Women fetched water from the well, baskets containing water jars slung on long poles across their shoulders. Cooking fires sent up wisps of smoke that leeched the dawn from the sky.

Brigette rose on one elbow, smiling sleepily. Seeing her like that on the rice mat, in that hootch, in that setting, I was struck by how different our worlds were. How different, but yet how familiar hers felt to me at that moment. I smiled back at her and went back to bed to hold her and make love to her so I could smell how she smelled in the morning when she was still warm from sleep.

"Mike," she noticed, "you are different here."

"It was good here," I said. "I would like for the good days to go on and on forever."

"They can, for goo'ness sake," Brigette chirped brightly. She tapped her forehead and looked wise. "You capture good things in head. You keep them there for all time to come. You want them again, you remember and them come back like on little movie screen. Remember this when you go back to wife in 'Nited States. In here, Mike, for goo'ness sake," she said, again tapping her forehead, "you can be anywhere you want, anytime you want."

Margie Lou Crowe had believed something like that too.

39

As I DROVE THROUGH THE BROWN WINTER FARMLAND TO Vinita, I played back in my mind the interviews I had had yesterday with Sheriff E.W. Cantrell and with the Lawsons, the foster family Dog was living with when he ran away to live in the woods.

"You want to know the truth, Mr. Kragel?" Sheriff Cantrell asked after I cornered him in his office at the towering old courthouse in downtown Muskogee.

He was a roly-poly man, more old than middle-aged, with long wisps of gray hair washclothed from one side of his head across the top to the other in an attempt to camouflage his baldness.

"The truth as opposed to what? A lie?"

"As opposed to the bullshit we normally feed the press."

"I've had my coffee. I can take it."

The sheriff chuckled. "I took you for a truth man."

"Don't get me wrong, Sheriff. I don't always let the truth stand between me and a good story. My guess is that you're not of the common opinion around Braggs that Johnny Able killed his girlfriend."

"The thought that he did has crossed my mind more than once," the sheriff admitted. "But unlike the common people, a law enforcement officer has to depend upon more than just his feelings. You have to understand small-town Okies, Mr. Kragel. They're a clannish bunch. When something happens, they're not going to believe one of their own did it. The first thing they blame is the outsider. Johnny Able was the outsider."

"You questioned him about the homicide?"

"I could have busted the kid right then, held him as a material witness if nothing else. Except—"

When the sheriff frowned, his forehead traveled up underneath the hair stretched across his dome. Behind him on a bulletin board hung an array of wanted posters and other flyers, including one for a chili supper Saturday night at the local VFW.

"Except what?" I prompted when the sheriff appeared to have lost himself in thought.

"I promised Shirley Crowe I wouldn't arrest him unless it was necessary. She says she's sure Able didn't do it. Frankly, I just don't know what's necessary in this case."

Sheriff Cantrell outlined how he had driven alone onto the military reservation to meet the kid. Able picked the time. It was at dusk when the waning light could deceive you into seeing things that were not real and missing things that were. Johnny stepped into the road and stood there until Cantrell saw him and braked. It happened so suddenly and so quietly, the kid appearing out of nowhere, that a chill gripped the sheriff's spine.

"I let him go," Sheriff Cantrell said. "He looked to have been in a fight. I thought maybe the victim left all those marks on him, but I took some hair samples from him and the State Crime Bureau said it wasn't his hair underneath her fingernails, although it *was* his hair we found on her clothing strewn in the bushes. But that's not enough to arrest him on. If we accept the premise that Able killed her, then we have to also accept that someone helped him. And you know what they call Able out there—the Wild Boy. As far as we know, the two Crowe girls were the only people the kid had even talked to for almost four years. Well, except for that one time he met up with Delbert Crowe.

"It's a real mystery," the sheriff concluded.

"Did you check out Delbert Crowe?" I asked.

"I thought about that too," Sheriff Cantrell admitted. "Crowe's a mean bastard and he treats those girls of his and his wife like shit. My deputies have been out there five or six times on domestic disturbances. It's always Crowe drunk and beating up on his family. But as far as saying the sonofabitch killed his daughter, I just can't say that. Actually, I can't say *who* did it. There's one thing, though, that I'm convinced of."

"And that's . . . ?"

"If Johnny Able *didn't* do it, then he knows who did. He just stood there and looked at me when I told him the law would handle it. The next thing I knew, he was just *gone.*"

The sheriff shook his head morosely.

"I've never seen anyone beat as badly as that girl was when we found her body," he said. "She bled so much from all the cuts that I doubt if she had a teaspoonful of blood left in her. Both her arms were broken, and one leg too. One of her ears was missing."

I glanced up quickly.

"Her ear?"

"Yeah. It looked like it had been torn off in the fight. Why?"

"Nothing."

The sheriff went on, but I wasn't really listening. "We had three more homicides in Muskogee County that same month," he said. "It was the worst month we've ever had for killings. We still haven't solved any of them, but it has always been Margie Crowe's I wanted to break most. That was on May twenty-one two years ago come this spring. One of these days I'll find out for sure who did it."

"Yeah. Good luck."

"That's what it'll take—luck."

When I left the courthouse I was thinking about the ears strung on Dog's belt in Vietnam.

The Lawsons said the name of the youngster who stayed with them for a winter and a part of one spring that year was

Johnny Alan Stroud. He was quiet, blond, skinny. They said the Welfare Department told them the fourteen-year-old's father was doing time for murder in a Colorado prison and his mother wasn't dead, she was an alcoholic. Juvenile Court took Johnny away from her and farmed him out to foster parents. The Welfare paid the Lawsons about three hundred dollars a month for taking Johnny in.

"We could use the money," Mr. Lawson said. "The kid was all right. He wouldn't hardly ever talk. Then one night he just took off. We notified the police, but we didn't hear a word about him until maybe three or four years later. An agent from the State Crime Bureau dropped by and said they'd learned Johnny Able was probably Johnny Stroud and that he might have been the one who killed that girl out at Camp Gruber. They asked me if I thought he was capable of it, from what I knew of him."

"What'd you tell them?"

"I said, 'Maybe he could. He was an odd boy. Quiet. Real odd."

40

CARL CAN'T'S PARENTS SEEMED MY LAST CHANCE TO UNRAVEL THE mystery of Johnny "Dog" Able and the murder of Margie Lou Crowe. But what could that shithead Carl Can't have known?

My foot pressed heavy on the gas feed. I was speeding when I passed a highway patrol trooper. He was busy with another violator, so he just wagged his finger at me in warning. I slowed down until I passed out of his sight over the next hill.

This was redneck country. Pickup trucks, rifle racks in the

back windows, bumper stickers that said: I'LL GIVE UP MY GUN WHEN THEY PRY MY COLD DEAD FINGER OFF THE TRIGGER.

Vinita was the site of the state sanatorium, the insane asylum. The attendant of a gas station near the railroad tracks and the rodeo arena told me with a sly smile that the nuts at the sanatorium were not the only nuts in Vinita. Each summer, he said, the townspeople got together to have a Calf Fry Festival at the fairgrounds.

"They fry a calf?" I asked, puzzled.

The pump jockey looked at me. "You a Yankee?" he asked. "You don't know what calf fries is?"

I had to plead ignorance.

"Calf fries is the bull's nuts," he said. "His balls. We call 'em mountain oysters."

"You *eat* them?"

"They's good." He laughed. The good ol' boys liked to josh the outsider. "We eat calf fries and have apple peeling contests and hairy leg contests. It's a family thing. Good fun. I wouldn't miss it myself. We have a Miss Calf Fry contest and a dance."

"What do they call Miss Calf Fry?" I asked, unable to resist. "Queen of the Balls?"

No wonder Carl Can't was so weird—growing up with nuts and eating nuts.

I found the Dubose house in an addition north of the main street downtown. There was a ploughed field behind and a cul-de-sac with little brick houses in a circle. A woman came to the door first. She had Carl's mousy appearance. She even had pimples, although she must have been in her fifties.

She emitted a little startled cry when I introduced myself, then immediately called to someone inside. Her husband came to the door and peered at me through the locked screen. Frank Dubose had Carl's habit of shifting his eyes across your face. Mrs. Dubose disappeared. I heard a back door slam.

It was obvious I wasn't going to be invited inside.

"That was a fine thing you wrote about Carl in the newspapers," Dubose said, his voice sad. "But like I told you before, Mr. Kragel, you were our son's friend and all but I still don't have anything to tell you. Isn't it enough that Carl had to die over there in that war? Can't you just let his mother and me forget about all that other? It's over with."

"It's not over with, Mr. Dubose," I argued gently. "It can't be over with until Margie Crowe's murder is solved. I think Carl knew something about it."

Dubose's gaze shifted across my face.

"Mr. Kragel, is it true what you wrote about our boy?"

They always wanted to know about their war dead. Had they suffered? What was it like? Had they died well?

"Carl saw the Vietnamese girl lying wounded in the road," I said. "He gave his own life attempting to rescue her."

That was the truth.

Dubose's face relaxed.

"It is true," he said.

"Yes."

"Mr. Kragel, do you know what that means to us? Carl was always a weak, sickly child. His mother spoiled him because of it. I'm not proud of some of the things Carl did, but I am proud of this. They put up a plaque in the high school with Carl's name on it. Vinita had a Carl Dubose day. Carl's a hero around here now. I'm not going to spoil that. I'm not going to let anyone else spoil it either."

His eyes stopped shifting. They met mine.

"Doesn't it matter to you that a girl was murdered?" I persisted. "Mr. Dubose, you know what happened, don't you? Carl told you something."

His eyes shifted. You could see in his face that the man was living with some kind of guilt.

"Mr. Kragel, what is it you really want? Revenge? Justice? Or is it just a journalist's macabre sense of curiosity?"

I felt like a muckraker. Old Prof Beardsley was right. I had to see the dark side.

"There's nothing to be gained digging around in the past," Dubose said. "Mr. Kragel, would it satisfy you to know that whatever happened to the girl is all but settled in a very decisive way?"

"I'd have to know how."

"The boy you mentioned to me? Johnny Able? I've been reading your articles about him. What's a sniper's chances of making it through the war?"

It was hard to say it, but I said it: "He may be dead now."

"Then it *is* settled. It's all over."

I was still puzzling over that when Dubose's eyes warned me of someone approaching from behind. I turned in time to find Mrs. Dubose and two men hurrying across the cul-de-sac. One of the men appeared to be an older, rougher version of Carl Can't. The other reminded me of Gorgeous George the wrestler. Gorgeous George picked up with one hand a power mower left on the lawn and placed it by the garage door.

The older, rougher Carl Can't stopped to regard me and take a drag off his cigarette.

"I opened your car door for you," he said.

"That was thoughtful," I said.

"Buffalo here wanted to jerk the door off," said the man, whom I took to be Carl's brother. "I talked him out of it."

"He looks capable," I admitted.

"You'll leave now," Carl's brother said. "You won't come back."

I turned to Frank Dubose, who still stood behind the screen door.

"Please?" he said. "Don't you understand? It's all over."

I shrugged. "It's not over until I say it's over," I shot back over my shoulder as I started walking to the rented Chevrolet. "I'm not leaving until I find out what happened."

I could be as stubborn as anyone.

41

A REDNECK WEARING A BASEBALL CAP WITH THE BRIM PUSHED UP in front and who looked like a recent escapee from the sanatorium sat down at the bar on one side of me, while another redneck on the other side plinked halfheartedly at a mandolin. A man and woman argued, their voices rising, at the tables by the pool table, and someone went out the back door into the cold night. The barmaid was freckled and about ten pounds heavier than a 1964 Buick.

So much for Vinita nightlife.

Walter Cronkite was announcing the CBS news on the TV behind the bar.

"I was trying to watch 'As the World Turns' this afternoon when they had to start talking 'bout Vietnam," the barmaid said, leaning her elbow on the bar next to me and turning so she could see the screen. "That's all they been talking 'bout all day. You can't watch nothing anymore because of Vietnam. I think everybody's 'bout to get tired of it always pushing off the good programs."

"It's a rotten inconvenience," I said.

"I was saying to my boyfriend the other day: 'Wesley,' says I, 'Wesley, why they keep showing all that shit on TV? Nobody wants to see American boys over there murdering them little Chinamen. It ain't right, so why they showing it?'"

I was trying to listen to Walter. I moved down one barstool with my drink.

"You could have told me to shut up," the barmaid grumbled.

"I could have."

Walter had that smooth, serious delivery as he explained how seventy thousand communist soldiers launched a surprise offensive just before dawn on the eve of Tet, the Vietnamese New Year. Fierce battles were raging now in Nha Trang, Saigon, Hue, Da Nang, and a hundred other South Vietnamese cities.

Americans at home, Walter said, were accustomed to the familiar images of U.S. troops being disgorged from hovering helicopters or slogging through dense jungle and across muddy rice paddies. With Tet, the fighting had shifted to a new arena—the supposedly impregnable urban areas.

The screen switched from Walter Cronkite to Morley Safer. He was crouching behind a wall, breathing heavily, looking excited, while gunfire popped like firecrackers in the background. Some footage ran of the U.S. Embassy in Saigon. I had been there a number of times. That was where I dropped off Carl Can't's body. The embassy was an ugly concrete pile shielded by thick walls surrounded by handsome pastel buildings left by the French.

The news footage showed a Marine racing past the camera. He stopped against the wall of the chancery building and tossed a pistol to someone on the second floor. Safer said a platoon of VC had blasted a hole through the wall that surrounded the embassy. The Saigon police guards fled. Cowardly little bastards. So far, five GIs had been killed in the embassy fighting.

The camera showed an MP lying on his back dead near a wall. The lens shifted to a dead VC in black pajamas and tennis shoes sprawled inside a flower garden.

Safer said the embassy had been saved, although GIs and ARVN were still fighting VC at the nearby radio station. There was still the distant popping in the background.

The TV screen shifted to a scene elsewhere in Saigon. It showed a bug-eyed South Vietnamese officer executing a prisoner who had his hands bound behind him. The officer raised a little snub-nosed pistol to the VC's head. The officer squeezed the trigger, and on international TV, for everyone in the world to see, the officer blew out the VC's brains. Cronkite said the executioner was Col. Nguyen Ngoc Loan, South Vietnam's police chief.

"Oh, good God!" the barmaid exclaimed, covering her mouth.

General Westmoreland appeared on the screen, looking grim. He commented that the North Vietnamese had very deceitfully taken advantage of the Tet truce to "create maximum consternation."

Maximum consternation? What kind of double-talk bullshit was that? The VC had come out to fight. That was the reason troops and supplies had been filtering into the south from Hanoi for the past several months.

I slid off the stool and leaned across the bar on my elbows. The biggest story of the war was unfolding in Vietnam— and here I sat on my ass in the middle of Oklahoma.

Good timing, Kragel.

Hank Baylor was probably jumping through his asshole, what with just him and Tom Stoud to cover the action for INS. He would have to depend on the freelancers and on what he could beg out of the AP.

I started toward the pay telephone, then returned to the bar. I couldn't get involved with that *there* when I hadn't even finished with *here*.

Walter Cronkite was back. He said what might be the fiercest battle of the offensive was developing in Hue where the enemy had raised the yellow-starred VC flag atop the Citadel, the ancient fortress in the center of the city. It appeared, he said, that the enemy was reinforcing himself and digging in. Marine units were being drawn from elsewhere and trucked or choppered to the city. The gooks would have to be dislodged by foot troops. The South Vietnamese government was refusing to allow aircraft strikes against the Citadel.

That could get nasty.

I hesitated as the thought struck me: *Brigette was in Hue.*

I walked to the back door of the bar and looked through the little window. A train was passing on the track. I saw it rushing through the winter night, and I saw the red lights flashing at the crossing. It was a long train.

Brigette was in Hue.

I paced back to the bar. I stood. I tossed off my drink.

Walter Cronkite had now turned to the war at home. He was talking over footage of antiwar student demonstrations on campus. Jane Fonda came on and said the righteous North Vietnamese people were merely defending themselves and their homeland against Yankee aggression.

Bitch. I liked her in *Walk on the Wild Side,* but I'd never watch another of her movies. Even if she did have a nice ass.

Baylor's last message to me said Brigette was back working at a hospital in Hue. I knew she had once been a nurse's aide, but I couldn't remember at which hospital. At least she hadn't gone back to the streets when I left. I tried to place from memory the locations of the Hue hospitals.

If I recalled correctly, there were three of them—two on the outskirts and one along the Perfume River near the Citadel. I remembered because I went to them once to interview peasants whom the VC had tortured along the DMZ.

I remembered the VC hung up the headmen by their heels and cut off their testicles. They strung up a pregnant woman and ripped her baby from her womb and showed it to her before she died. They gouged out eyes and cut off fingers and tongues and killed babies by rapping their heads against trees. It was a lesson to the villagers for cooperating with the government pacification projects.

I'd never watch another of that bitch Jane Fonda's movies.

Civilians as well as soldiers were dying in this war. If Brigette was in Hue, she was in the thick of the fighting.

I ordered another Tom Collins and tossed it off quickly.

For goo'ness sake. For goo'ness sake.

"What's happening to you?" the barmaid demanded.

I looked at her. I got up and walked out.

It was cold outside. I pulled my coat together and buttoned it. I stepped away from the lighted doorway and into the darkness of the parking lot. It was a circular area around a little wooded space in the center.

My senses must have been dulled by the drinks and my return to Stateside peace. I didn't catch the shadows separating out of the little wooded space until it was too late. Some giant grabbed me from behind, pinned my arms to my sides, and lifted my feet off the ground. Another shadow flitted in front and began working out on me with his fists. I heard my own ribs cracking. My nose flooded with blood and I choked on it. I thought I was going to drown on my own blood.

I fell to the ground and someone kicked me while I gasped for breath.

"Leave it be, mister," said a voice that sounded far away. "Get the hell out of Vinita and stay out. Next time, you're a dead man, mister."

42

DEAD MAN, MY ASS.

At Craig County General a pretty nurse named Nita helped an intern patch me up. The intern stifled yawns because he said he couldn't get used to the graveyard shift. Nita giggled when I told him that was a poor choice of words. Together they wrapped my ribs and took eleven stitches in my right eyebrow. My eye swelled until it was only a slit. I still had all my teeth though.

A policeman came as required to take the assault report. His belly flopped out over his gun belt. About what I expected for a hick town Okie cop.

"You didn't see who did it, right?" the policeman said.

"It was too dark."

"That right they didn't rob you?"

"I still have my two dollars."

"You've really pissed *somebody* off," the policeman decided.

"Eating bull nuts and beating up strangers seem to be big sports in your friendly little town."

"You won't prosecute them?"

"No."

The policeman closed his notebook and left. He seemed annoyed. Probably he had been parked in an alley somewhere catching a nap.

It dawned on me when the stores opened and I went to a hardware store that I was behaving the same way Dog would have. Taking care of things myself.

"It's solid oak," the salesman said. "Put an ax head on this handle and you can chop a rick of wood with it every day for the next ten years."

"You've convinced me. I'll take it."

"Looks like you've already been in a car wreck," the salesman said. "It looks painful."

"Only when I swing an ax handle."

Frost on the windshields of the parked cars gave back an alive glow to the early morning sun when I drove onto Flint Circle. An old Ford pickup was warming up for its owner to drive to work, its windshield wipers scraping at the frost and its tail pipe emitting white smoke. I stopped in front of the Dubose house and got out. I heard a door slam across the circle, and then another. I figured there'd be a welcoming party waiting to greet me.

I waited. I knew telephones were ringing and that Frank and his wife were likely peeking through their curtains. I stood with my door open watching the house, one foot propped on the seat inside, my back to the circle. I listened for footsteps. I grinned a little when I heard them.

As the grunts said in Vietnam, it was payback time.

My timing had to be just right.

I waited.

"Boy, you sure are hardheaded," a voice said from behind.

"That's what my ol' mammy always said," I replied, not looking.

"Didn't your ol' mammy also tell you to keep your nose clean and not sass your betters?"

"I must have missed that part in my upbringing."

"Then I suppose it's another lesson you'll need."

"And you're the one to give it, right, sport?"

The footsteps approached. I reached inside the car, then spun around with the ax handle gripped in both hands. The quick movement hurt my ribs, but it was worth the pain to see the expression on the faces of Buffalo and Carl's brother. I had been pugil stick champion of my old division at Fort Benning, Georgia. I still wasn't too old to use a stick.

I took out the dim-witted Buffalo first when he charged to grapple with me. I swung like hitting a home run and demolished his right knee. As he went down, I followed up with a short hard chop to the groin and finished him off with an uppercut in the face with the blunt end of the oak handle. He brayed like a wounded mule and sprayed the side of my car with blood droplets. He lay in a fetal position holding himself and yowling with pain.

The salesman was right. It *was* a sturdy handle.

A back spin brought me within striking range of Carl's brother, who had stopped to stare at his downed partner. The ax handle sank two inches into his solar plexus. He grabbed himself and dropped to his knees. He turned blue and desperately gasped for air.

I took a step back, the ax handle still at the ready.

They weren't getting up.

"The game getting a little rough for you good ol' boys?" I taunted.

Buffalo gurgled and writhed on the street, smearing blood. Carl's brother toppled onto his side next to Buffalo.

"That'll be enough," a voice said.

Frank Dubose came walking across his lawn. He stopped well out of range.

"There won't be any more need for your ax handle, Mr. Kragel," he said. His son was starting to revive. "Pete, take Buffalo to the emergency room. Use the pickup."

"He . . . he . . . The sonofabitch broke my ribs," Pete panted.

"I can't really say I blame him—after last night. Mr. Kragel, you can put up the handle."

His eyes shifted from me to the downed men to the pickup truck warming up in the crisp morning. He sighed deeply. His breath came out in a misty baloon.

"You really don't give up, do you, Mr. Kragel?" he said.

His voice sounded sad, resigned. He waited a minute, thinking.

"I guess it really don't matter anymore," he said at last. "It's not worth anybody getting hurt over. Mr. Kragel, you are a determined man. We heard you were nosing around old courthouse records all yesterday afternoon. I think it's about time this whole affair was laid to rest. It won't change the fact now that my son died a hero."

"Paw . . . ?" Pete said, struggling through his pain.

Frank Dubose ignored him.

"Mr. Kragel, will you come inside a minute?" he asked. "I suppose you knew Carl always kept a journal, a diary? He's been writing in one daily since he was fifteen years old. I'm going to show you something we've kept a secret. . . ."

The man looked relieved, like someone had just lifted his pickup truck off his shoulders.

Pete was on his feet. He was staggering and weak, but he was up and trying to get Buffalo up. I followed Frank Dubose into the house where Carl Dubose had grown into Carl Can't.

I dialed the telephone.

"Sheriff Cantrell, this is Mike Kragel. It's important. You said there were three other unsolved homicides that followed Margie Crowe's. Can you tell me about them?"

I imagined the sheriff's brow moving up underneath his thin strands of hair.

"I need details," I said.

"I guess it won't hurt to give you what we got," he replied. "Two were Muskogee boys and the third was from Vinita. The Vinita boy hung around Muskogee with the other two."

"Yes?" I said.

"We found the Vinita boy—Eddie Randol—in his car out on the Shawnee Bypass on June eight. He'd been shot in the head. It looked like he was picked off while he was driving.

"On June thirteen we found Rod Goodsell shot in his front yard.

"Two nights later Roy Betchan's brother found him on the street in front of their house."

"Sheriff, the three of them were friends? Who else did they hang around with?"

"They had several associates, but the one they were with mostly was another Vinita boy. He had an odd last name. Let's see . . ."

"Dubose?"

"Yes. Carl Dubose."

"All three were shot with a twenty-two caliber rifle?"

"How did you know that? But, yes, and all from long range. Whatta you have going, Kragel?"

"Sheriff, I don't know if I can tell you just yet. But I will later. Was there anything else unusual about the homicides?"

"I'll say. More weird than unusual. All three of them, Kragel—their ears had been cut off."

43

MIKE KRAGEL DISPATCH, 3 FEB 68:

Chicago (INS)—When American GIs returned from World War II, they came home en masse to ticker tape parades and celebrations. The war was over.

The same thing, to a lesser degree, was true of Korea. The war was over and Americans welcomed their fighting men home.

There are no parades for the returning Vietnam veterans. The war is not over. It is still escalating after four years of fighting.

When U.S. Army Sgt. Brian Epperson got off the plane in Los Angeles, he was with ten other servicemen returning after combat duty in southeast Asia.

"There was a bunch of spaced-out hippies having a demonstration outside the passenger terminal," he recalled. "They carried signs that said things like: HELL NO, WE WON'T GO and BABY KILLERS SHOULD NOT LIVE. The hippies were the enemy too. The police came and escorted us through them. I think it was for *their* protection, not *ours.*"

The ten servicemen split up in Los Angeles to go to hometowns in places like Springfield and Tallahassee and Nogales. Epperson was the only serviceman aboard the flight to Peoria, Illinois. He went into the men's room to change out of his uniform as soon as he landed.

"They made me feel like I ought to be ashamed of it," he said.

Epperson's buddy, former Marine PFC John Tandy, was a member of the Force Recon operating near the Cambodian border.

"One day I'm in combat," he said. "Then"— blinking his eyes—"like that I'm back in the world. I went over by myself as a replacement, I came back by myself. It was probably the loneliest time of my life when I got off the plane at home. My family didn't understand what was wrong with me. I should be happy to be home, but nothing seemed to make sense anymore. Everything was petty. Everything got on my nerves. Old high school friends would come by and want to go to the Tastee Freeze or drag Main or something and I'd think about my buddies in Nam eating beans 'n weenies out of a can, getting rained on and shot at.

"I felt guilty because some of my buddies got it over there and I was home already with all my legs and arms intact. It seemed the world *here* wasn't real; I left the real world back *there.* I've got fired off three jobs because I can't get my mind back here from there."

After a few weeks of trying to go it alone, trying to pick up lives left behind in order to pull a one-year tour of duty in the Republic of Vietnam, veterans seek each other out at places like the American Legion, the Veterans of Foreign Wars, and the Vietnam Veterans Association. They feel they cannot talk about the war to anyone who wasn't there. No one else understands.

"My wife divorced me a month after I got home," former Navy SEAL Brett Heleander added. "She said I wasn't any fun anymore. We were high school sweethearts, but she said I was too old for her now."

Former Marine rifleman Kevin Harper is afraid he is going crazy.

"I can't be sane," he said. "I miss the war, so I must be crazy. It was the most exciting time of my life. I feel like everything after that is anticlimatic, that I've seen the high points at twenty and everything else for the rest of my life is downhill."

"It was the most important part of my life," agreed ex-navy riverboat gunner's mate Claude Duchan. "I miss my buddies. They were closer to me than brothers. I keep wondering how they're doing. I don't want to go back, but I don't want to be here either."

Restless, the returning veterans seek out each other in order to talk about their experiences, to share common fears and anxieties while they cope otherwise alone with returning to the "real" world.

But for some of them, maybe even for most of them, at least for now, the "real" world is not the United States of America.

"Everything that was important to me I left back in the Nam," admitted Army Sgt. Gordon Lewis. "I've just reenlisted. I'm going back to Vietnam."

Part
Three

Part
Three

44

IF YOU WERE ONE PLACE, YOU WANTED TO BE ANOTHER, AND IF YOU were there you wanted to be here. The curse of the journalist. Never satisfied until you were where things were happening. And then still wanting to be somewhere else.

"Mike, I knew when you left you wouldn't stay put in Chicago," Hank Baylor said, preening his handlebar mustache and chewing on his cigar.

He stood to the side of the window in the INS office and peered out. Nothing remained of the building across the street except a gutted framework filled with ashes. Before Stoud left for Khe Sanh again he showed me a stray bullet hole in the side of what used to be Carl Can't's desk.

"It was all that *urgent* crap," I said. "And then when I couldn't contact anyone at the office . . ."

Baylor grinned. "You couldn't resist the call of the bugle," he said. "Well, as the grunts say, the doo-doo has come down."

The gooks had been chased out of Da Nang, but not before the Continental Palace took a 75mm round through the French Fuck. VC had holed up for a while in the room

Brigette and I shared. They trashed the place. The lizard was smart enough to haul ass out of Dodge. Either that or the gooks ate him.

"You look liked warmed-over pastrami," Baylor said.

I hadn't shaved or changed since Chicago. Black stubbly stitches took the place of my shaved eyebrow, and my eye had turned greenish gray, like the skin of a dead man in the sun. I felt worse than I looked.

Baylor regarded me carefully. "Mike," he said, "I'm sorry about Brigette. You couldn't have known. No one would ever have thought it of her."

"Goddamn cunt," I said with feeling.

I looked away.

Bill Lange had been the source of the *urgent* message I received through the Chicago INS office. I was already in Saigon before I managed to get through to INS Da Nang. Baylor simply announced that he would have Lange meet me at the Da Nang air base.

"He'll explain everything," Baylor said.

The sniper commander came striding stocky and measured across the tarmac when I stepped off the C-130 from Saigon. Behind him were the burned hulks of two F-105 jets that had been pulled off onto the grass strips to clear the taxiways. VC sappers had broken through the wire the first night of Tet.

"Dog's dead," I said.

I just knew it was true.

"Where'd you hear that?" Lange asked.

"I assumed . . ."

"You assumed wrong," he snapped. He hesitated. "It's about Brigette."

I stared at him. The man no longer looked old; he looked *ancient.* Like a scarred old bulldog that you're about ready to take to the vet to have put to sleep. He had the veteran's one-hundred-yard stare in a ten-foot room. His jungle utilities were bleached almost white and his boots were worn white too. The cigar he chewed on was cold.

When I found my voice, I murmured uncomprehendingly, "Brigette? What does she have to do with this?"

Besides, what made him think I got hung up on a gook cunt just because he had?

"Let's step over here," Lange said.

We separated ourselves from the wide-eyed FNG replacements and a horde of newsmen who were swarming in-country to cover the Tet offensive. It was monsoon season in Vietnam and the skies were overcast. It was still hot.

I could tell Lange had not been sleeping nights.

"Mike, I create these killers and then things happen to 'em," Lange said from some deeply felt well of sorrow. "Do you remember Collins who turned catatonic? Do you remember Dougherty's spotter, the kid from Alabama whose hair turned white when Dougherty got wasted? Mike, I remember every one of 'em. I remember 'em every minute I'm awake. I should. I created 'em. I created all these killers and sometimes I can't shut 'em off, and sometimes they shut themselves off like Collins did. But sometimes it's worse than that. Sometimes it's much worse. Mike, I created *Cho Linh hon*. And now that I have . . ."

"Bill, you're rambling. What about Brigette?"

"That's what I'm getting to, Mike."

He took out his ONE SHOT-ONE KILL cigarette lighter, but his hands were too unsteady to light his cigar. Finally, he gave up.

"Mike, I was hesitant about Dog at first because he was such a baby. I thought he couldn't take the killing either and the same thing would happen to him that happened to Collins. Was I ever wrong. I've created something evil, Mike. Killing is all Dog lives for now. He's got eighty-nine confirmed kills and his body count is the only goal he has. Mike, Dog is worse than Collins. At least Collins had a conscience to escape from."

"Bill, you were telling me about Brigette."

"Listen to me, Mike. Dog doesn't develop many loyalties, and the ones he does develop are unnatural. Like toward me, for example. Mike, I realize now that it was Dog who killed Steinke because Steinke was going to bring charges against me. He shot Judy, too, because he thought Judy was a spy and that she betrayed me. See what I mean about his loyalties?"

What did all this have to do with Brigette?

"Mike, the only other person Dog feels loyalty toward is you. He talks about you almost like you were his father. What I'm trying to tell you is that I sent Dog to Hue. I sent him there because that's where he stood the best chance of getting killed—*and I wanted him to get killed.* I've lost contact with him now and I can't call him back. Mike, I swear to you that I didn't know Brigette was in Hue when I sent him."

Suddenly I understood. But I didn't understand.

"Why would he want to kill Brigette?"

"For you," Lange said. "He thinks it's for you. And for me and Judy. If Dog isn't killed first and if Brigette survives the fighting, then Dog is gonna find her and waste her just as sure as God made little green apples. Mike, I'm telling you because I know. Judy Wong wasn't the spy. *Brigette is the spy.*"

My goddamned guts felt like a train clacking over loosely jointed rails.

"Hue is developing into the biggest fight of the entire war," Baylor said. "It's going to be bigger than Dak To even."

Stoud covered Dak To; that was right after I was wounded in the Hai Van. B-52s flew three hundred sorties against the commies who besieged the marines there, but the commies kept the attack going for twenty-two days.

Stoud had that one, but I wanted Hue for myself.

"You can have Hue," Baylor said. "It's going to be a bitch. But, Mike, listen. I want copy. The story comes first. Like you say, it don't mean nothing what happens to Brigette. You are no squaw man, right?"

I was no squaw man. I wanted back in the war, that was all. That was what I did—wars. That was what I was—a part of war.

"Get the hell back to your war then," Sharon had said in the lawyers' office when she finished signing the divorce papers. "Mike, you don't belong here. You never have."

I didn't either. I belonged to Vietnam with its heat and the rain and the gooks and the dying. It stank of dead fish, rot, and human shit, and I hated it. I loved it too. Figure that one. It was like ol' Rudyard Kipling said. Where else but in the land of the Lotus Eaters did the dawn come up like thunder? That was because, where there was war, *everything* was like thunder. No mewling little dawns and piddling sad broads who left their dogs tied to fire hydrants or who drank by themselves in empty bars at one A.M. In war, the only thing that had meaning was your life as you lived it right now, and the only reason that had meaning was because you risked it.

Baylor said, "You may get your chance in Hue to write your Top Stick's obituary after all. He'd make a great subject for a novel."

"I'm never going to write a novel," I said. "Hank, do you know which hospital Brigette's working in?"

Baylor was still at the window. After a moment of silence, he said, "Mike, you're a journalist."

"Which hospital?"

"It's surrounded by the enemy," Baylor said presently. "But then, she *is* the enemy, isn't she?"

He turned from the window to look at me. He shook his head and sighed.

"City Hospital between *Cercle Sportif* and the Citadel. Right on the river."

"I know where it is."

"Mike, think journalist. Think copy. You could get another Pulitzer out of this."

"The thing about you, Hank, is you don't realize everything is a trade-off."

You gave the other fella what he wanted because he gave you what you wanted.

I had laughed in Lange's face.

"Brigette's no more of a fucking spy than I am," I said.

The captain looked like he was breaking the news of a death in the family. "If anybody understands how you feel, Mike, *I* do," he said.

He took something out of his pocket and put it in my hand. Old memories clogged every sensor in my brain as I stared at Brigette's abalone shell comb, the one that always reminded me of rainbows. How many times had I lain in bed watching Brigette at the mirror combing her long black hair?

"I remember Brigette always wore this in her hair," Lange said. "It was unusual enough that I noticed. I asked her once to let me look at it, remember?"

"It's hers," I acknowledged.

"Judy *wasn't* the spy," Lange said. The relief in his voice made me hate him momentarily. "Judy told me once that Brigette was always pumping her for military details, especially after the times when Judy came out to Hill fifty-five. It didn't dawn on me then that—"

"Where did you get the comb?" I demanded.

Lange explained.

Division, he said, came down with an order for a special sniper mission. The target was a French homosexual who stayed on after Dien Bien Phu to build one of the largest rubber plantations in the country. He survived by playing footsy with the local Vietcong. A GI captured by the VC managed to escape and pass on to G-2 how he and apparently other captured American grunts were taken to the Frenchman's plantation for interrogation. The Frenchman was a sadist who enjoyed torturing Yank POWs, few of whom survived.

If that wasn't enough to have the Frog assassinated, then the fact that he had set up an elaborate intelligence network in Da Nang was.

"It's dangerous. It may be more risky than going after the general you wasted that time," Lange briefed his top shooter. "Monsieur DeFrange is apparently very important to the VC. His plantation is kept surrounded and guarded."

"When?" was all Dog wanted to know.

"They want him hit tomorrow night. He's supposed to be

meeting one of his agents at the plantation house. They want both of them taken out if you get the chance, but he's the primary target. Your target folder includes maps, aerial and ground photos, weather reports, photos of the target, and everything else you'll need."

"Why not just call in an air strike?"

"Because DeFrange is a 'neutral.' You can't call in air strikes on neutrals. Your mission is classified top secret."

The Ghost Dog slipped through the VC patrols that guarded the plantation. Two more guards in black pajamas stood picket among the stately palms of the Frenchman's front yard. Lights shone through double windows thrown open for the evening breezes. Dog caught glimpses of the target as DeFrange moved about inside the house. He was a heavyset man, Dog noted through his rifle scope, even heavier than his pictures indicated. He had meaty pouting lips, and dark hair pomaded to his skull. His hair looked like patent leather. He wore a purple smoking jacket.

Dog burrowed into a brushy hide two hundred yards from the house, at such an angle that he could easily watch the target and keep the sentries in view at the same time.

The Frenchman was obviously waiting for someone. Every few minutes he got off the sofa and either went to the door or looked out the window. Dog practiced placing his cross hairs square over the big man's heart.

Dog waited for an hour in his hide before a Peugeot using only its running lights came along through the royal palms that lined the long driveway from the road. It stopped in front of the house. Through his scope Dog watched a young Vietnamese woman get out of the backseat. She was attractive and dressed traditionally in an *ao dai*. Her driver waited in the car with the engine running while Monsieur DeFrange admitted her to the house.

The couple sat on the expensive sofa in the main room and talked animatedly for a few minutes. The woman kept turning so that her back was toward the sniper who waited in the dark outside watching through the wide windows. Dog thought he could kill both of them with a single shot if he got them lined up in the right position. If she moved four inches to her right, just eased forward a bit, he could place a 172-grain bullet through her head and into the face of the Frenchman. Two pink mists with one shot. It would be a first for him.

Even Pablo Rhoades had not made a shot like that.

Dog waited patiently, watching intently through his scope. He made his decision when the woman stood up to leave. The two-for-one shot was out. He centered his cross hairs on DeFrange's nose, then dropped them smoothly to the Frenchman's heart. The Frenchman gallantly took the woman's hand, smiling like his face was oiled.

Dog killed DeFrange with a bullet through the heart. Both man and woman dropped out of sight below the window frame.

Dog swung his rifle and picked off both sentries before they could recover from their surprise. The Peugeot took off along the lane between the trees like it had been goosed by a giant. Dog let it go.

"His orders were to take the shot, then *di-di,*" Lange said. "But he'd die in order to claim his kill's ears. The woman escaped, but she lost the comb while she was crawling on the floor to get out the back door."

"Who else knows about this?" I asked.

"I let it slip, Mike. I told Dog the girl in the house was Brigette Nguyen. Nobody else knows. Just you, me, Dog. And Dog is going to kill her because of you and because of me and Judy Wong."

45

I TALKED CAPTAIN LANGE OUT OF ACCOMPANYING ME TO THE combat base at Phu Bai where the 5th Marines were staging against Hue. The man was being eaten away by guilt and sadness. If the brass had any sense at all—and you could never accuse officers of that—they'd medevac Lange home. You saw Lange's kind of sadness and guilt in soldiers just before they bought the farm. It made them careless.

I came into Phu Bai by chopper where the skies were overcast and it was raining lightly. The chopper pilot worked his pedals and skirted wide of Hue. Black smoke curled up into the wet air above the MACV compound and the city treasury building. It didn't take much imagination to envision the house-to-house fighting going on down there.

To the southwest I saw the Hai Van Mountains where the sniper shot me in the leg and where Dog and I held each other in the rain.

I had no need of a son.

The Perfume River meandered through the city. I thought I saw the yellow-starred VC flag flying over the ancient old fortress on the river, but we were too far away to be sure. I picked out *Cercle Sportif* where three broad promenades cut through the concentric circles. I strained my eyes and found the square three-story City Hospital with its courtyards and sandstone wall.

There didn't seem to be any fighting there yet.

My gaze followed the Perfume River to where it bisected a long stretch of pristine white beach. A convoy of OD green six-bys crept along the beach, looking like a disjointed caterpillar. The six-bys were full of leathernecks bound for the battle.

"Can you see the Citadel?" the pilot asked through my helmet intercom, pointing.

"Yes."

"It's insane," he said. "Modern fighting men with all their machines of war have been ordered to attack a three hundred-year-old medieval fortress using no weapons that will destroy it. Take Hue, we're told, but take it *gently*. Fucked up!"

I'd have to remember that quote.

I kept watching the hospital, as though hoping even at this distance to catch a glimpse of Brigette at one of the windows.

Fuck her. I always felt guilty about using her. Turns out she was probably using me.

For goo'ness sake.

Why should I give a damn if Dog blew out her brains and cut off her ears?

The wind sighed and coughed, whipping sheets of water. The rain made an ambient hiss, like a noisy snake undulating through the streets of Hue City. The night was inky, cloying. Who would have thought it could be so cold in the tropics?

I stood inside next to a paneless window and watched it rain. The fight for the north side of Hue continued out there. I heard the sharp bang of a grenade a street over, preceded by a subdued flash that bounced off the lowering clouds. An M16 stuttered on full automatic. Alpha Company of the 1/5 was still in contact, but I could hear Second Platoon of Baker Company moving around me in the darkness of the house.

"Fifty percent alert," Lieutenant Thompson told his platoon, whispering. "I don't want any of you fuckers asleep that ain't supposed to be asleep."

I heard box springs creaking as the off-watch grunts piled onto a bed still in their wet clothes and muddy boots.

Copeland on the other side of the window from me stirred slightly; I felt rather than observed the movement. Copeland was the grunt with the stylized Marine Corps emblem on his helmet with *Semper Fidelis* replaced by the slogan *Simply Forget Us.* Today he had seen his buddy get it.

It happened right after we crossed the first canal from the village of An Cuu into the maze of two- and three-story buildings on the outskirts of Hue. A sniper from one of the buildings up the street picked off Copeland's buddy. He shot him through the legs with a machine gun, then left him writhing and screaming in the street as bait.

Copeland had to be restrained to keep him from rushing into the street to save his friend. Three other grunts piled on Copeland and dragged him into a house whose residents had fled. One of the grunts picked up a gold elephant and stuffed it into his ruck.

The gook shot Copeland's buddy again after a few minutes, after he saw the bait wasn't going to work. The machine gun bullets splattered blood and flesh. I heard Copeland screaming inside the house where the other grunts held him. It was like the bullets were tearing into his own flesh.

I wondered what Copeland was thinking now as he stared into the wet ink of the night. It was better, I thought, being a journalist than a grunt. All a journalist had to do was be an observer. A journalist wasn't a part of things. The lenses of his cameras and his own mind kept him removed from the action.

Earlier, Lieutenant Thompson asked, "How long have you been doing this shit?"

"All my life so far," I said.

We were crouched in a drainage ditch full of slimy water, pinned down by gooks with B-40 rocket launchers. We were waiting for a 106mm recoilless rifle to be brought up on a "mule" to blast the gooks out of a row of houses across the street and down the block. The fighting was trashing the little French houses of the well-to-do citizens of Hue City.

Thompson was from New York and would have looked more appropriate at a formal dinner than crouched here with filthy gutter water swirling around his ass while he calmly smoked a cigarette. His men of the Second Platoon, what remained of them, were scattered up and down the drainage ditch. One of them crawled up to the edge of the ditch, stuck his M16 over the top without exposing his head, and sprayed the gook stronghold with a burst. He was answered by a rocket that swooshed low over the ditch and exploded on the other side.

"Hold your fire!" Lieutenant Thompson shouted. "The one-oh-six'll be here shortly. We'll have payback."

The lieutenant's radioman sprawled on his back on the muddy bank of the ditch with his boots trailing in the water. He watched us blankly while he monitored the radio, the hand piece propped on his shoulder next to his ear. The lieutenant smoked. He glanced up and down the ditch at his men.

It was a lull for us, but everybody else was still fighting. Heavy sounds of battle came from the streets on the other side of the ditch as the Marines pushed toward the Citadel. A gook body in NVA khaki lay in the ditch with us. It stank. Flies swarmed over it in a black cloud, even in the misting rain.

It still had its ears.

"I've watched you," Lieutenant Thompson said. "You're a cool hand, Kragel. Everybody's ducking and running and shit and there you are everywhere with your eye glued to your camera."

"Haven't you heard?" I said.

"Heard what?"

"A camera distances you from the fighting. You're not really there at all. They can't shoot you if you're not there."

"I think I'll get me a camera," Thompson decided.

"Journalists are spectators," I said. "We're not participants."

He looked at me. He looked away again.

"You're here squatting in this filth getting shot at just like the rest of us. Why don't you go home? I'd damn sure go home if I had the chance."

I paused. "I am home," I said.

It dawned on me that Dog had once declared the same sentiment.

"Most of the newsmen come out, get their pictures, then haul ass," Lieutenant Thompson said. "They never know diddly squat about war."

Another rocket exploded with a flash bang. The explosion was followed by screams for "Corpsman! Corpsman!"

"Oh, shit!" Thompson said.

He started running hunched over down the ditch, splashing water. I followed with my cameras around my neck and my beat-up old camera bag flapping.

I took pictures of the wounded grunt while his buddies and a corpsman patched him up with a tourniquet and rolled him into a poncho for carrying. His head was snapping from side to side in agony. His face was gray. He had lost a leg. I took pictures of his leg still in the boot where it stood in the mud.

Through the lens you saw things you ordinarily didn't see, but it sterilized them and kept them at bay. It kept you apart from the war.

Only another journalist would understand that.

I heard sounds coming from Copeland in the darkness of the house where Second Platoon was bivouacking for the night. I heard the men snoring where they were piled up like puppies on the bed and on an overstuffed sofa and on the floor, but it was the sounds Copeland made that caught my ear. I listened and after a moment I realized what it was.

I stared into the wet night while Copeland cried. I stared hard and I didn't want to listen to the poor bastard because it reminded me of nights when Brigette held me against the nights, because they were the bad times, and I did not want to remember them.

Goddamn her.

What was I going to do about her, and about Dog and her, and about Dog and the murders he committed?

It was part of my nature to procrastinate. I recognized it and knew it and lived with it. Somehow, if you left things alone long enough, they seemed to work themselves out. Maybe Dog would get himself killed and I wouldn't have to do anything.

I listened to Copeland's muffled sobbing and shivered inside my utilities. I wanted to tell him to shut the fuck up, but I didn't.

After a while, fatigue overcame me and I slid down along the wall until my knees were against my chin. I hugged my knees for warmth. I couldn't sleep, but it was like sleep. From out of the city somewhere, through the hissing monsoon rain, a rifle shot penetrated the fog that piled up inside my head.

I jerked awake.

After you have been in combat you learn to distinguish between the sounds of different weapons—between the Mattie Mattell chatter of an M16, for example, and the harsher, slower *bark! bark!* of a Chicom AK-47. The shot I heard came from a sniper rifle. It was a single high-pitched bang whose echo reverberated through the street canyons. I recalled the sound Dog's Winchester Model 70 made when he shot the gook sniper through the face in the Hai Van.

I dropped my head on my knees and shivered again.

46

MIKE KRAGEL DISPATCH (WITH UNDEVELOPED ROLLS OF FILM from the fighting in Hue), 12 Feb 68:

Vietnam (INS)—Hue—not far from the DMZ—is a lovely old town of temples and palaces. Three hundred years ago the emperor Gia Long reconstructed the city and built a fortress, the Citadel, to replicate the seat of his Chinese patron in Beijing. Because of its cultural and political significance to the Vietnamese people, the city has remained a kind of neutral ground for both sides in the war. Ho Chi Minh's NVA regulars have been known to drink in the same bar with ARVN from the South.

No one expected fighting in Hue.

All that changed during the early morning hours of January 31, the beginning of Tet, the Vietnamese lunar New Year.

Communists crashed into the city from three directions, catching the ARVN home forces with their pants down. Communists attacked MACV headquarters, overran the treasury building, and hoisted the VC flag above the Citadel.

"The ARVN don't have the courage of American boys," said a battalion commander of the 5th Marines. "They get their bacon in the fire and start crying for us to come pull it out for 'em. If the ARVN had half the guts the VC do, this war'd already be won."

So far, three U.S. Marine battalions from the 5th Marines have been consigned to liberate Hue. There are indications the enemy intends to hold the city to the last man. Hue has become a political statement to the North Vietnamese.

"They want to demoralize support in the United States for the presence of U.S. troops in Vietnam," said a spokesman for the U.S. Embassy, "and break the will of South Vietnam to continue to resist. Hue has become a statement. The longer the enemy can hold out, the more powerful the statement."

So far, the communists have held the city for nearly two weeks, resulting in heavy fighting. Gradually, however, enemy troops are being compressed toward the center of Hue, toward the vicinity of Cercle Sportif where all boulevards converge, and toward the Citadel across the Perfume River from Cercle Sportif. U.S.

commanders expect the NVA and VC to prepare a last ditch stand at the Citadel.

The South Vietnamese government demands that the Citadel not be destroyed.

"Figure that," said Lt. Wayne Thompson, a marine platoon leader. "We're to storm the walls like knights of the Crusades. It wouldn't surprise me if they took our rifles away and issued swords and pikes."

The first Marines into Hue crossed the Perfume River aboard landing craft while enemy soldiers peppered them with small arms fire from both shores. The Marines entered from the north and cautiously threaded their way through the streets.

All fighting in Hue leads toward the Citadel.

The weather has remained cold and clammy with a low overcast that has made the use of tactical air support almost impossible.

According to intelligence recovered from captured enemy soldiers, the communist political cadre had made a long list of so-called cruel tyrants and reactionary elements prior to the attack. Reports indicate that because of this list thousands of Vietnamese civilians have been executed by the communists in Hue in the worst bloodbath of the war.

Those executed range from pedicab drivers known to cater to American army and Marine officers to city officials and the district police chief's concubine.

The VC had instructions to arrest all foreigners in Hue except for the French, apparently because of de Gaulle's criticism of U.S. foreign policy.

Marines sweeping into the city from the north report finding scores of dead civilians lying where they have been clubbed to death or executed by communist firing squads.

The city is a scene of desolation, of utter destruction. The streets are filled with burnt-out trucks and tanks and overturned automobiles still smoldering. Bodies lie everywhere, most of them civilian. They are bloating and starting to decay. Black flies are everywhere, like scuttling clouds.

The smoke and stench of death have blended like in a horror movie. It is a horrible smell. It permeates your clothing, the hair in your nose. You can taste it when you breathe, when you eat your C rations. It is like you are eating and breathing death.

All that is missing in the movie is the weird music to tell you when something is about to happen, when an enemy sniper is about to pick off your point man, when a rocket is going to explode and rip the legs off your squad leader.

More than eighty Marines have died in the fighting and another three hundred have been wounded.

It is close house-to-house fighting. Sometimes the enemy is only ten to twenty yards away. One Marine inside a house killed a VC sniper on the roof.

It is a shadowboxing type of fighting, ducking in and out of buildings, watching everywhere for looming shadows and ambushes. Everyone's knees and elbows are bloody from all the getting up, running, and falling again.

"It's bad," said Lance Cpl. Tom McBryde, "but at least they're coming out to fight. It's not like in the bush where the only time you see the little . . . is when they're dead. Come to think of it, *dead* is the best way to see them."

Lieutenant Thompson's Second Platoon, Baker Company, Second Battalion, may be the first unit to come within range of the Citadel. His men are fighting their way up one of the broad promenades that leads to *Cercle Sportif* and the railroad bridge across the river to the ancient fortress.

Pinned down temporarily by an enemy machine gunner hidden in a government office building ahead, the lieutenant directs two of his men to circle the building and place LAW (Light Antitank Weapon) rockets through third floor windows.

The machine gun goes silent when the rockets explode.

The lieutenant and his men drag their casualties out of the street. There are two Whiskies and one Kilo, two wounded and one killed.

The lieutenant calls for a medevac, which in Hue is a six-by truck. The body is placed in a black bag to go to an assembly point in the rear, while the wounded are evacuated to a Battalion Aid Station.

Then Second Platoon saddles up and moves out. By nightfall the Marines expect to see the rounded domes of the Citadel.

"It's going to be a *real* fight here on in," Lieutenant Thompson predicts.

47

GRENADES BANGED AND M16S AND AK-47S DUELED. I CHANGED lenses on the Nikon, switching from a wide-angle to a 135mm telephoto. My hands felt stiff and swollen. I fumbled, but I made the change.

I wanted close-up shots of Lieutenant Thompson. His men called him "Kick Ass" Thompson. He was leading the platoon against a Benedictine chapel occupied by a VC squad.

I panned until I found Thompson, opening the lens a couple of stops to compensate for the overcast and the smoke. Thompson had his back to a wall. There was a hole blown in the wall next to him. Through the lens it was like watching a war movie. His face underneath his helmet was tense and smoke stained and scratched, but it was composed. I still thought he looked like he should be wearing a tux.

I clicked off a few frames. Then, ignoring the puddles of water, I crawled around to the end of the building where I could watch the fight unfold. I found myself looking down the throat of the dangerous broad avenue that ran straight as a bee's flight toward *Cercle Sportif.* I saw some treetops above buildings maybe a half mile away, and I knew that was the park at the *Cercle.*

Beyond the park was City Hospital by the river.

A dead Marine lay in the street next to a disabled tracked vehicle. Somebody had stripped off its .50-cal machine gun. I brought the telephoto to my eye and recognized the dead Marine as Copeland. Poor sad bastard.

I snapped close-ups of his body. He lay in a puddle of thick blood. I snapped a close-up of his helmet rightside up in the blood with his epitaph scrawled on it: SIMPLY FORGET US.

Thompson yelled at Rock and Boogie at the other end of his building. Boogie was a diddy bopper from Watts who called whites "honkies" and said he was in the Marines getting training for when the race war started in the United States. Rock was an Alabama redneck; he and Boogie were inseparable, an odd couple. Thompson shouted orders at them and they darted around the end of the building out of sight into some yards and across some bamboo fences. Boogie was carrying his M-79 "blooper" and a bandoleer of grenades for it.

Thompson then sent Big John's squad snooping and pooping down the opposite end of the street in my direction. The rest of the platoon poured cover fire into the chapel across the avenue while Big John's men scurried across in front of me. Some green tracer rounds streaked among them and skittered off the pavement, but everyone in the squad made it across. The snuffies fanned out among the buildings.

I took pictures of a machine-gun crew setting up an M-60. Crew-served weapons always made for good action shots.

The war was all around me and I was taking pictures and

making notes. It was like old times. I was a part of it, but still separate from it. I wasn't carrying any baggage with me on this one.

Fuck Brigette. The traitorous bitch deserved to lose her ears.

The M-60 opened up on the chapel. Red tracers arced out into the avenue, then snapped back into the church. The bullets gnawed at the plaster walls. Dust enveloped the building. The machine gunner found his range and poured lead through the church's high narrow windows.

From the opposite side of the church, Boogie tested his range with the blooper. His first grenade exploded outside next to a statue of a Catholic saint, knocking off the saint's right arm. His next two rounds found a window.

"Fuck them dinks *up!*" somebody yelled.

No more fire came from the chapel. It had thick, wide doors made of burnished mahogany. Bullets had patterned it with splinters.

I took shots of "Kick Ass" Thompson and his raggedy-ass grunts approaching the church with their rifles at the ready. Smoke poured out the shattered windows. The one-armed saint looked down on the soldiers with eternal benevolence. McHenry paused and crossed himself in front of the saint, then crossed himself again, quickly, at the threshold before he flung open the door and flitted inside. Tinbloom the Jew went in with him as cover.

Rock and Boogie came up. The black man sat down next to the church wall and took a can of C-rat beenie-weenies out of his utility pocket and stuck a plastic spoon in his mouth and started opening the can.

"Beans, beans, wonderful fruit," Rock chanted, "the more ya eat the more ya poot."

"Poot?" Boogie said with disgust, looking up. "You weak-ass white boys might *poot*. Us soul brothers *fart*—loud, long, an' continuously."

Lieutenant Thompson stood by the door. "Boogie, god-damn. Can't you wait until later to eat?"

"I is hongra, Lieutenant."

"You're always hungry. Christ."

"Don't swear in church, Lieutenant," Rock cautioned. He was redheaded with freckles. "Ya nevah know when ya might piss off the Lawd."

A rifle shot banged inside the chapel, interrupting the conversation. Thompson crouched. Rock ducked around the corner of the building. Boogie took a bite of beans. I took a shot of Boogie grinning at the camera with his mouth full.

"Yeah!" Boogie said.

"Mac? Tin?" Thompson shouted into the church.

"Everything's A-OK," McHenry called from inside. He came to the doorway. He looked tired and whiskered. His M16 hung at the end of his arm. He took out a cigarette, cursed because it was wet, and then cursed again when he tried futilely to make a match strike.

"They was just two of 'em left, Lieutenant. The others must have *di-di'd* out the back. One was still alive," McHenry said.

He grinned. "Tinbloom took care of the sorry cocksucker."

Thompson looked around.

"Okay, you pogue baits, inside," he ordered. "Chow break while we wait for a truck to pick up Copeland. Rock, you and Boogie watch the front. Mac, take Tin with you and check around out back."

The grunts crowded eagerly inside. It was starting to rain again. They dropped their rucks around the walls and dropped with them. They didn't even glance at the two gook corpses. They opened their C-rats.

"Lieutenant, I think you ought to see this," Tinbloom said, coming inside from out back.

Tinbloom wore glasses on a small, boyish face. His grandparents had died in the Nazi concentration camp at Auschwitz. I followed him and Thompson out the back door, down some stone steps, and around behind a large plastered building. McHenry was standing there, looking, just looking.

Hordes of flies rose in an angry buzz from a pile of bodies next to the building. The wall had obviously been backdrop for a firing squad; it was cratered with bullet holes and splashed with dried blood and bits of brains and bones and flesh. The bodies were all clad in brown or black robes—the Benedictine monks.

"They didn't have to kill these poor dumb assholes," McHenry said.

My eyes raked across the pile of dead flesh. I'd seen stiffs like this before. In Korea, dead Chicoms were so thick in the trenches sometimes that we walked on them instead of in the mud. I looked at the dead monks in distaste.

I was going to take pictures of the massacre to document it, but then my eyes fastened on the woman. The Nikon dropped from my suddenly numb fingers and banged against my chest on its strap.

I stared.

"Isn't this some shit, Kragel?" Thompson said. "Kragel?"

The dead woman was a little apart from the others. She lay facedown in the short grass. She was small and young and her long black hair sprayed out around her head and down her back. Her legs were slim. They had been shapely.

I kept staring. It was the length of her hair and the shape of her body and the traditional *ao dai* she wore. The garment was peach colored with Vietnamese suns and symbols. It had a big bow on the rear. The bow was crushed and blood smeared, but it was there.

I stared.

Odd how the brain works at such times. Instead of its conjuring up Brigette out of the past, it brought forth Sharon. Sharon.

Sharon was right there, saying, "You're always just an observer, Mike."

She was signing the divorce papers. Her lawyers Greed, Sloth, and Avarice watched disapprovingly, but they didn't say anything. Sharon must have warned them I was crazy.

"Sharon," I said, "it doesn't do any good to tear at each other."

"There have been times when I wanted to rip you apart,"

Sharon admitted. "But not now, Mike. Not now. I just want you to face up to reality."

I didn't need this shit.

"The *real* world?" I scoffed. "This shit is the *real* world? I don't need your skim-milk reality."

"Mike, you poor sad sonofabitch."

"You've really changed," I said.

"You haven't," she shot back. "You're Peter Pan in Never Never Land where you never have to grow up to face responsibilities."

"Sharon, goddamnit . . ."

"Mike, you poor slob. Open your eyes. I still love you. I always will, at least a little."

She had me trapped.

"You won't let yourself accept a woman's love," she said, getting into it. They always had to have the last word. "You won't let yourself become a part of anything, Mike, not really. You're always the outsider, the perpetual observer. You use your camera like a shield to fight back the world. I've heard you say it a hundred times that a camera makes you an observer instead of a participant. I didn't realize how true that was until now.

"Don't stop me, Mike. I want my say. I'm not being vindictive. I'm giving you love the only way you've left to me. As soon as you start getting involved with anyone or anything, as soon as you drop that shield of yours that protects you from being anything other than an observer, then you run like holy hell. You ran from me, you're running from that Vietnamese girl. You've run from everyone who has ever tried to get close to you. Mike, you have to stop running before it's too late. Don't be like your father."

I saw him, my dad, the day he left home. He was running away. I cut across the pasture and I watched him as he drove the long narrow road through the hardwoods.

My dad was crying.

"Sharon, you have your divorce," I said.

"You're afraid to be anything but an observer," Sharon said, "because to be a participant in life demands an

229

investment, a commitment. The only thing you'll ever invest in is a new camera. You poor sad sonofabitch. You and that kid you write about—the sniper."

Was the sniper the only thing I wrote about that anyone read?

"He shoots them with a gun," Sharon said. "You shoot them with a camera. Each of you fights back the world in his own way."

Lieutenant Thompson touched my arm. It startled me.

"Kragel, do you know this woman?" Thompson asked.

I stepped quickly across and around the dead monks. I ran to the woman and knelt by her side. I grabbed her. Her body was stiff and her blood had dried and stuck her to the grass so that there was a sound like cloth tearing when I rolled her over. The eyes were open and fixed. The gentle rain fell on her face.

"Kragel . . . Mike, is there something wrong? Do you know her?"

I started laughing with relief.

"I thought I knew her," I chuckled, out of control. I looked up at Thompson, at Tinbloom standing next to him.

"It's not her!" I cried. It was raining in my face and I loved the feel of it. I loved the sound of my words, and so I kept saying them. "It's not her. *It's not her!*"

I kept Copeland's M16 when the truck came for him. There was no reason for it. I just took the rifle and slung it over my shoulder and removed his extra magazines from their pouches and stuffed them into the cargo pockets of my utilities.

I took his helmet too. I washed the blood off it in a gutter running with water and glanced one time at the SIMPLY FORGET US. Then I grabbed off my bush hat and plopped the helmet on my head. It was the first time I had worn a helmet since Korea. Lieutenant Thompson looked at me.

"There's always room for one more in hell," he said.

48

THE NEARER WE DREW TO THE CITADEL, THE FIERCER THE ENEMY resistance. After holing up for another restless night, this time in a tourist souvenir shop a half block from the Benedictine chapel, the grunts were already up and fighting. Screaming men and arcing tracers filled the misty morning. I smelled fish sauce and abandoned camphor-wood cooking fires. I smelled cordite, and I smelled death.

Baker Company had orders to take and hold *Cercle Sportif* and secure the hospital at the near end of the railroad bridge. I peeped out a window of the souvenir shop. The avenue opened in front, leading toward a splash of green at the end that was the park. The yellow-starred VC flag rippled above the Citadel beyond.

Lieutenant Thompson was on the radio, kneeling with his radioman among carved elephants and wooden Buddhas and little chalk temples and bronze replica knives. The platoon members had ransacked for what they wanted, stuffing their rucks, then discarded everything else as piles of trash on the floor. Here and there were burnt circles on the floor where the men had heated Ranger coffee and ham-and-eggs C-rats over heat tabs.

I continued my observation while Lieutenant Thompson called for artillery to pound the park at *Cercle Sportif.*

An abandoned Russian tank sat in the avenue at the circle. Earlier, at dawn, it ran out of ammunition. So did a U.S. M-48 tank. The two steel monsters started ramming each other. They backed off and charged, clanging and rattling, and collided like steel-armored prehistoric monsters.

Firing ceased on both sides to wait the outcome of the contest. Some VC farther down the street came out into the open to watch and cheer their champion; some marines on the other side did the same thing. I took pictures.

The tanks feinted and charged and crashed into each other with a ferocity that belittled the efforts of common foot soldiers. When the Russian tank lost a track and started smoking, its three-man crew piled out of it and fled toward the inner *Cercle,* looking back over their shoulders. Marines yelled and cheered and gave the Bronx honk, but nobody fired on the VC.

The VC scurried back to their holes and the gyrenes found theirs and the fighting took up where it had left off. The damaged American tank limped back to friendly lines, its commander waving and grinning from his open hatch and accepting a hero's welcome.

Looking through binoculars, I saw the VC had built defenses in depth across the park, past a picturesque French fountain located in the center of the *Cercle,* and on into the courtyard of City Hospital. Enemy machine guns, 51s, commanded all approaches. Bursts of fire had bogged down Thompson's advance and likely the advance of the rest of Baker Company in their streets on our right and left flanks.

Radio traffic was heavy; firing was heavy. Big John's squad was plunging a steady stream of M-60 tracers into the *Cercle* past the Russian tank.

Boogie had taken over Sergeant Edwards's squad this morning after Edwards ran into a booby trap and lost an arm. Boogie's squad was spread out among the buildings on the opposite side of the street from Big John's. They didn't have a machine gun, but they were rattling away with their M16s.

"We are going to kick ass," Thompson said.

He rushed to the window and peeped out with me. His radioman behind him switched to the platoon freq on the PRC-25. Thompson radioed Boogie and Big John to hold their squads under cover. Mana was coming from heaven in five.

It came like refrigerators hurled through the air. The

105mm shells exploding at the end of the avenue cracked with such terrific energy that they seemed to steal all the air. They rattled and broke what glass remained in the nearby houses. I ducked instinctively. So did Thompson. We grinned sheepishly at each other, but we didn't stick our heads up again. We sat next to each other underneath the window with our backs to the wall and our helmets so close they banged. The radioman was a kid of about eighteen; his hands trembled and he got as near Thompson as he could.

The barrage continued for five minutes.

"It won't strike the hospital," Thompson said.

"Some rounds are long," I replied.

"They aren't that long. You can tell by the sound."

"I have to be at the hospital with the lead element," I said.

"I thought you were just an observer," Thompson chided.

"I want to observe from up front."

"If you get any nearer up front you'll be sitting on Uncle Ho's lap."

The barrage lifted. The avenue was charged with smoke and dust. You couldn't see across the street.

"Kragel, she'll be all right," Thompson said. I had told him about Brigette. "My men don't fire on civilian women, even if that fucking hospital is treating enemy wounded."

I hadn't told him Brigette *was* the enemy.

"Let's go!" Thompson yelled, jumping to his feet and running outside. "Second Platoon, let's go, let's go, let's go!"

Second Platoon linked up with Third Platoon near the smoking Russian tank, where the advance bogged down again.

Third Platoon's commander was a young Annapolis graduate named Greystone Junger III. "The *Third*," he emphasized in his precise New England accent when Thompson introduced us and omitted the appellation. Junger's men called him Greystone Junger the Turd.

The two platoon commanders established a joint command post in a hotel lobby a hundred yards to the rear of the fighting at the *Cercle*. Baker Company commander was working his way over to take charge. He had ordered Second and Third to hold fast until he arrived with First Platoon's heavy weapons.

"Mike Kragel," Junger said, concentrating. "You're the grunts' journalist the enlisted men worship. Tell me, Mr. Kragel, why is it you so despise officers?"

"Some officers," I corrected.

"Most," he said.

"Most," I agreed.

"Why?"

"I suppose it's because I'm antiauthoritarian. I hated my father. It has nothing to do with the fact that most officers are pretentious assholes."

Thompson turned away from the map table to keep Junger from catching his grin.

"We're just fighting this war under orders like everyone else," Junger said.

"Punching your career tickets," I said.

I didn't need this shit.

"Were you in the military, Mr. Kragel?"

"Korea."

"Enlisted or officer? Or do I need to ask?"

"I turned down a commission. I couldn't pass the required course on ass kissing."

"That explains it," Junger said smugly. "That's why you make heroes of the grunts."

"All my heroes are cowboys."

"We encountered one of your heroes from the ninth yesterday. That's a weird duck."

The only 9th Marines in Hue were Lange's snipers.

"That boy is a candidate for somebody's psych ward," Junger said.

He frowned and concentrated on a tourist street map of the combat zone. There were no military maps available.

Thompson was standing looking toward the door that led out of the hotel into the street. A gyrene had pulled a rattan sofa with cushions next to the door to sit on while he kept guard. It was raining again. Rain skittered across the open doorway and made a puddle at the Marine's feet. The sound of heavy firing came from the *Cercle*.

I walked to the door and looked out. Through the gray veil of rain and fog and smoke that hung over the city I vaguely made out the tall red-tiled roof of City Hospital beyond the *Cercle.*

"Better keep your head down, sir," the Marine said.

"I'm no *sir,*" I said. "I work for a living."

The Marine grinned.

I walked back to the map table where the two lieutenants were busy devising attack strategy.

"We can walk directly over them," Junger was saying.

Thompson shook his head. "Not without sustaining heavy casualties."

"Some casualties are to be expected. They're acceptable."

What a turd.

"Where was he?" I asked Junger.

He looked up. "Who?"

"The Marine from the ninth."

"Oh. 'Vietnam's most feared sniper.' Isn't that what you call him in your articles? He looks like a spoiled grade school dropout. I can't believe some North Viet hasn't yet collected that reward on his head. He doesn't look like much, Mr. Kragel. Are you sure you didn't simply create him out of words and ink?"

He chuckled at his wit, then fell suddenly silent. He looked nervous.

"There is a Marine Corps regulation against mutilation of the enemy dead," he said. "All those ears on his belt. I guess he thinks he's Wyatt Earp or something with those two pistols and his rifle. I was going to write him up for violation of regulations . . ."

"What happened to him?"

"The little fuck was so damned polite. 'I have a job to do, sir,' he said. The last I saw of him he had just climbed down from the top of a Buddhist temple where he made two shots and killed two enemy soldiers who had one of my squads pinned down. He went up and cut off their ears. I have that report directly from my squad leader. I'm still going to write him up when this is over."

"Where was this?"

"Four or five blocks over. Why? Are you going to write another hero story about him? Don't worry, Mr. Kragel. Your hero is around somewhere—mutilating bodies, no doubt."

49

BAKER COMPANY COMMANDER CAPT. SHARKY BILBO ARRIVED AT the hotel command post with one sleeve torn off and a filthy blood-stained bandage wrapped around one huge bicep. He was unshaved and his dark beard made hollows in his cheeks. His eyes were caves.

"Lieutenants, you've been sitting on your asses all morning," he said to Thompson and Junger. "I want that hospital taken before sunset. Lieutenants, is that clear?"

Baker Company hurled itself at *Cercle Sportif* again and again, but the entrenched enemy fought back desperately. I saw some Marines fall in the street as Thompson's platoon charged across toward the shell-cratered lawn of the park.

One of them fell screaming with blood spurting from the end of his arm where his hand used to be. The other lost his head; it just disappeared when a rocket went through it. His helmet flew thirty feet into the air on impact. The body stood there for a second with no head. Ol' Ichabod Crane's headless horseman, dismounted, was leading the charge. The helmet banged in the street and went rolling toward the Russian tank before the body toppled over and spasmed in the street.

I didn't recognize the headless man until Boogie screamed. "Holy shit! Them motherfuckas!" He ran out into the open yelling and spraying the vicinity of a Cupid statue with his M16 on full automatic.

236

Boogie emptied his M16. Then he threw it down and picked up the body of his redneck buddy from Alabama, Rock. Green tracers zipped all around him. It was a heroic sight—Boogie carrying the headless Marine out of the street, walking, with his back turned contemptuously to the enemy while they hurled everything they had at him.

"Motherfuckas!" Boogie yelled until he was hoarse. "Motherfuckas!"

I could no longer just *watch*. I spotted a gook in a hole in some hedges by the Cupid statue. I dropped my camera on its strap around my neck. I took up Copeland's M16. I emptied a full magazine into the hedges. "Motherfuckers!" I cried in echo to Boogie's cries.

Afterward, I zipped up my cameras and slapped a fresh magazine of ammunition into the M16. The camera lenses were no longer keeping the war back.

"I see you've really joined the war, Kragel," Lt. "Kick Ass" Thompson said.

Baker had thirty percent casualties by sunset. Four Marine bodies lay unrecovered in the street. Bilbo said he'd get them out after nightfall. "No Marine of mine is gonna lie out there like that all night."

A Marine observer on the top floor of the hotel command post said the enemy was having his problems with casualties too. He watched the Vietnamese littering their casualties to the hospital. Women, some of them nurses and aides in white or blue, ran out of the hospital and helped carry the wounded gooks inside.

What was I going to say to Brigette, to do, *if* we broke through to the hospital, *if* she was still there, and *if* I got there ahead of Dog and his rifle and she was still alive and I was?

"The gooks ain't taking their wounded to the hospital's front door no more," the CP observer reported later to Captain Bilbo. "I heard two or three shots from a hunting rifle. One of our guys must have been on top of the buildings. It's a thousand meters across that park, but whoever was shooting picked off a slope with every shot. It had to be that shooter from the ninth. Captain, that fella is *deadly.*"

"He's undisciplined. He's uncontrollable," Lt. Greystone Junger the Turd said.

Bilbo lifted an eyebrow. "How many confirmed kills have *you* made today, mister?"

"Well . . ."

"That's what I thought. Lieutenants, you still haven't made a present to me of that park and the hospital. It's already dark. We should be getting in some replacements. You know what your job is at first light. We have to occupy this position in order to reach the river and the Citadel."

"This whole thing is insane, sir," Lieutenant Thompson said.

50

NIGHT SETTLED LIKE A DAMP BLANKET. THE FIREFIGHT TAPERED off to a jittery rifle shot or a grenade bang now and then. The troops in squads and fire teams occupied buildings along the street facing *Cercle Sportif*. At the hotel, the command post compressed itself into a tight circle of officers, NCOs, and radiomen around a map-strewn table in the lobby. Someone erected poncho walls around the table to contain the flickering light of a single candle on the table.

"It's insane," Thompson said.

"It's war," Bilbo replied tersely.

"What's so important about that old fort?" Thompson continued. "Cap'n, you know I'm willing to kick ass. But this . . . ? Let them keep the Citadel. As soon as they find out we don't want it either, they'll disappear. That's the sensible way."

"But it isn't the Marine Corps way, right, sir?" Lieutenant Junger interjected.

Kiss ass.

It was dark away from the table, but you could still make out the shapes of things, like the potted palm in the lobby. I made my way wearily off a hallway to a room that had apparently been the manager's office. Grunts occupied most of the other lower-floor rooms on the buddy system, one sleeping and one on watch, but I had earlier claimed this one for my own since it was of no tactical importance, having no windows or openings to the outside.

I closed the door and lit a candle from my camera bag and stuck it to the center of the desk with its own hot wax. I swept papers onto the floor, dumped Copeland's helmet and rifle onto the office sofa, and pulled up a chair. I took out my spiral notebook and looked at it with pen poised. I was going to catch up on my notes.

I saw Brigette's face instead. I heard her voice. "For goo'ness sake."

I got up and paced the room.

Guys like Horton fell for slanteyes and then they couldn't go home anymore.

Where the fuck *was* home?

Brigette betrayed me. She used me. "Biness is biness, for goo'ness sake."

Yeah. Business is business.

I took out the abalone shell comb Bill Lange gave me. It reflected the candlelight like a piece of rainbow in my hand. I closed my fist around it. I slumped at the desk clutching the comb like a psychometrician seeing across the divide into the past and the future. I could see the past, but not the future.

"One day, Mike, you go home to wife in 'Nited States. Brigette must be practical, for goo'ness sake."

"I can never love you, Brigette."

"Brigette have heart big enough for you and me, Mike."

"No heart's that big."

She turned from combing her hair at the mirror, that long

black silky hair with its fresh Oriental scent. The voyeur lizard peered through the door glass in the morning light. Traffic was already heavy on Duc Phon Street. I walked over to Brigette, both of us still naked. I wrapped her tiny body in my arms from behind.

"Baby-san," she murmured softly, almost sadly. "Mike and Brigette separate and apart from war. Mike and Brigette have separate place war not come to."

I sniffed Brigette's comb to check if she might have left some lingering scent on it. She hadn't. I rose wearily and walked to the closed door. There was nothing but darkness and death and silence beyond it. The candlelight flickered after me. I left the door closed.

There had to be more to life than a pension and a place to retire to at the end.

I went back to the desk.

I wondered if my dad found out what happened to you at the end. He drove crying down the long narrow road through the hardwoods, and then I didn't see him again until Mom died.

I flew back home from the Cuban invasion training camp in Guatemala and looked at Mom in her coffin. Aunt Cora selected the dress Mom wore. Dad came in and I didn't recognize the tall old man who stopped beside me. I didn't look at him more than a glance until he bent over the coffin and a tear dropped and splattered gently on the dead woman's cheek. Then I looked at him. He looked old and used up. It was almost like looking at a mirror image of myself, only thirty years older.

It was an awkward moment. Neither of us knew what to say for a long time. We just stood there in the viewing room of the funeral home, the two of us side by side, and gazed down at Mom while that awful music wept in the background.

"Son?" he said finally.

I didn't answer.

"Son, I'm sorry for everything."

I still didn't know what to say.

"I always loved your mother," he said. "And I always loved you."

Then he turned silently and left. He sat alone in the back row during services and slipped out after the final prayer. I often wondered what happened to him.

There had to be more to life than that.

"Mike, you are never satisfied," Sharon complained during those periodic times when I was home. "You're restless and edgy. Can't you be like other men?"

"How are other men?"

"They watch TV and relax. They go to ball games and stop for a beer with buddies and send their wives roses."

"I can't do that."

"I know. There is a dark side to my Michael."

"What do you mean by that?"

"Just that there's a dark side. There must always be conflict and war in your life. When there isn't, your life has no meaning. You pace."

"I pace?"

"You're pacing now. Like a hungry tiger behind bars. Mike, you're going again?"

"Sharon? Sharon, Hank Baylor has been transferred to the INS office in Vietnam. He's asked me to come."

"I don't know how much longer I can keep waiting for you, Mike. I get lonely."

"I have to go," I said.

"I know," she said. "I always know."

A machine gun stuttered a few broken phrases outside the hotel. I paced in the hotel office, then returned to the candlelight at the desk and placed Brigette's comb so that it picked up the candle flame. I stared at it, remembering.

It was a night for remembering.

The office door opened so silently that it was only a whisper. It whispered again in closing. I looked up quickly, half rising.

Dog stood just inside. His patrol cap was pulled low, but the flame from the candle still reflected in his eyes, deep inside them like embers burning at the back of caves. His utilities hung loose on his lean frame, bunching only around his web gear and the two .45s in holsters. The deadly rifle hung at the end of his arm. The heavy string of ears on his belt included a number of fresh ones.

We stared into each other's eyes.

51

DOG SILENTLY TOOK IN THE ROOM, HIS SHIFTING EYES STILL LIKE embers in caves. He survived by constant awareness of his surroundings. His eyes found Brigette's comb on the desk. His gaze returned to meet mine.

"Johnny?" I said cautiously.

"Mike?"

It was tentative. It hadn't been that way after the Hai Van, but now I felt uncomfortable in the kid's presence, like at the beginning. It was like when you knew too much about a person, things you shouldn't know, and the person *knew* you knew.

My stare dropped to the string of ears on his belt. Dog's moved back to Brigette's comb.

"You know about her?" Dog said bluntly. He seldom wasted words.

I still hadn't decided what to do with the secrets I gathered in Oklahoma. At the time, solving the mystery had been enough. But now Brigette was involved in the consequences of both Dog's future actions and mine. Our collective parts had led us to this point. I had to do something now, something dramatic, if I hoped to alter all our futures. No procrastinating on this one, Kragel.

"I know about her," I said. "And more. Carl Can't recognized you that day on the road—and you recognized him. Now I know why."

Dog's expression remained flat, unchanged. His head nodded slightly. I rummaged in my camera bag and took out a sheaf of papers that I had been carrying around, trying to decide what to do with them. I handed Dog the pages from Carl Can't's old journals.

"Start with May twenty-two," I said. "Ol' Dog reads, right?"

Dog moved to the candlelight and positioned himself as he read so that he faced the door. I watched him. His expression remained flat. I could almost quote Carl's entries from memory:

May 22: It was an awful thing, I don't want to think about it, but I can't not stop thinking. Eddie and Rodney and Roy and me, we swore a pact. We swore it in our own blood that we would never tell anybody about it.

But I have to let it out somehow. I mean, I really tried to stop them. We were there partying and listening to the car radio, and I tried to talk them out of hurting the girl when they saw her come out of the woods. But they were just drunk enough not to listen.

They hit me in the face with their fists and made me sit in the car while they did things to the girl. They did it in the headlights of the car where we could all see. She fought them, but they beat her until she stopped.

What could I do against three of them?

"Is that the reason you didn't kill Carl Can't when you killed the others?" I asked.

Dog glanced up.

"Johnny, what happened to Margie . . . It shouldn't have happened, but it did. Now, it's over with, Dog. It's all over."

"Sir," he said, reverting to the formality that worked for

him to keep others at a distance. "Sir, it will never be over with."

He read on:

> I'm so ashamed. A skinny blond kid must have heard the screaming. He ran out of the woods and he fought Eddie and them until Roy hit him with a big stick. I should have helped him more. I got out and tried, but they hit me too, and I got back in the car.
>
> The boy and girl both looked like they were dead. Rodney tied a piece of wire around the girl's neck and dragged her over into the bushes while Eddie and Roy dragged the boy.
>
> They were scared. They said if I said anything I'd go to prison too because I was with them and the law would say I was guilty too.
>
> Oh, Lord, I hope they aren't dead!

Dog glanced up from the journal. He sank heavily onto the chair and I saw the hurt in his face. It was like the hurt I felt in him when we were in the rain on the Hai Van and he said Margie's name.

"I wish you hadn't found this," Dog said, and he was once again in control.

"It had to come out sooner or later."

"But it shouldn't have been you. I had a feeling when you left Nam that we'd meet again."

"Johnny, it can all be finished now, over with. If you'll let it."

Dog's lips thinned. "It'll be finished," he said, "when I am dead."

A thin bitter smile crossed his face.

"Mike—" His voice broke, just a hairline. "Man *is* an island, Mike. Life is war. Margie Crowe was the only human being I ever fully trusted."

"Kid . . . ?"

He was reading again. I let him, directing him to the important parts. Maybe reading it, facing it, would help purge it from his soul.

May 23: It was in the papers today. The girl died. It didn't say anything about the boy. Rodney called to warn me to keep my mouth shut.

June 9: They found Eddie Randol shot in Muskogee. The police said it was like a sniper or something, but nobody has any idea of why he was shot.

June 14: The sniper shot Rodney Goodsell in his front yard last night. The police still say they don't know who did it or why, but I know.

It was because of what we did. It was the skinny blond boy. Roy said the boy was wild or something, that he was crazy. Roy is scared titless. He said as soon as he can get some money, he's going to leave Oklahoma and go to Florida. He said I should go with him if I don't want the crazy boy to kill me too.

I didn't have anything to do with it. I tried to stop them. Roy said that wouldn't make any difference to the crazy boy.

June 17: The sniper got Roy Betchan last night. I knew about it before it was in the papers. The crazy blond boy was here last night too. He woke me up in my room. He had a rifle and he wouldn't let me move or look at him. It was dark, but I knew who it was.

I knew he was going to kill me, too, but all he said was something like, "I'm going to let you live. Every day you live you'll remember that you were a coward."

Oh, God, he's right. I am a coward. I'll do anything to make it up, what I let happen to them that night. There's got to be something I can do to make it up.

"Carl Can't was a shithead," I said, "but he had his own hell to deal with. His dad was right. Whatever else Carl was, he died a hero on the road to Bien Hoa. He tried to make up for what happened."

"He just died, sir, that's all," Dog said. He held up the journal. "You returned to Vietnam to show me this?"

I looked away. "There were other reasons."

Dog picked up Brigette's comb. He turned it slowly over and over in his hands. My gaze locked on it.

"You didn't go to the police," Dog said. "Why?"

"I'm not sure I know. I wanted to talk to you first, I suppose. Johnny, the world is all fucked up, but listen to me, kid. You've been at war long enough. It's up to you and me to end it for you together. Turn yourself in and tell them what happened. I'll go with you. Any jury in the world will let you off on temporary insanity."

"I wasn't insane," Dog said. "The Bible talks about the Law of the Jungle, an eye for an eye, a tooth for a tooth. That's *not* the Law of the Jungle. It's the law of Moses, of civilized man. I know. It was far more civilized living in the woods than it has ever been since I came out to join your world."

I glanced at the string of grisly objects on his belt.

"I learned quickly," he said, reading my look. "They take from me, I take from them."

"It has to end," I said.

"I'm not finished here yet."

I was tough and had seen it all, but my blood ran cold. I leaned over the desk toward Dog. The movement made the candle flicker shadows across his face. I recoiled a little from what I read through the shadows. Bill Lange was right. This kid was ancient inside, older than all of us put together. I thought I smelled dust and dryness and air so old you couldn't breathe it.

"Your hundred kills," I scoffed, saying it leaving me disgusted as it never had before. "Is killing a woman going to make you better than Pablo Rhoades?"

"Women don't count," he said without emotion.

"Goddamnit, kid! She counts to me. Just like Margie Crowe counted for you."

I thought I had him, but then he stood up and carefully replaced Brigette's comb on the desk.

"Johnny, the killing can stop, here, now, for you. What happened to Colonel Steinke, to Judy Wong . . . What happened in Vietnam stays in Vietnam, a part of the war best forgotten. But the others in Oklahoma. That was not war. You can go home, but I know now it has to be taken care of. I won't hide it for you, Johnny."

"Mission first, people second," Dog said. "Isn't that what they teach us, that the mission always comes first? It was your woman's fault that Judy Wong had to die. It almost destroyed Captain Lange. I have a mission to perform."

"It was *you* who killed Judy Wong," I said, my voice rising. "It wasn't Brigette."

He strode softly around the desk and toward the door. He paused.

"Mike . . . ?" he said.

I waited. He turned on me those bleached eyes with the fire in the caves.

"Mike," he said without emotion. "I have to do what I must."

"Why?"

That seemed to stump him. "I have no father," he said presently, looking at me with his strange eyes.

I wanted to shout angrily at him for saying that. I wanted to, but I didn't know why I wanted to.

Maybe he was crazy. Maybe war made us all crazy.

"Mike," he said, "one of us, either you or I, cannot leave Hue alive, not with what you know. I won't be put in jail."

The Winchester Model 70 took on life of its own. It mesmerized me in the candlelight. I watched it uncoil in the sniper's hands. This time there was no 135mm lens between me and it. I recalled long ago on Hill 55 how I asked him if it was unloaded.

"Of course, sir," he had replied. "I would never point a loaded rifle at someone I didn't intend to kill, sir."

Dog peered unblinking through the scope at me in the tiny room. I stared back at him.

I thought about lunging for Copeland's M16 on the sofa, but I knew I could never reach it.

"I'm not going to let you kill Brigette, Dog," I said, and it was said and the decision made.

Dog lowered the rifle. He walked to the door.

"Mike . . . ?"

I thought he was going to say *I'm sorry.*

"Mike, there has to be a hundredth kill," he said.

Then he was gone into the city, and the city was rotting and falling around us.

52

CAPTAIN BILBO FOLLOWED JUNGER THE TURD'S ADVICE AFTER all and attacked head-on. At dawn, what was left of Baker Company charged across the promenade and managed to obtain a toehold in the park. It was raining a little, and the clouds were low and gray and intrusive.

Boogie at the head of his squad fell behind a statue of an elephant carrying an ornate *howdah.* He fell flat on his back and tried to get up and couldn't. His face was so black it was blue, especially with the rain misting on it. Tinbloom slid down next to us on the grass while the rest of the squad continued pouring fire past the fountain. Tinbloom had lost his glasses.

"Boogie Man, you all right?"

"Dude, do it look like I's shuckin' an' jivin'?"

Tinbloom helped me drag the squad leader to better cover in a shell crater behind the elephant. The crater held six inches of muddy red water. Doc Brown made a broken field run across the park that would have done the Jets proud. He looked at Boogie's wound. There was a tiny round hole in the soldier's ribs. It didn't bleed but a drop or two, but the corpsman said Boogie was bleeding inside. Boogie was out of the fight.

"You honkies has got a real cluster fuck here," Boogie said. "Journalist-man, you is a cool dude. Get these her muthas' sorry asses outa dis park befo' it become they graveyard."

Big John and his squad to the right flank of the elephant had killed the VC who occupied a sandbagged trenchline and now occupied the trenches themselves. I heard First Platoon farther over among the dwarf shade trees where they were shouting at each other and shouting at the enemy. Boogie's radioman crawled over from an abandoned foxhole and said Third Platoon was reporting heavy firing coming from the hospital ground.

"Journalist-man, is you a part of this shit or ain't you?" Boogie asked.

What the hell. I grasped Boogie's arm. "I'm a part of this shit," I said. "Doc, get two men to carry Boogie back to the casualty pickup point, then hightail it back here. Radioman, come with me. Contact Six Actual and tell Lieutenant Thompson that this squad is going right down the middle of the park to the hospital walls. Is that clear?"

"Yes, sir."

"Then let's go! Let's go!"

"It don't mean nothin', dude," Boogie said, grinning past his pain.

"The hell it don't," I said back.

I was no longer simply an observer. Not only was I participating, I was *leading*.

The Marines accepted it. They jumped up by fire teams, one maneuvering while the other lay down cover fire, leapfrogging like that past the enemy trenches and the big fountain and the hedges. I started yelling and screaming like a madman, and the squad took it up. It was like a race across a torn-up park. A dozen raggedy-ass leathernecks bore down into the throats of the defenders.

Second Platoon heard and saw, and then First Platoon on our right flank. At first, one or two Marines joined the squad. Then little groups of them. First Platoon on line burst out of the dwarf shade trees. Second Platoon followed in its sector. Everybody was firing from the hip and screaming like a banshee. The fucking gooks must have thought we were crazy. And maybe we all were, a little. War itself was craziness and the way you survived it was by being crazy too.

Some gooks in black wearing pith helmets ran across in front of me carrying long tubelike RPG-7 rocket launchers. One of them knelt in the open and pointed his tube at me. He wasn't fifty meters away. I sprayed him from the hip and the 5.56mm rounds flipped him over backward.

How was *that* for participation?

Tinbloom paused to fire into a spider trap. Doc Brown ran by carrying a wounded grunt on his back.

First Platoon reached the other side of the park first, chasing a half-dozen gooks. The gooks ran into the broad street that circled the back side of *Cercle Sportif,* what had once been Hue's greatest tourist attraction. The Marines mowed them down. The scroungy little bastards went down in the middle of the street like bags of rags.

There were more enemy soldiers in the hospital set back near the river, with the ancient Citadel and its rain-drooping VC flag in the distant background. The hospital gooks opened up on the charging Marines with hand-held mortars and small arms fire.

I had lost Copeland's helmet in the madness. My hair was soaked. I tasted the water streaming down my face. It tasted salty. I wiped at my face. My hand came away bloody.

I paused for just an instant on the gentle slope of the grassy park where it swept down to the broad street that separated the park from the hospital grounds. A head-high sandstone wall enclosed the three stories of the hospital. The building was white with small rows of windows and a gabled red-tiled roof.

Brigette was in there.

I saw a puff of smoke emit from a top-floor window. I heard the bang of the rocket exploding in the park, a scream.

The attack was bogging down. The Marines were starting to mill in the open.

"Marines!" I shouted. "Let's kick commie asses!"

I slapped a fresh magazine into my M16 and charged again. The adrenaline was pumping. I ran past the Marines, picking up Tinbloom and then Big John and his squad.

That started it again. Second Platoon erupted across the street toward the hospital, firing M16s from the hip, screaming and yelling. Lt. "Kick Ass" Thompson charged past me with the platoon. Momentum carried us to the sandstone wall.

Nothing was going to stop us now. Nothing was going to stop me.

"Grenades! Use grenades!" Lieutenant Thompson shouted at the line of Marines behind the wall.

Grenades sailed into the narrow courtyard between the wall and the hospital's wide front doors where the gooks, like gophers, had dug fighting holes. Grenades began exploding in the courtyard, filling it with deadly singing shrapnel. Shrapnel peppered the other side of the wall. I heard screaming and shouting in Vietnamese.

Another puff of smoke came from the top floor corner window and a section of our wall exploded. I grabbed a man with a LAW rocket and pointed out the window.

"Easy shot," he said.

He sighted with the tube on his shoulder. The LAW gave a high-pitched squeal. A fiery ball of smoke arced high in the air and plummeted through the enemy window. The entire upper corner of the building exploded in a tremendous bang of dust and smoke.

"Takes care of that shitbag," the Marine said.

The wall gave me a breather. I crouched behind it while chaos ruled and I looked around. The Marines, the by-God Crotch—I admired these tough, filthy, cursing, mean, beautiful bastards. Courage, as journalists liked to say, was commonplace. Or perhaps it was just foolhardiness. Whatever it was, I was one of the bastards, a combat soldier again. I felt *alive.* In combat, every minute is an hour and an hour is a day and there was no yesterday and there certainly might be no tomorrow. You were alive for the moment, and you were more alive than you would ever be again.

In combat, everything was contradiction and chaos, but everything seemed to fit nonetheless. Everything became so simple. For me, there was only one goal—reach Brigette. What happened after that couldn't concern me now.

The VC were retreating from the front courtyard by fleeing through the hospital and out the back door. The Marines went over the wall. A wounded grunt in the courtyard gripped a .45 pistol in each hand. There was a growing spread of blood on his shoulder. He stood erect in the courtyard snapping shots with his .45s, engaging in his own fight at the OK Corral.

A gook in a foxhole thirty feet away shot at him. The Marine, who had lost his helmet and had fiery red hair, walked slowly toward the gook, right down Main Street. The gook kept firing. The redheaded Marine cocked one .45 and brought the pistol down to the level. He fired one shot. The gook's face exploded.

"Yahoo!" the Marine yelled. *"Yahoo!"*

He turned to engage another enemy soldier who stuck his head and rifle around the corner of the building.

A member of "Big" John's squad scurried among the fallen VC shooting them again to make sure they were really dead.

"They ain't dead till they're dead!" he cried.

In the midst of the fighting Doc Brown knelt over a wounded Marine. He had an IV started. He hung the IV fluid on the toe of a dead gook whose foot he propped against a tree.

The Marines, the by-God Fighting Crotch.

Lieutenant Thompson, Tinbloom, and I were the first liberators inside the hospital. Beyond the wide entranceway was a tiled foyer with hallways branching off in three directions. A VC lay facedown in the foyer in a pool of fresh blood, through which his fleeing comrades had tracked, leaving the floor smeared with bloody tennis shoe and sandal prints.

I kicked the remaining glass shards out of the front door to permit Big John to head his squad inside. Most of the firing had ceased. Marines outside were cordoning off the building and setting up their own defenses as Big John's ragged squad entered the hospital in a rush to start the floor-by-floor, room-by-room search.

"There are civilian women in here!" I yelled, reminding the Marines.

I had barely uttered the warning before a round zipped by so close it seemed to steal the air I was breathing. The bullet gave a kind of *cr-a-a-ak!* as it went by. It splatted into the tile floor next to the dead gook. I dropped to the floor with Thompson beside me.

"Sniper," he breathed.

My heart ratcheted against my ribs. That wasn't *just* a sniper out there, was my first thought. That was the deadliest sniper in Vietnam, *Cho Linh hon,* carrying out his threat to make me his hundredth kill.

The poor little sonofabitch. The thought kept racing through my head. Dog no longer knew when to stop or where to draw the line.

Lieutenant Thompson's face was next to mine on the floor.

"You're bleeding," he said.

"I've bled before."

"Are you hit, Kragel?"

I glanced at the doors through which the shot had come from the direction of friendly lines. Dog was watching. He had been watching all along. He could take me out any time he wanted. Then why had he deliberately missed? What was he doing?

"I've got to get to Brigette if she's still here," I said.

We crawled away from the door and stood up next to the wall in the hallway. The floor was slippery with blood. It smelled like zinc or mercury or some kind of wet metal.

Big John's squad was bursting from room to room on the

first floor, dragging out bandaged enemy soldiers and taking them prisoner in the hallway. Even the seriously wounded ones who could not walk were dragged from their beds and cots and pallets and dumped in the hallway. They moaned softly and stared at the Americans who guarded them. The Americans stared back; they were still wanting to kill. The Vietnamese remained perfectly motionless, except for their eyes.

"Kragel, you can be my platoon sergeant anytime," Lieutenant Thompson said. "Hell. You can be my company commander. When you joined the war, you *joined* it."

"It's not over till it's over. Till the fat lady sings."

"She's singing!" Thompson hooted, still on a high from the action. "Goddamn, she's singing."

I flinched as a shot echoed from the second floor. A minute later a Marine tossed a gook corpse over the stairwell. It splattered blood on the first floor. The prisoners watched with fear-filled eyes.

"Gook tried to stab me with scissors," the Marine called from above.

"Fuck," said another grunt. "We oughta go through this place like a dose of salts through a goose. Kill 'em all and let God sort 'em out."

I raked my gaze across the Americans. "There are civilians in here, Lieutenant. Tell them."

"There'll be no shooting unless it's necessary," Thompson ordered. "All of you. Is that clear?"

"We ain't seen no fuckin' civilians, Lieutenant."

I started frantically up the stairway, taking three steps at a time. I heard Thompson behind me.

"Take it easy, Kragel," he panted. "All the women and civilians are probably holed up in a room somewhere."

Some of the Marines were still searching the second floor of the hospital while the rest had proceeded on to the third floor. Tinbloom and a Georgia black grunt called Peaches found a locked door. Peaches kicked it open and darted inside.

"Skipper, take a look at this," Tinbloom called as Peaches marched a group of people out of the room at gunpoint.

Some of the people were French doctors while the rest were nuns in white and some Vietnamese nurses and aides wearing blood-splattered blue with white collars. There were about twenty people in all. They looked frightened. The French doctors were protesting angrily.

"Shut yer traps," Peaches growled. "Lieutenant, they been treatin' the gooks. We oughta waste the lot of 'em."

Peaches glared at his prisoners.

I trotted down the hallway toward them, my eyes searching. I looked them over.

"Is this all of them?"

"I'll check again," Peaches volunteered. "Tin, keep your eye on these traitorous cocksuckers."

I went with Peaches when he slipped back inside the room. It was an operating room dimly lighted with kerosene lanterns because the electricity had been knocked out in the fighting. There was a dead VC naked on the OR table with his thoracic cavity exposed.

I squinted in the poor light.

"Dinks," Peaches said.

There were two of them squatting like villagers in the opposite corner, both women dressed in the blood-splattered striped uniforms of nurse's aides. They clutched each other and watched us with eyes as round and frightened as those of cornered animals.

Brigette stared at me. Tears began to run down her cheeks.

53

AN HOUR AFTER THE FALL OF THE HOSPITAL I WAS LEADING Brigette through Hue's deadly streets, back through the debris, human and otherwise, left in the wake of the Marine advance on the Citadel.

Fuck the Citadel and the Pulitzer and fuck Hank Baylor and the war most of all.

The two of us together. We slipped past *Cercle Sportif* and past the disabled Russian tank. The corpses littering the city from the last two weeks of fighting left an awful stench that the wet lowering clouds and the drizzle held trapped in the rubbled streets. Hue had become a graveyard with its corpses exposed.

Brigette gasped and retched. The corpses were everywhere, covered with black flies. You could hear the busy hum of the flies and smell the rot before you came to it.

"Your friends," I said to Brigette, trying to control the anger that kept trying to bubble to the surface.

"Mike . . . ?"

"Not now. Wait until we're out of hell. The way I feel right now, I love you but I'd zap your pretty ass if you started confessing."

"Mike, oh, my Big Shoot."

I thought I heard something. I shoved Brigette against a wall and pressed myself next to her. I fingered the trigger of Copeland's M16. Lieutenant Thompson had given me extra full magazines in pouches to clip to my web belt. I had a full canteen also and two grenades. Copeland's Simply-Forget-Us helmet was gone, so I had gone back to my old patrol bush hat.

I waited, holding my breath to listen to movement in the courtyard of the neighboring house. Brigette's hand crept to my arm and gripped it.

"There may still be snipers out there," Lieutenant Thompson said when I informed him of my plan to take Brigette and return to the rear.

He didn't know the half of it.

He glanced at Brigette with her pretty tear-stained face. "At least you knew what you were fighting for," he said wearily.

I instructed Brigette to change into trousers if she could find a pair. "If not, take some from one of the prisoners. And hurry, goddamnit!"

Thompson watched her leave the room. She returned wearing a baggy pair of black pajamas speckled with dried bloodstains. I made her get rid of the black top. She came back with a light blue nurse's blouse. It was a little better. I didn't want some trigger-happy grunt back at battalion headquarters mistaking her for the enemy.

If we made it that far.

Thompson gave me one of the tourist street maps.

"I can't spare any men to go with you," he said, looking in the direction of the Perfume River and the Citadel on the other side. "I hope you know what you're doing, Kragel. It's dangerous out there by yourselves."

I shrugged. It could be even more dangerous if we didn't go.

I hadn't had time to analyze my plan completely. War seldom gave you the luxury. All I could be sure of was that Dog was out there somewhere watching and waiting. It was his deadly rifle that could have ended my life at the hospital door. I *felt* it. But for some reason, that singleness of purpose that had made *Cho Linh hon* the most dreaded name in I Corps had faltered when it came to shooting me. At the last instant, he had pulled off his aim, as he had not pulled off from Colonel Steinke, Judy Wong, the three boys from Muskogee, and nearly a hundred others.

I had watched the kid on the Hai Van, learning enough

about him and his techniques to know I was no match for him. I realized instinctively that survival depended upon separating Brigette and myself from the Marines and trying to make our way back to the rear. As long as we were with the platoon, Dog had all the time he needed. And I couldn't expose his crimes without at the same time exposing Brigette as a spy. I hadn't come all this way to have Brigette end up in a South Vietnam prison camp.

Dog would follow us. I was sure of that. I knew him. But maybe we could lose him in the city, or maybe we could make it back before he regained his determination.

It was a chilling thought. The only reason I wasn't already dead was because *Cho Linh hon* couldn't make up his mind whether or not to actually kill me.

Christ!

Whatever happened in this odd triangle was going to happen out there in Hue. It was something I had to handle myself. On this one I couldn't just take pictures and go on to write about it.

Sharon, how was that for an investment, a commitment?

I hesitated at the door of the hospital, catching my breath before consigning us to the city. I took deep breaths and looked at Brigette next to me, her hand clasping mine hard, trusting me even though she didn't understand and I didn't have time to explain.

"Good luck," Thompson said.

Brigette and I burst through the hospital door and past the sandstone fence, running hard through the scattered bodies in the courtyard. Doc Brown lifted a solemn hand in farewell as we headed back the same way I had just come.

Funny how in life you went back over the same old ground so much.

Now we were alone in the middle of destruction, and there were noises in the next courtyard.

Brigette shook her head desperately when I motioned for her to remain where she was and to stay quiet. I had to pry her hand from my shirt sleeve. I made a face at her and an angry gesture and, trembling, she stayed with her back pressed against the wall as though becoming part of it.

I eased down the wall, the mist of rain hissing in my face. The noises continued.

I came to a low mortar-and-bamboo fence that separated the courtyards. Taking a deep breath, I eased an eye over the top, the M16 ready.

Two cur dogs looked up at me, startled. Their faces were bloody. One lifted his lip in a snarl. They were eating a corpse.

I snapped my head away.

—————————— **54** ——————————

IT FELT LIKE WE WERE THE ONLY TWO PEOPLE ALIVE IN A CITY abandoned after some major catastrophe. The sounds of battle pursued us from the rear near the area of the river and the Citadel, but here our footfalls echoed in the streets and the clouds settled over us like a wet blanket, dampening our moods and lending an air of foreboding to the way and time ahead. The only thing we saw alive was an occasional dog loping down the street. The dogs were not starving.

A rooster somewhere crowed. It was a sound so incongruous in these surroundings that Brigette and I froze and looked at each other.

It was slow going. We moved from building to building, our eyes searching for enemy soldiers. At the same time I was acutely aware of the fact that we would not see Dog. The only announcement of Dog's presence would come when one of us fell with a bullet through the heart.

We moved away from the promenade, and selected alleys

and side streets that provided no long-range shots. If and when anything happened, I wanted it to happen within range of my M16.

I wanted a chance at least.

The rain was bringing night early. When I called a rest break inside an abandoned house, I could barely make out the subjects of framed pictures on coffee tables and wall shelves in the living room. Brigette and I huddled together on the floor behind a rattan sofa where I could keep watch over the door and a window.

Brigette was brimming with questions. Why had we taken off alone through the city when there was still fighting?

"The VC won't harm *you,*" I replied, more sarcastically than I intended.

We were whispering and our voices hissed. I felt her body stiffen next to mine.

"Mike, there things you no understand," she whispered hoarsely. "Brigette could not tell you then."

"Business is business."

She hesitated. "It biness in beginning," she said. "Mike? Mike?"

I looked at her. Her face was a soft oval in the gathering dusk.

"Mike, it not just biness at end."

I looked away. To have something to do and gather my thoughts, I left her behind the sofa and crawled to the window. Curtains still covered it and there was still glass. I did not disturb the curtains when I peeped out the window around the edges. Dog would notice movement like that. I knew he was out there.

The intensity of the rain was increasing. Rain drummed against the red tile roof of the house. I watched it skittering in sheets in the narrow streets between the rows of little houses where the more well-to-do citizens of Hue had lived. There had not been much fighting on this street; it simply looked deserted. It looked wet and dark and deserted.

I thought of Dog in the Hai Van when the rain came in the night. He huddled next to me, and then he was like a little boy cradled in my arms.

I crawled back to Brigette. Our clothing was wet, but I could feel her warmth through the thin fabric.

"He won't come tonight," I said, more to myself than to her. "We'll stay here until dawn. It'll be too dark in a few minutes to move."

I felt Brigette grow more fearful beside me. The least I owed her was an explanation. It was her life too. The rain pounding on the roof kept our voices contained inside the house.

"Old Professor Beardsley warned me about muckraking on the dark side of human nature," I began. "Brigette, do you remember *Cho Linh hon?*"

"All Vietnamese people know *Cho Linh hon.* There is great fear of him. You write much about him, for goo'ness sake."

I didn't need to see Brigette in the dark to know the smooth shape of her face, the lips like one of her nipples, the sloe-almond eyes, the delicate scar across her nose that gave her face character and intrigue.

"Why you talk 'bout *Cho Linh hon?*" Brigette asked, her voice unsteady.

"When I was in America I found out something about him that can send him to prison. For that he may kill me."

"Mike!"

"That's not all. Brigette, he's in Hue now, out there somewhere. He's not just after me. I suppose I don't have to tell you why *you're* his target too."

Her breath caught. "No," she said. I waited, but she left it at that for a long pause.

"Cho Linh hon evil man," she said at last. "He kill because him like to kill. Mike, is it true he the one kill Judy Wong?"

"He thought she was a spy." My voice tinged with bitterness. "But she wasn't the spy, was she? You were."

She let silence hang again.

Then she said, "Mike, how you find out this?"

I reached into my pocket and pressed the abalone shell comb into her tiny hand. I felt her give a start, as though bitten by the comb.

"Mike . . . ?"

"Just don't lie about it, Brigette. You used me."

"We use each other."

It was true.

"Mike," she said. "Look at Brigette."

"It's too dark."

"You and Brigette, Mike. One no need sun to see the other."

I looked at her.

"Brigette Vietnamese, you American," she said. "Everybody take side in war. Each do what think is right, for goo'ness sake. Mike, I tell you now what happen. Mike, Judy Wong not just Judy Wong. Judy Wong my sister."

"Your *sister!*"

She pressed near to me. She shivered.

"Papa him fight French," she went on, her voice turning flat. "French kill him at Dien Bien Phu. American bomb kill mother of Judy Wong and Brigette. Our brother is VC kill by American soldier at Nha Trang. Ho Chi Minh not enemy of Brigette's family. Boo-coo American come from other side of ocean Brigette's enemy. Whole family dead except for Judy Wong and Brigette."

"Is that how you got the scar—Americans?" I asked.

"When American bomb village, Judy Wong my sister lose half one foot. I cut on face. But mother dead. VC come to village and talk."

"And Judy Wong and you came to Da Nang to look for paramours to spy on." I finished for her, because her confession was painful to hear. "Then Judy Wong and you were *both* spies."

"First we work hospital in Hue, then we go Da Nang. Mike, you no enemy now," Brigette whispered. I felt her breath, tasted it. "You not enemy for long time, for goo'ness sake. Brigette almost die when you leave. Brigette think you not come back. I go to Frenchman to tell him Brigette not want spy no more. Judy Wong dead, for goo'ness sake. Brigette only one in family left.

"Brigette at plantation when *Cho Linh hon* shoot Monsieur DeFrange. I know it *Cho Linh hon* because I hear he cut off Frenchman's ears. Then I come Hue work in hospital again. I not want to take side in war no more."

"Yes," I said.

"You not Schopenhauer?" Brigette asked. She touched her face to mine. I felt warm tears.

"I'll deal with it," I said. "But not now."

One thing at a time. First, I had to get Brigette and me through the night and through tomorrow. After that I'd worry about being a squaw man.

"Cho Linh hon shoot us, take ears," Brigette despaired. "Mike, Brigette die and go to ancestors without sadness. But first, you must tell Brigette you love me."

I couldn't. I still felt betrayed.

"Brigette know you love me, for goo'ness sake," she said. "You come back from other side of world to fight for Brigette. Brigette know Mike love me. Brigette know."

The most I could do was put my arm around her, as I had Dog so long ago. I drew her near and held her. Holding her beat back the terrible dread of uncertainty while I listened for the sound of movement in the rain outside.

"I can't help it," I whispered. "I feel for the kid. I'm afraid of him, but I can't hate him even though I know he's out there right now watching us. There's a bond between us. He feels it, too. As long as he feels it, he won't kill us."

I stopped. I held Brigette tighter.

"He'll be waiting for us out there somewhere tomorrow," I said. "If he's made up his mind . . . Brigette, we may have only one chance. I may have to kill him. If I can."

55

DAYLIGHT CAME NOT LIKE THUNDER; IT SLITHERED IN. THERE would be no sun. Heavy clouds rested on the rooftops, but the rain had stopped. It did not smell fresh following the rain like it should; there had been too much dying on this killing ground.

Grasping Brigette's hand and carrying the M16, I led the way cautiously through Hue's destruction. I paused at each house and carefully scrutinized the way ahead, listening, smelling, looking, before I committed us to the dangerous journey across to the next house.

Noon, if all went well, should bring us to the route the Marine trucks used coming from Phu Bai. The trucks brought out supplies and reinforcements, new meat for the grinder. They took out the old meat that had already been ground up.

There was just one thing between us and escape.

I kept seeing his eyes the way I had seen them that first day through the Nikon lens. Bleached out by the sun. Intense.

"Something happens to them," Bill Lange had said. "Collins went catatonic to escape. Others don't want to escape. They can't stop killing."

Lange was wrong. Dog killed and killed and kept killing because killing *was* his escape. Johnny Able had gone catatonic inside *Cho Linh hon. Dog* was the killer, the most feared sniper in Vietnam. *Johnny Able,* who shone through only briefly now and then, was the boy in the woods who loved Margie Crowe.

* * *

"Mike!"

I grabbed Brigette and thrust her behind a pile of debris and rubble and dropped next to her. I had to keep my mind on business before I lost my business.

The Vietnamese hadn't spotted us. Peeping through an opening in the rubble, I watched him but remembered not to stare. Staring awakened a man's instincts.

The VC slipped down the street toward us, but on the opposite side. He was dressed in black pajamas and tire tread sandals and carried a Chicom AK-47 with a banana clip. At first I thought he might be point for a patrol. Then I realized he was alone and even more frightened than we. He was just a kid of maybe fourteen or fifteen, with the wide eyes of a kid at Halloween.

We were in a little business district of a few neighborhood shops. The VC broke open the door of one of the shops and went inside and came out eating something. He looked up and down the street with nervous flitting motions of the head. I crouched lower. I fingered the trigger of my M16.

The child VC proceeded cautiously down the street. I watched him come to a street intersection. As he paused to check things out, his body suddenly leaped into the air and went skittering like a rag doll. An instant later the crack of a single high-powered rifle shot cracked and reverberated through the streets.

The sound of the sniper shot still hung over the VC flopping his arms and legs in his death throes when I jerked Brigette to her feet. I led the way running down an alley, then broke off onto a side street. When she started lagging behind, I hustled her into the back courtyard of a house where she could catch her breath while I tried to think.

We huddled together behind an elevated rock garden filled with flowers. Brigette held onto my arm with both hands. She was hyperventilating from panic.

"Quit it!" I snapped. "Take deep breaths. Deep."

I was forty years old and every muscle in my body seemed to be rebelling. My eyebrow with the stitches in it burned. The scab from the glass cut on my cheek had broken off and the wound was bleeding again. I hadn't shaved in a week. I smelled.

I didn't need this shit.

"Cho Linh hon take our ears, Mike!" Brigette gasped.

"I'll be damned if he will," I growled.

Only desperate men, or lost men, or a sniper like the Ghost Dog prowled these mean streets alone. The shooting of the VC kid was no chance encounter between lost enemies. How well I remembered the sound of Dog's Model 70 from the Hai Van. And how better for Dog to express his contempt for me as worthy prey than to pick off an enemy while he knew I watched.

Did it mean that the cat-and-mouse game he had played with us since we left the hospital was over?

The way I saw it, I had two options.

Brigette and I could continue to run and extend the chance that he was still wavering over his decision to kill us. I looked at Brigette. Could I further risk her life, and mine, on the whims of a kid with blood as cold as the rain that fell during the night?

Or, I could stop procrastinating and face what I had to do.

It suddenly struck me.

Dog was the perfect killing machine, but like everything human he possessed the one great flaw that kept him human. Repeatedly, he had risked his life after a successful kill in order to collect his grisly trophies—at Thieu Bien with an enemy force breathing down his neck, on the Hai Van, after the Lotus Bitch and the Frenchman. The ears on his belt proved to him that he was better than Pablo Rhoades, that he *was* the Top Stick.

Cho Linh hon would never leave a kill without collecting its ears.

I stood up. "Brigette, I want you to wait for me here."

"No! Mike, I not care to live no more without you."

"Goddamnit, I don't have time to argue. Our living may depend on the next few minutes. I'll be back. I promise. Hide here and don't move."

"Cho Linh hon will kill you!"

I pried her fingers loose one at a time from my clothing. "Hide. Don't move."

Stalking a predator brought into play every sense you possessed, including the sixth. I strained to use every rusty skill I had ever learned about hunting men as I crept through the rubble, taking a different route back to the freshly slain VC. I circled wide, then approached the corpse from the opposite direction.

I toyed with, then dismissed, the idea of taking Dog prisoner when he came for his trophies. Dog always said he would save the last bullet in his last pistol for his own brain. The only way Brigette and I were going to survive this encounter, one in which I was greatly outmatched, was for me to kill Dog along with the kid Johnny Able who had retreated to hide inside *Cho Linh hon*.

I steeled myself for the ordeal.

When I drew near to the new corpse, I dropped to hands and knees, then to my belly. I crawled along a bamboo fence, worked my way between two houses where there was a dead child of about three or four lying in a crib of flies on the veranda, scrambled elbow after elbow across a narrow, muddy alley, and wormed my way into a patch of weeds. My heart thudded, but my mind was clear and focused. I had one thing on it—survival.

From the weed patch, I commanded a clear view of where the VC fell in the street. He lay well within M16 range. He seemed undisturbed. If I knew Dog, he would wait and watch before he showed himself. And, then, when he did, I would kill him by surprise from hiding like he had killed all those whose ears now dangled from his belt.

A wave of revulsion at the deed I had assigned myself rolled up out of my stomach like bile. Zapping gooks and chinks you did not know was one thing. It was combat. It was another thing altogether to kill an American you did know. Especially if you had held that American in your arms like the son you never had.

I dropped my head on my arms to settle my nerves and

regain control. When the nausea passed, I lifted my head and pressed my cheek against the black plastic stock of the M16. I pinned the open sights on the dead soldier.

I waited. It was just a matter of time.

56

THERE WAS NO PROLOGUE WHEN THE ACTION BEGAN, NO DRAMATic music to warn you of impending peril. It was just coldly matter-of-fact and sudden. It was almost like when I was wounded on the Hai Van, except this time it was no snakebite. It knocked the breath out of me. It was like a great stake came out of the sky and pegged me to the ground.

Then I heard the report of the rifle and felt my muscles wildly convulsing. The world went into slow motion out of which I was able to extract and digest only shreds of reality. It was like being in one of those dance halls where the flashing black lights reveal action in stop-motion snatches.

I heard a woman screaming. *Goddamn, she followed me. Go back run run di-di go . . .*

Her long hair was flying as she bolted toward me in her black pajamas and nurse's top.

I was operating beyond consciousness, on automatic pilot. My instincts picked up impressions.

Long black hair. Screaming my name. Gray clouds. Weeds.

Another rifle shot! Dog was killing us.

No! The shot missed.

Brigette grabbing me. Pulling. I was too heavy for her. She was weeping, bellowing with awful grief and pain.

We were targets.

Grab her. Hold her. Die on top of her so maybe Dog'll think she's dead too. He doesn't take a woman's ears.

He took the Lotus Bitch's.

Pulling at me. Movement somewhere else. A blur.

A third shot! Someone fell on top of me. It wasn't Brigette.

Not Brigette? Who?

Being dragged quickly out of the weeds. Brigette had one arm.

Who had the other arm?

Dog had the other arm.

Dog?

Pulled into a building. Bins of rice and tubers. Some canned goods on shelves. Shattered glass on the floor.

The world started slowing down again. The world returned to perspective as I caught my breath at last. Breathing was painful. I felt warm blood from where I had been shot in the lower back, but I could move my legs. My spine was safe.

Brigette was all over me trying to cradle me in her arms, thrusting her body between me and the skinny Marine. She was screaming at Dog in Vietnamese. Dog looked at her, then sat back on his haunches in the debris of the Hue shop. He wore his pistols and his web gear and his patrol cap pulled low over his almost-colorless eyes. And he wore his ears on their parachute cord.

It was a moment before I could speak. *"It wasn't you!"* I cried in surprise. "Then *who?"*

Dog was breathing hard with his mouth open. A pinkish froth issued from between his lips. I had seen that before. A lung shot.

While Brigette and I watched, Dog sank back on himself and seemed to grow so much smaller. He became a little boy again, the orphan in the wilderness that I had held in my arms in the Hai Van. My heart went out to this kid whose aloneness in the world seemed suddenly so haunting and marked.

Dog dragged himself backward and slumped with his

back against the bottom of a row of shelves. His rifle lay across his legs. Brigette kept it up in Vietnamese while I watched Dog, mesmerized.

"Brigette, hush!"

"Mike . . . Mike!"

"I'm going to live, Brigette. I've been shot worse. Brigette, patch him up quickly."

A sucking chest wound didn't give you much time.

"No, Mike! He *Cho Linh hon*. He kills us. He kill us."

"He's not *Cho Linh hon;* he's Johnny Able. He didn't shoot me. Fix him."

Dog held up his hand weakly. He glanced toward the window facing the street.

"There isn't enough time," he said, coughing up more foam.

The two of us, wounded, looked into each other's eyes for a long moment.

"Johnny," I said. "I don't understand you."

A kind of thin smile touched his bloody lips. He was very pale through his tan.

"What you see . . ." he stammered, "is all there is of . . ."

He didn't have the strength to finish.

"That's not all there is of Johnny Able," I said. "There is much more."

For a moment he seemed to recover. He tried to scoot across the floor on his haunches, but he collapsed, breathing heavily, coughing.

"Mike?" he said. It was barely audible. I pulled myself near him. Brigette held on.

"Mike, the gook sniper will try . . . finish us off. He knows . . . he hit us. Help me . . . to the door. He'll . . . he'll be watching the window . . ."

It surprised me to discover I hadn't the strength to drag his thin body across the floor. Brigette helped. The three of us pulled ourselves across the floor through the broken glass and spilled rice. Dog had spotted a hole torn into the bottom of the front door. Probably from a grenade explosion outside, or maybe a Marine kicked it.

Dog was fading fast. He couldn't lift his rifle.

"Mike, you . . . you have to be . . . sniper now. I . . . I can't do it. You have to . . ."

"Johnny," I said, "you did the same thing that shithead Carl Can't did—getting it to save somebody else. You wanted us dead anyhow. Why didn't you let the gook sniper finish us off? Then you could have killed him."

Maybe Dog couldn't answer that one, so he didn't try.

I looked at him. I realized how it must have happened. He killed the spotter, then settled down to wait for the sniper to reveal himself. Only, I showed up first. The angle must have been all wrong for him when the sniper opened up on me. Unable to get a shot off at the Vietnamese sniper, he could either let Brigette and me die in the street, or . . .

He could expose himself to save me like he had before when I was wounded on the Hai Van.

The sniper's third shot found *Cho Linh hon*.

"What made you do it, Johnny?" I asked him.

Was it because *he, Cho Linh hon*, wanted to kill me himself?

He still could not answer. "Find the . . . sniper, Mike," he said.

I looked at him. I looked at Brigette. I picked up the Winchester and lay on my stomach with it. Dog lay on one side of me, Brigette on the other. I felt blood oozing from my side where the bullet exited. I was stiff and the wound was painful, but I could still handle the rifle. It felt heavy and smooth and clean and mechanical. The three of us side by side peered through the hole at the bottom of the door at the row of buildings across the street down the block. There was no movement.

"See . . . like a hotel or rooming house? He's . . . he's somewhere in . . . somewhere. I was waiting him out . . . trying to spot him when you . . . The other man . . . the dead one . . . was his spotter."

I peered through the 8X Unertl scope. The windows jumped out at me. I scanned them slowly, searching.

"Wait," Dog coached. "Have patience. . . . He'll glance out two . . . maybe three times . . . Then when he gets . . . bold . . ."

The rifle felt clean and deadly in my hands. It felt powerful. It made *me* feel powerful. I glanced at Dog. I knew he understood what I was feeling.

I returned my eye to the scope.

There was a flash of movement in the rifle scope. I waited, tense, expectant, and in spite of my wound I was thrilled by this most deadly game. I could see how you could get hooked on it.

"How many now?" I asked Dog.

He understood.

"I . . . I . . . Mike, I needed . . . one more," he muttered, and his breathing was becoming ragged, shallow.

"Ninety-nine kills," I said. "Top Stick," I said.

I could have been his one hundredth kill, but I didn't want to think about that.

Another movement in the window down the street.

"He's about ready," I said.

"M-Mike, you have to kill him," Dog stammered. "If not . . . he . . . he kill you."

"I know."

"Thats the way . . . it is," Dog said.

Brigette clutched my shirt, breathing heavily.

The moment the VC showed himself, I knew Bill Lange was right. The first thing you saw were the eyes. They jumped right out at you through the scope.

This soldier was older than the other by a few years. I was glad of that. His hair was cropped close and black around a thin Oriental face. He had a few thin hairs on his upper lip. There was a mole above his right eye. He peered intently out his window in our direction, but I realized he had not located us.

Staying too long in the window was his mistake. I was going to kill him. I felt so very powerful, knowing I controlled life and death.

I stroked the trigger very gently, remembering all the old marksmanship techniques I had learned in army boot camp over twenty years before.

The rifle cracked.

I brought the weapon down quickly out of recoil to find I had made a brain shot. The gook was doing the chicken. He kicked himself out the window. When he hit the street below he continued to flop around for a few more seconds.

I dropped my head on my arms; Brigette's arms came around me. I wanted her to hold me.

After a moment, I thought of Dog and turned toward him. He lay on his side with his head in the broken glass. His pale eyes were slitted. His lips were stained red and the red had spread up his face and dried. He spoke, spitting more froth.

"Every bondsman by . . . by his own hand . . ." he said, and he tried to smile.

"Johnny . . ."

"Mike . . ."

"Johnny, would you really have killed me?"

There was nothing left of the kid.

Afterward, I always preferred to believe that he wouldn't have.

57

MIKE KRAGEL DISPATCH, 25 FEB 68:

Vietnam (INS)—The other grunts called him Dog, as in Bird Dog, because of his uncanny ability to sniff out the enemy. The North Vietnamese and the Vietcong called him *Cho Linh hon*—Ghost Dog—because like a ghost he prowled the jungles of Vietnam killing the enemy one accurate shot at a time with his powerful Winchester hunting rifle.

His real name was Johnny Able, 20-years-old.

Lance Cpl. Johnny Able, USMC, died early last week during the fighting for the ancient capital of Hue in Vietnam.

Able was an orphan who from the age of fourteen lived alone in a bunker on an abandoned army post in Oklahoma. When he was eighteen, his girlfriend was brutally assaulted and murdered. She was the only person he ever let close to him.

Johnny Able joined the U.S. Marine Corps soon after that. He was a natural at shooting, having hunted meat constantly to feed himself in Oklahoma.

When he graduated from the Marine sniper school, he made a vow to kill one hundred enemy soldiers in order to top the record previously held by Marine Gunnery Sgt. Pablo Rhoades. Rhoades had ninety-three confirmed kills.

In testimony to his prowess and stealth in the forests and to his shooting skills, the North Vietnamese Army offered the equivalent of three years' pay as reward to the soldier who brought in the body of *Cho Linh hon.* Wanted posters bearing Able's picture were plastered in every village.

"Corporal Able was the greatest sniper of the war," said his commander, Capt. Bill Lange. "There was something about the kid. He was a loner, but yet there was something . . . unique. I don't know what it was. You just had to know him. There will never be another like him."

One hundred fifty marines and four hundred Republic of South Vietnam troops died in the twenty-five-day battle for Hue that started on the eve of Tet. More than five thousand communist soldiers were killed.

The man known as Dog died not as Dog the sniper but instead as Johnny Able the man.

He had ninety-nine kills, one away from reaching his goal, when INS journalist Mike Kragel was pinned down and seriously wounded by enemy sniper fire on a deserted street in Hue.

Able could have remained safely under cover and shot the enemy sniper for his hundredth kill.

Instead, the Marine sniper received a mortal wound when he dashed into the open and, with a Vietnamese nurse's aide, dragged Kragel to safety.

In saving the journalist's life, Johnny Able gave his own.

"He knew the chances," Kragel said. "He deliberately gave up his own life in order to save mine. Cpl. Johnny Able's one hundredth kill was—*himself.*"

THE BEST **MEN'S FICTION**
COMES FROM **POCKET BOOKS**

BOOMER Charles D. Taylor ❑ 74330-9/$5.50

THE 100TH KILL Charles W. Sasser ❑ 70320-X/$6.50

BRIGHT STAR Harold Coyle ❑ 68543 0/$6.50

DARK WING Richard Herman, Jr. ❑ 53493-9/$6.50

DEEP STING Charles D. Taylor ❑ 67631-8/$4.95

A TIME OF WAR Michael Peterson ❑ 56787-X/$6.50

FINAL ANSWERS Greg Dinallo ❑ 73312-5/$5.50

FLIGHT OF THE INTRUDER Stephen Coonts
❑ 70960-7/$6.99

RAISE THE RED DAWN Bart Davis ❑ 69663-7/$4.95

RED ARMY Ralph Peters ❑ 67669-5/$5.50

SWORD POINT Harold Coyle ❑ 73712-0/$6.99

THE TEN THOUSAND Harold Coyle ❑ 88565-0/$6.99

38 NORTH YANKEE Ed Ruggero ❑ 70022-7/$5.99

UNDER SIEGE Stephen Coonts ❑ 74294-9/$6.99

RED INK Greg Dinallo ❑ 73314-1/$6.50

AS SUMMERS DIE Winston Groom ❑ 52265-5/$6.50

TO KILL THE LEOPARD Theodore Taylor ❑ 89025-5/$5.99

Simon & Schuster Mail Order
200 Old Tappan Rd., Old Tappan, N.J. 07675
Please send me the books I have checked above. I am enclosing $_____ (please add
$0.75 to cover the postage and handling for each order. Please add appropriate sales
tax). Send check or money order–no cash or C.O.D.'s please. Allow up to six weeks
for delivery. For purchase over $10.00 you may use VISA: card number, expiration
date and customer signature must be included.

POCKET
BOOKS

Name _____

Address _____

City _____ State/Zip _____

VISA Card # _____ Exp.Date _____

Signature _____ 213-08